Byron A. Dunn

Raiding with Morgan

Byron A. Dunn

Raiding with Morgan

1st Edition | ISBN: 978-3-75237-613-5

Place of Publication: Frankfurt am Main, Germany

Year of Publication: 2020

Outlook Verlag GmbH, Germany.

Raiding with Morgan

BY

Byron A. Dunn

PREFACE.

General John H. Morgan was one of the most picturesque figures in the Civil War, an officer without a peer in his chosen line. During the two years of his brilliant career he captured and paroled at least ten thousand Federal soldiers, and kept three times that number in the rear of the Federal army guarding communications. When we consider the millions of dollars' worth of property he destroyed, and how he paralyzed the movements of Buell, we do not wonder that he was considered the scourge of the Army of the Cumberland.

General Morgan was a true Kentucky gentleman, and possessed one of the kindest of hearts. The thousands of persons captured by him almost invariably speak of the good treatment accorded them. The following incident reveals more clearly than words his generous spirit. In reporting a scout, he says:

"Stopped at a house where there was a sick Lincoln soldier, who died that night. No men being in the neighborhood, his wife having no person to make a coffin or bury him, I detailed some men, who made a coffin."

The adventures of Calhoun as a secret agent of the "Knights of the Golden Circle" opens up a portion of the history of the Civil War which may [pg 8]be almost unknown to our younger readers. During the war the whole North was honeycombed with secret societies, whose members denounced Lincoln as a usurper and a bloody monster, and maintained that the government had no right to coerce the South. They resisted the draft, encouraged desertions, and embarrassed the Federal Government in every way possible. In secret many of the leaders plotted armed rebellion, the liberation of Confederate prisoners, and the burning of Northern cities. They held out inducements to the South to invade the North, and there is but little doubt that Morgan was lured to his destruction by their representations.

Shortly after the close of the war the author met a gentleman who had served on the staff of General Breckinridge. This officer affirmed that he carried a message from Breckinridge to Morgan, saying that the former had positive information that forty thousand armed "Knights" stood ready to assist Morgan if he would invade Indiana. Everything goes to show that Morgan relied on these reports, and it was this belief that induced him to disobey the orders of General Bragg.

It is an interesting question whether General Breckinridge was really privy to the plans of the "Knights," and whether he secretly encouraged Morgan to disobey orders, hoping that the appearance of a Confederate force in the North would lead to the overthrow of the Lincoln Government and the independence of the South. The author [pg 9]has taken the ground that

2

Breckinridge was fully cognizant of Morgan's intended move.

This volume mentions only the greatest of the General's raids, and the author has tried to narrate them with historical accuracy as regards time, place, and circumstances. In stating the number of his men, his losses, and the damage he inflicted on the Federals, the General's own reports have been followed; these, as was to be expected, differ widely in many cases from those of the Federal officers.

The tale of the exploits of Calhoun is substantially true, though the hero himself is fictitious, for every one of his most notable feats was accomplished by one or other of Morgan's men. It was Lieutenant Eastin, of Morgan's command, who killed Colonel Halisy in single combat. Calhoun's achievements in the escape from the Ohio Penitentiary were actually performed by two different persons: a sharp dining-room boy furnished the knives with which the prisoners dug their way to liberty; Captain Thomas H. Hines planned and carried to a successful termination the daring and ingenious escape. Captain Hines fled with General Morgan; and every adventure which befell Calhoun in "The Flight to the South" actually befell Captain Hines. The Captain's marvellous story was published in the January number of "The Century," 1891, and to this narrative the author is indebted for the leading facts.

A. A. DUNN.

August 1, 1903.

[pg 10]

CHAPTER I.
AFTER SHILOH.

The great battle of Shiloh had been fought, and victory had been snatched from the hands of the Confederates by the opportune arrival of Buell's army.

The Southerners had lost their beloved commander, slain; a third of their number had fallen. Although defeated they had not been conquered. They had set forth from Corinth in the highest hopes, fully expecting to drive Grant's army into the Tennessee River. This hope was almost realized, when it suddenly perished: twenty thousand fresh troops had arrived upon the field, and the Confederates were forced to retreat. But they had fallen back unmolested, for the Federal army had been too severely punished to think of pursuing. Both armies were willing to rest and have their decimated ranks filled with fresh troops.

Of all the Southern troops engaged at Shiloh none felt their defeat more keenly than the Kentucky brigade under the command of Colonel Trabue. They had fought as only brave men can [pg 16]fight; they left one-third of their number on the field, killed and wounded. Defeat could not demoralize them, and it fell to their lot to cover the retreat of Beauregard. They had stood like a wall of adamant between their fleeing army and the victorious Federals. No charge could pierce that line of heroes. With faces to the foe, they slowly fell back, contesting every inch of ground.

Fondly had they hoped that Grant would first be crushed, then Buell annihilated, and their march to Nashville would be unopposed. From Nashville it would be an easy matter to redeem their beloved Kentucky from the ruthless Northern invaders.

It was but a few days after the battle that there was a social gathering of Kentucky officers at the headquarters of General John C. Breckinridge. Conspicuous in that group of notable men was one whose insignia of office showed him to be only a captain. But he was already a marked man. He had greatly distinguished himself in Kentucky and Tennessee as a daring raider and scout, and at the battle of Shiloh he had rendered invaluable service at the head of a squadron of independent cavalry.

It was but natural that in such a gathering the situation would be freely discussed. "It looks to me," said Breckinridge, with a sigh, "that if we are forced to give up Corinth, our cause in the West will be lost. I am in favor of holding Corinth to the last man."

[pg 17]

"What is your opinion, Morgan?" asked one of the officers, turning to the captain of whom we have spoken.

Thus addressed, John H. Morgan modestly answered: "The General will pardon me if I differ with him somewhat in his opinion. Corinth should be held, as long as that can be done with safety to the army. But Corinth itself is of little value to us, now that the railroad between here and Chattanooga is in the hands of the enemy. It is not worth the sacrifice of a hundred men."

"What! would you give up Corinth without a struggle?" asked the officer, in surprise.

"Not if a battle offered a reasonable hope of victory," replied Morgan. "What I mean is, that the place should not be held so long as to endanger the safety of the army. Corinth is nothing; the army is everything."

"Then you believe, Captain, that Corinth could be lost, and our cause not greatly suffer?"

"Certainly. The further the enemy advances into the South, the more vulnerable he becomes. Even now, give me a thousand men, and I can keep forty thousand of the enemy busy protecting their lines of communication."

"Morgan, you are joking!" exclaimed several of the officers.

"No joke about it. I expect to see old Kentucky before many days; and if I do, there will be consternation in the ranks of the Yankees."

"Do you think you can reach Kentucky with a [pg 18]thousand men?" asked Breckinridge, in a tone which showed his doubt.

"I shall make the attempt with less than half of that number," replied Morgan, coolly.

A murmur of surprise arose, and then Trabue asked: "Will Beauregard let you make the hazardous attempt?"

"Yes, with my own squadron, but he will risk no more men in the venture."

"Well, good-bye, John, if you try it," said one of the officers, laughing.

"Why good-bye, Colonel?"

"Because the Yankees will get you sure."

"Perhaps!" answered Morgan, dryly, as he arose to go.

"The whole South will ring with the praises of that man one of these days," remarked Breckinridge, after Morgan had made his exit.

"A perfect dare-devil. I am proud he is a Kentuckian," remarked Trabue.

Not knowing the flattering words spoken of him, Morgan wended his way to his headquarters, where he was informed by the orderly who took his horse that a young Confederate officer had been waiting for some time to see him.

"He said he must see you," continued the orderly, "and if necessary he would wait all night."

"All right, I will see what he wants," replied Morgan, as he turned and entered his headquarters. There he was greeted by a young man, not much [pg 19]more than a boy, who wore the uniform of a Confederate lieutenant.

Morgan gave him a swift glance, and then exclaimed: "Bless my heart! if this isn't Calhoun Pennington, son of my old friend Judge Pennington! I am more than glad to see you. I have heard of some of your exploits, and often wondered why you did not seek to take service with me. Let's see! You were on the staff of the late lamented Governor Johnson, were you not?"

"Yes," replied Calhoun; and his voice trembled, and tears came into his eyes in spite of himself, as he thought of the death of his beloved chief.

"A grand man, a brave man," said Morgan, gently. "Now that he has gone, what do you propose doing?"

"That is what I have come to see you about. General Beauregard has offered me a position on his staff, but I wanted to see you before I accepted."

"What! a position on the staff of General Beauregard! That is a rare honor for one so young as you are. Of course you are going to accept?"

"I do not know yet; I am to give him an answer in the morning, as I said I wanted to see you first. Great as the honor is which has been offered me, I feel it is a service which would not be agreeable to me. I much prefer the freer life of a scout and ranger. Perhaps you may know, I have done much of this kind of work. I have even performed more dangerous tasks than that of scouting, and I confess I rather like it."

[pg 20]

Morgan mused for a moment, and then suddenly asked: "Are you not a cousin of Frederic Shackelford, son of the late Colonel Richard Shackelford of our army?"

Calhoun's brow clouded. "Yes," he answered; "but why do you say the late Colonel Shackelford? Uncle Dick is not dead."

"Is that so? I am rejoiced to hear it. It was reported he was among the slain."

"He was desperately wounded," answered Calhoun, "but he did not die, and he is now a prisoner in the hands of the Yankees. Uncle Dick is a hero; but as for that traitor cousin of mine, I hate him!" and again Calhoun's brow grew dark.

"I have no reason to love him," laughed Morgan, "but I cannot help admiring him. He it was who discovered our well-laid plans, and forced me to flee from Lexington, as a thief in the night."

"Aye!" answered Calhoun, "but for him and that brute Nelson, Kentucky would now have been out of the Union. But that is not all. Had it not been for the same two traitors there would have been a different story to tell of Shiloh. Grant's army would now have been prisoners, Buell's in full flight, and our own pressing northward to redeem Kentucky. Had there been no Nelson, Buell's army would not have reached Grant in time to save him from destruction. If there had been no Fred Shackelford I should have borne the news to General Johnston that Buell would join Grant by the fifth, and Johnston would have made his [pg 21]attack a couple of days earlier. I was bearing the news to Johnston that Nelson would reach Savannah by the fifth when I was captured."

"Captured?" echoed Morgan, in surprise.

"Yes, captured, and by no less a personage than my cousin Fred Shackelford. But for this I would have reached Johnston by the second; as it was, I did not reach Shiloh until the morning of the last day of the battle."

"Then you escaped?" queried Morgan.

"No; my cousin let me go, after he had held me until he knew my information would be of no value. I was dressed in citizen's clothes. He could have had me hanged as a spy. I suppose I ought to be thankful to him, but I am not." And Calhoun shuddered when he thought how near he had been to death.[1]

"That was kind of him," said Morgan; "and you ought to be thankful to him, whether you are or not. To tell the truth, I took a great fancy to young Shackelford, and tried hard to get him to cast his lot with me. But as I failed to get him, I believe you would make a splendid substitute. You still think you had rather go with me than be on Beauregard's staff?"

"A thousand times, yes. I had rather go with you as a private than be a lieutenant on the General's staff," answered Calhoun, with vehemence.

[pg 22]

Morgan's eyes sparkled. "That is the finest compliment I ever had paid me," he said, "but I cannot allow the son of my old friend Judge Pennington to serve in the ranks as a private soldier. Yet my companies are fully officered now. Let's see! How would you like to go back to Kentucky?"

"Go back to Kentucky?" asked Calhoun in surprise.

"Yes, to recruit for my command. Do you think you could dodge the Yankees?"

"I believe I could. I could at least try," answered Calhoun, his face aglow with the idea.

"The case is this," said Morgan: "I am going to make a raid in a few days, and am going to try to reach Kentucky. My present force is small—not much over four hundred. I do not look for much help from the Confederate Government. Those in authority do not regard with much favor independent organizations. To augment my force, I must in a great measure rely on my own efforts. I know there are hundreds of the flower of Kentucky youths eager to join me if they had the opportunity. You are just the person to send back to organize them. When can you start?"

"In the morning," answered Calhoun.

Morgan smiled. "Good!" he said. "You are made of the right material. We will make full arrangements to-morrow. Good night, now, for it is getting late."

Thus dismissed Calhoun went away with a light [pg 23]heart. He was to be one of Morgan's men. It was all he wished.

The next morning Calhoun informed General Beauregard that while sensible of the great honor which he would bestow on him by appointing him a member of his staff, yet he believed he could be of more service to the South by casting his fortune with Morgan, and he had concluded to do so.

"While I greatly regret to lose you," replied the General, "I believe you have chosen well. To one of your temperament service with Morgan will be much more congenial than the duties of a staff officer. In fact," continued the General, with a smile, "I think you resemble Morgan in being restive under orders, and prefer to have your own way and go where you please. A command or two of partisan rangers may do, but too many would be fatal to the discipline of an army. Morgan may do the enemy a great deal of mischief, but after all, the fate of the South must be decided by her great armies."

"True, General," replied Calhoun, "but if Morgan can keep thousands of the enemy in the rear guarding their communications, the great armies of the North will be depleted by that number."

"That is true also," answered Beauregard; "and for that reason Morgan will be given more or less of a free rein. I have recommended him for a colonelcy. Convey to him my regards, and tell him I heartily congratulate him upon his last recruit."

General Beauregard's kind words touched Calhoun deeply. "Thank you, General," he replied, with feeling. "I trust I shall never prove myself unworthy of your good opinion. May God bless you, and crown your efforts with victory!"

After parting with Beauregard, Calhoun lost no time in reporting to Morgan. He found his chief in command of about four hundred men, rough, daring fellows who would follow their leader wherever he went. A more superb body of rough-riders was never formed.

Calhoun was introduced to the officers of the squadron, and when it became known that he was going back to Kentucky to recruit for the command—although many of the officers wondered why their chief had selected one so young—they gave him a hearty welcome. But when it became known that he was the son of Judge Pennington, of Danville, that he had already won renown as a daring scout, and had been offered a position on the staff of General Beauregard, their welcome was doubly enthusiastic.

To this welcome there was one exception. One of Morgan's officers, Captain P. C. Conway, had applied to Morgan for permission to go back to Kentucky on this same duty, and had been refused. He was a short, thickset, red-faced man with a very pompous air. His weakness was liquor; yet he was a brave, efficient officer. What he considered an affront was never forgiven, for he was of a revengeful disposition. It was consistent with his [pg 25]character that he should become a mortal enemy of Calhoun.

When he was introduced to Calhoun he merely bowed, and did not offer to give his hand.

"I believe I have heard of Captain Conway," said Calhoun, with a smile. "I have heard a cousin of mine speak of him."

"Why, yes," spoke up Morgan, with a twinkle in his eye, "Captain, Lieutenant Pennington is a cousin of your particular friend, Captain Fred Shackelford, of the Yankee army."

Conway fairly turned purple with rage. "Lieutenant Pennington has no reason to be proud of his relationship to that sneak and spy," he snorted.

"I have no more reason to love my cousin than you," replied Calhoun, with some warmth. "He may have played the spy; so have I; but sneak he is not, and I would thank you not to use the term again, traitor though he is to the South and his native state."

Conway glared at him for a moment, but there was something in Calhoun's eye which told him that if he repeated the term it might cause trouble, so he snapped: "Well, spy and traitor, if those terms suit you better; but it may be of interest to you to know that I have sworn to see that precious cousin of yours hanged, and"—with a fearful oath—"I will see that he is."

With these words he turned on his heel and stalked away.

"Shackelford's name has the same effect on [pg 26]Conway that a red rag has on a mad bull," laughed Morgan. "He can never forget that trick your cousin played on him."

"Ah! I remember," said Calhoun; "Fred told me all about it. Conway may take a dislike to me simply because I am Fred's cousin. I noticed that he greeted me rather coldly."

"I reckon he will not carry his hatred so far as that," replied Morgan, "yet it may be best not to mention Shackelford's name to him."

But Morgan might have changed his mind if he had heard Conway talking to a brother officer.

"Just to think," he fumed, "that the Captain picked on that young upstart to go back to Kentucky to recruit instead of one of us. I volunteered to go yesterday, and he put me down. To my mind, Pennington is no better than that sneak of a cousin of his, and Morgan will find it out some day."

"Better keep a still tongue in your head, Conway," dryly replied the officer, a Captain Matthews, to whom Conway was complaining. "Morgan will give you hell if he finds you are trying to create dissatisfaction."

"I am not afraid of Morgan," muttered Conway, but he said no more.

In the mean time Calhoun was hurriedly making preparations for his journey. Many of the officers and men were engaged in writing letters to send back by him to the dear ones in Kentucky. Morgan intrusted to him several important communications to prominent Southern sympathizers.

[pg 27]

Just as Calhoun was ready to start, Morgan gave him his secret instructions.

"What I now tell you," he said, "is too important to commit to writing. You may be captured. For hundreds of miles you must ride through a country swarming with Yankees. You will need discretion, as much or more than you will need courage. Much depends on your success. I intend to make a raid north about the first week in May. If possible (and I think it is), I shall try to reach Kentucky. My force when I start will not reach five hundred. If I could be joined by a thousand when I reach Kentucky, I believe I could sweep clear to the Ohio River. But with the short time at your disposal that will be impossible. But join me at Glasgow with all you can. I expect to be in Glasgow by the tenth of May at the latest."

"All right," replied Calhoun, "I will try to meet you there at that time, with at least one or two good companies."

Little did Morgan think at the time how badly he would need those companies.

At last all was ready, and amid shouts of "Good-bye" and "Success to you," Calhoun vaulted into the saddle and rode away eastward.

[pg 28]

CHAPTER II.

THROUGH THE LINES.

At the time Calhoun started for Kentucky, General Halleck was concentrating his immense army at Pittsburg Landing, preparatory to an attack on Corinth. Federal gunboats patrolled the Tennessee River as far up as Eastport. General Mitchell held the Memphis and Charleston Railroad between Decatur and Stevenson, but between Corinth and Decatur there was no large body of Federals, and the country was open to excursions of Confederate cavalry. In Middle Tennessee every important place was held by detachments of Federal troops. To attempt to ride through the lines was an exceedingly dangerous undertaking, but that is what Calhoun had to do to reach Kentucky. He expected to meet with little danger until he attempted to cross the lines of General Mitchell, which extended along the railroads that ran from Nashville southward. The country through which he had to pass was intensely Southern, and the Yankee cavalry did not venture far from the railroads.

When Calhoun left Corinth, he rode straight eastward, until he reached Tuscumbia, Alabama. Here he found little trouble in finding means to cross the Tennessee River. Once across the river he took a northeast course, which would take him [pg 29]through Rogersville. Now and then he met small squads of Confederate cavalry. They were scouting through the country, and did not seem to be under very strict military discipline, doing much as they pleased.

Now and then he came across a party of recruits making their way to the Confederate army at Corinth. They were mostly country boys, rough, uncouth, and with little or no education. They knew or cared little of the causes which had led up to the war; but they knew that the Southland had been invaded, that their homes were in danger, and they made soldiers whose bravery and devotion excited the admiration of the world.

In order to find out what General Mitchell was doing, and as nearly as he could, to ascertain the number of his forces, Calhoun resolved to ride as near the line of the Nashville and Decatur railroad as was prudent. As he approached Rogersville, he learned that the place had just been raided by a regiment of Yankee cavalry, and the country was in a panic.

Approaching the place cautiously, he was pleased to ascertain that the cavalry, after committing numerous depredations, had retreated to Athens. He now learned for the first time of the atrocities which had been committed on the defenceless inhabitants of Athens, and his blood boiled as he listened to the recital. No wonder the citizens of Rogersville were in a panic, fearing that their fate might be the same.

[pg 30]

"The whelps and robbers!" he exclaimed; "how I should like to get at them! But their time will come. Never will the South lay down her arms until every Northern soldier is driven in or across the Ohio."

In Rogersville Calhoun met with a Doctor Jenkins, who was especially well informed as to the strength and positions of the Federal army, and as to the feelings of the citizens.

"At first," said he, "the result of the battle of Shiloh greatly discouraged us, and the slaughter was horrifying. But we are getting over that now, and every true son of the South is more determined than ever to fight the war to the bitter end, even if we see our homes in flames and the country laid waste. How is it that Kentucky does not join hands with her sister states?"

"She will, she must," cried Calhoun. "Already thousands of her sons are flocking to the Southern standard. It needs but a victory—a Confederate army to enter her territory, and the people will rise *en masse*. There are not enough traitors or Yankees in the state to keep them down."

"Do you think Beauregard can hold Corinth?" asked the Doctor.

"He can if any one can. He is a great general," answered Calhoun. "But Morgan thinks the loss of Corinth would not be fatal if the army were saved. 'Under no consideration,' says Morgan, 'should Beauregard allow himself to be cooped up in Corinth.' "

[pg 31]

"I reckon he is right," sighed the Doctor; "but may the time never come when he will have to give it up."

"Amen to that!" answered Calhoun.

From Rogersville Calhoun made his way north. He ascertained that the railroad which Mitchell was engaged in repairing was not strongly guarded, and he believed that with five hundred men Morgan could break it almost anywhere between Athens and Columbia.

Near Mount Pleasant he met a Confederate officer with a party of recruits which he was taking south. He sent back by him a statement to Morgan of all he had learned, and added: "Taking everything into consideration, I believe that Pulaski will be the best place for you to strike. I have no fears but that you can capture it, even with your small force."

Calhoun met with his first serious adventure shortly after he had crossed the railroad, which he did a few miles south of Columbia. Thinking to make better time, he took the main road leading to Shelbyville. He was discovered by a squad of Federal cavalry, which immediately gave chase. But he was mounted on a splendid horse, one that he had brought with him from Kentucky. He easily distanced all his pursuers with the exception of three or four, and he was gradually drawing away from all of them, except a lieutenant in command of the squad, who seemed to be as well mounted as himself.

HE EASILY DISTANCED ALL HIS PURSUERS.

[pg 32]

"Only one," muttered Calhoun, looking back, as a pistol-ball whistled by his head; "I can settle him," and he reached for a revolver in his holster. As he did so, his horse stepped into a hole and plunged heavily forward, throwing Calhoun over his head. For a moment he lay bruised and stunned, and then staggered to his feet, only to find the Federal officer upon him.

"Surrender, you Rebel!" cried the officer, but quick as a flash, Calhoun snatched a small revolver which he carried in his belt, and fired.

Instead of hitting the officer, the ball struck the horse fairly in the head, and the animal fell dead. Leaving the officer struggling to extricate himself from his fallen horse, Calhoun scrambled over a fence, and scurried across a small field, beyond which was a wood. A scattering volley was fired by the foremost of the pursuers, but it did no harm, and Calhoun was soon across the field. Mounting the fence on the other side, he stood on the top rail, and turning around, he uttered a shout of defiance, then jumping down, disappeared in the wood.

The foremost of the Federals, a tall, lanky sergeant named Latham, galloped to the side of his commander, who was still struggling to extricate himself from his fallen horse. Springing from his saddle, he helped him to his feet, and anxiously inquired, "Are you hurt, Lieutenant?"

"The Rebel, the Rebel, where is he? Did you get him?" asked the Lieutenant.

[pg 33]

"Get him!" drawled the Sergeant, "I think not. He got across that field as if Old Nick was after him. But once across he had the cheek to stand on the fence and crow like a young rooster. I took a crack at him, but missed."

"Why didn't you pursue him?" demanded the officer, fiercely.

"What! in those woods? Might as well look for a needle in a haymow. But are you hurt, Lieutenant?"

"My leg is sprained," he groaned; "but the worst of it is, Jupiter is dead. Curse that Rebel! how I wish I had him! I would make him pay dearly for that horse."

"Here is the Rebel's horse. I caught him!" exclaimed one of the men, leading up Calhoun's horse, which he had captured. "He looks like a mighty fine horse, only he seems a little lame from his fall."

"That is a fine horse," said Latham, looking him over, "but he has been rode mighty hard. Wonder who that feller can be. I see no signs of any other Reb. He must have been alone. Say, he was a Jim-dandy whoever he was. I thought you had him sure, Lieutenant."

"So did I," answered the Lieutenant, with an oath. "When his horse threw him I had no idea he would try to get away, and ordered him to surrender. But quick as a flash he jerked a revolver from his belt, and fired."

"Better be thankful he hit the horse instead of you," said the Sergeant.

[pg 34]

For answer the Lieutenant limped to a stone, and sitting down, said: "Examine that roll behind the saddle of the horse. Perhaps we can find out who the fellow was."

Sergeant Latham took the roll, which was securely strapped behind Calhoun's saddle, and began to unroll it as carefully as if he suspected it might be loaded.

"A fine rubber and a good woollen blanket," remarked the Sergeant. "Looks mighty like those goods once belonged to our good Uncle Samuel. Bet your life, they are a part of the plunder from Shiloh. Ah! here is a bundle of letters."

"Give them to me," said the Lieutenant.

The Sergeant handed them over, and the officer hastily glanced over them, reading the superscriptions.

"Why," he exclaimed, in surprise, "these letters are all addressed to persons in Kentucky. What could that fellow be doing with letters going to Kentucky? We will see." He tore open one of the letters.

He had read but a few lines when he exclaimed, with a strong expletive, "Boys, I would give a month's pay if we had captured that fellow!"

"Who was he? Who was he?" cried several soldiers in unison.

"He was—let me see—" and the Lieutenant tore open several more of the letters, and rapidly scanned them—"yes, these letters make it plain. He was a Lieutenant Calhoun Pennington, and he [pg 35]was from the Rebel army at Corinth. I take it he was on his way back to Kentucky to recruit for the command of a Captain John H. Morgan. Morgan—Morgan, I have heard of that fellow before. He played the deuce with us in Kentucky last winter: burned the railroad bridge over Bacon Creek, captured trains, tore up the railroad, and played smash generally. These letters all seem to be private ones written by the soldiers in Morgan's command to their relatives and friends back in Kentucky. But he may have carried important dispatches on his person. We let a rare prize slip through our fingers."

"Can't be helped now," dryly remarked Sergeant Latham. "If you had captured him it might have put one bar, if not two, on your shoulder-strap."

The Lieutenant scowled, but did not reply. All the letters were read and passed around. Three or four of them occasioned much merriment, for they were written by love-lorn swains whom the cruel hand of war had torn from their sweethearts.

"Golly! it's a wonder them letters hadn't melted from the sweetness they contained," remarked Sergeant Latham.

"Or took fire from their warmth," put in a boyish looking soldier.

"Not half as warm as the letter I caught you writing to Polly Jones the other day," laughed a comrade. "Boys, I looked over his shoulder and read some of it. I tell you it was hot stuff. 'My dearest Polly!' it commenced, 'I——' "

[pg 36]
But he never finished the sentence, for the young soldier sprang and struck him a blow which rolled him in the dust.

"A fight! a fight!" shouted the men, and crowded around to see the fun.

"Stop that!" roared the Lieutenant, "or I will have you both bucked and gagged when we get to camp. Sergeant Latham, see that both of those men are put on extra duty to-night."

When things had quieted down, others of the letters were read; but some of them occasioned no merriment. Instead, one could see a rough blouse sleeve drawn across the eyes, and a gulping down as if something choked the wearer. These were letters written to the wives and mothers who were watching and waiting for their loved ones to return. These letters reminded them of their own wives and mothers in the Northland, waiting and praying for them.

Suddenly the Lieutenant spoke up: "Boys, we have been wasting time over those letters. That fellow was making his way back to Kentucky. He has no horse. What more natural than that he would try and obtain one at the first opportunity? That old Rebel Osborne lives not more than a mile ahead. You remember we visited him last week, and threatened to arrest him if the railroad was tampered with any more. It was thought he sheltered these wandering bands of Confederates who make it dangerous to step outside the camp. If we push on, we may catch our bird at Osborne's."

[pg 37]
"If not, it will at least give you a chance to see the pretty daughter," remarked the Sergeant.

"Shut up, or I will have you reduced to the ranks," growled the Lieutenant.

The subject was rather a painful one to the Lieutenant, for during his visit to the Osbornes the week before, when he tried to make himself agreeable to the daughter, the lady told him in very plain words what she thought of Yankees.

"It's nearly noon, too," continued the Lieutenant, after the interruption, "and that spring near the house is a splendid place to rest our horses and eat our dinners; so fall in." The Lieutenant slowly mounted Calhoun's horse, for his fall had made him sore, and in none the best of humor, he gave the command, "Forward!"

The plantation of Mr. Osborne was soon reached. It was a beautiful place. The country had not yet been devastated by the cruel hand of war, and the landscape, rich with the growing crops, lay glowing under the bright April sky. The mansion house stood back from the road in a grove of noble native trees, and the whole surroundings betokened a home of wealth and refinement.

From underneath a rock near the house gushed forth a spring, whose waters, clear as crystal, ran away in a rippling stream. It was near this spring that Lieutenant Haines, for that was the officer's name, halted his troops.

"Better throw a guard around the house," he said to Sergeant Latham, "for if that Rebel has [pg 38]found his way here, he may make a sneak out the back way. After you get the guard posted, we will search the house."

As the Sergeant was executing his orders, Mr. Osborne came out of the house, and approaching the troop, to Lieutenant Haines's surprise, gave him a cordial greeting.

"I cannot say I am rejoiced to see you again," he exclaimed, with a smile, "except you come in peace. I trust that the telegraph wire has not been cut, or the railroad torn up again."

"Nothing of the kind has happened," answered the Lieutenant.

"Then I reckon I am in no danger of arrest, and I trust you will take dinner with us. It is nearly ready."

The invitation nearly took away the Lieutenant's breath, but he accepted it gladly. As they were going toward the house, Mr. Osborne remarked, carelessly, "I see you have thrown a guard around the house. Are you afraid of an attack? I know of no body of Confederates in the vicinity."

"The truth is," replied Haines, "we ran into a lone Confederate about a mile from here. We captured his horse, but he succeeded in escaping to the woods, after killing my horse. I did not know but he might have found refuge here; and, excuse me, Mr. Osborne, but I may be under the necessity of searching your house."

"Do as you please," replied Mr. Osborne, coldly; "I have seen no such Confederate; but if I [pg 39]had, I should have concealed him if I could. But do not let this circumstance spoil our good nature, or our dinner."

Just then they met Sergeant Latham returning from posting the guard. "Sergeant, you may withdraw the guard," said the Lieutenant; "Mr. Osborne informs me he has not seen our runaway Confederate."

The Sergeant turned back to carry out the order, muttering, "Confederate! Confederate! The Lieutenant is getting mighty nice; he generally says 'Rebel.' "

If Lieutenant Haines was surprised at the cordial greeting he had received from Mr. Osborne, he was more than surprised at the reception he met from Mrs. Osborne, and especially the daughter, Miss Clara.

Miss Osborne was a most beautiful girl, about twenty years of age. No wonder Lieutenant Haines felt his heart beat faster when he looked upon her. When he met her the week before, she treated him with the utmost disdain; now she greeted him with a smile, and said, "I trust you have not come to carry papa away in captivity. If not, you are welcome."

"Nothing of the sort this time, I am happy to say," exclaimed the Lieutenant, with a bow, "and I hope I shall never be called upon to perform that disagreeable duty."

"Thank you," she answered, with a smile. "Now, you must stay and take dinner with us while your men rest."

[pg 40]

"The Lieutenant tells me he met with quite a little adventure, about a mile below here," said Mr. Osborne.

Miss Osborne looked up inquiringly. Before more could be said Mrs. Osborne announced that dinner was ready, and the Lieutenant sat down to a most sumptuous repast.

"What was Lieutenant Haines's adventure you spoke of?" at length asked Miss Osborne of her father.

"Better let the Lieutenant tell the story, for I know nothing of it," answered Mr. Osborne; "but he spoke of searching the house for a supposed concealed Confederate."

As Mr. Osborne said this, Miss Osborne gave a little gasp and turned pale, but quickly recovering herself, she turned a pair of inquiring eyes on the Lieutenant—eyes that emitted flames of angry light and seemed to look him through and through.

Lieutenant Haines turned very red. "Forgive me if I thought of such a thing," he replied, humbly. "Your father has assured me he has neither seen nor concealed any Confederate officer, and his word is good with me. Make yourself easy. I shall not insult you by searching the house."

A look as of relief came over the face of Miss Osborne as she answered: "I thank you very much. I shall never say again there are no gentlemen among the Yankees. But tell us of your adventure. I thought I heard firing about an hour ago. Was there any one hurt?"

[pg 41]

"Only my poor horse; he was killed," answered Haines.

"Ah! in the days of knighthood to be unhorsed was to be defeated," exclaimed Miss Osborne, gayly. "You must admit yourself vanquished!"

Haines laughingly replied: "I am sorry to disappoint you; but as I captured my enemy's horse and he fled on foot, I cannot admit defeat."

"Then your enemy was a solitary knight?" queried Miss Osborne.

"Yes, but to all appearances a most gallant one."

"Strange," she mused, "who he could be, and what he could be doing in this section. The place for true knights, at this time, is at Corinth."

"From letters captured with his horse, I take it he was from Corinth," said Haines. "From those letters we learned that his name was Calhoun Pennington, that he was a lieutenant in the command of Captain John H. Morgan, a gentleman who has given us considerable trouble, and may give us more, and that he was on his way back to Kentucky to recruit for Morgan's command."

"You say you captured letters?" queried the girl.

"Yes, a whole package of them. They were from members of Morgan's command to their friends back in Kentucky. The boys are having rare fun reading them."

"I suppose it is according to military usages to read all communications captured from the enemy," [pg 42]remarked Miss Osborne with a slight tinge of sarcasm in her tone, "but it seems sacrilege that these private letters should fall into profane hands."

"Some of them were rich," laughed Haines; "they were written by loving swains to their girls. There were others written to wives and mothers, which almost brought tears to our eyes, they were so full of yearnings for home."

"Lieutenant, there was nothing in those letters of value to you from a military standpoint, was there?" suddenly asked Miss Osborne.

"Nothing."

"Then I have a great boon to ask. Will you not give them to me?"

"Why, Miss Osborne, what can you do with them?" asked Haines, in surprise.

"I can at least keep them sacred. Perhaps I can find means of getting them to those for whom they are intended. Think of those wives and mothers watching, waiting for letters which will never come. Oh! give them to me, Lieutenant Haines, and you will sleep the sweeter to-night."

"Your request is a strange one," said the Lieutenant; "yet I can see no harm in granting it. You can have the letters, but the boys may have destroyed some of them by this time."

"Thank you! Oh, thank you! You will never regret your kindness. I shall remember it."

"I only ask you to think better of Yankees, Miss Osborne; we are not all monsters."

Dinner was now over, and Sergeant Latham [pg 43]came to report that the hour for the halt was up, and to ask what were the Lieutenant's orders.

"Have the troop ready, and we will return to camp. I see nothing more we can accomplish here," answered the Lieutenant.

The Sergeant saluted and turned to go, when the officer stopped him with, "Say, Sergeant, you can gather up all those letters we captured and send them up here with my horse."

"Very well," said the Sergeant, but he muttered to himself, as he returned, "Now, I would like to know what the Lieutenant wants of those letters. I bet he has let that girl pull the wool over his eyes."

In a few moments a soldier appeared leading the Lieutenant's horse.

The family had accompanied Lieutenant Haines to the porch. Stepping down to where his horse was, he said to the soldier, "You may return and tell Sergeant Latham to move the troop. I will catch up with you in a few moments. Did you bring the letters?"

"Yes, sir," answered the soldier, saluting, and handing the package to his commander.

"Very well, you may go now."

Lieutenant Haines stood and watched the soldiers while his order was being obeyed, for he did not wish to have any of his men see him give the package to Miss Osborne.

After his troop had moved off, Haines placed the bridle of his horse in the hands of a waiting colored boy, and returning to the porch where Mr. [pg

44]Osborne and the ladies still stood, said: "That is the horse I captured from my foe. He is a beauty, isn't he? Jupiter was a splendid horse, but I do not think I lost anything by the exchange. Here are the letters, Miss Osborne; you see I have kept my promise," and he reached out the package to her.

But before she could take them they were snatched from Haines's hand, and a stern voice said, "I will take the letters, please."

Had a bombshell exploded at Lieutenant Haines's feet he would not have been more surprised, and his surprise changed to consternation when he found himself looking into the muzzle of a revolver. Lieutenant Haines was no coward, but he was unarmed save his sword, and there was no mistaking the look in Calhoun's eye. It meant death if he attempted to draw his sword.

As for Mr. Osborne, he seemed as much surprised as Lieutenant Haines. Miss Osborne gave a little shriek, and then cried. "Oh, how could you betray us!" and stood with clasped hands, and with face as pale as death.

Mr. Osborne was the first to recover from his surprise. "I know not who you are," he said, "but Lieutenant Haines is my guest, and I will have no violence. Lower that weapon!"

Without doing so, Calhoun answered, "If I have done anything contrary to the wishes of those who have so kindly befriended me, I am sorry; but I could not withstand the temptation to claim my own. As it is, I will bid you good day."

[pg 45]

Thus saying, he dashed past them, and snatching the bridle of his horse from the negro boy, he vaulted into the saddle and was away at full speed.

For a moment not a word was spoken, and then Lieutenant Haines turned on Mr. Osborne and said, bitterly, "I congratulate you on the success of your plot. I will not be fool enough again to take the word of a Southern gentleman."

Mr. Osborne flushed deeply, but before he could reply, his daughter sprang in front of him, and faced Lieutenant Haines with flashing eye.

"I will not have my father accused of deception and falsehood," she cried. "He knew nothing of that Confederate being concealed in the house. I alone am to blame, and I told you nothing. I strove to entertain you and keep you from searching the house, and I accomplished my purpose."

"And you got those letters from me to give to him?"

"Yes."

Lieutenant Haines groaned. "It may be some satisfaction to you," he said, "to know that this may mean my undoing, disgrace, a dishonorable dismissal from the service."

22

"I shall take no pleasure in your dishonor," she exclaimed, the color slowly mounting to her cheeks. "I did not intend that Lieutenant Pennington should show himself. It was his rashness that has brought all this trouble."

"How can I return to camp without arms, with[pg 46]out a horse? It would have been a kindness to me if your friend Lieutenant Pennington had put a bullet through my brain."

Mr. Osborne now spoke. "Lieutenant Haines," he said, "my daughter speaks the truth when she says I knew nothing of the Confederate officer being in my house. Had I known it, I should have tried to conceal him, to protect him; but I should not have invited you to be my guest. As my guest, you are entitled to my protection, and I shall make what reparation is in my power." Then turning to the colored boy who had stood by with mouth and eyes wide open, he said, "Tom, go and saddle and bridle Starlight, and bring him around for this gentleman."

"Surely you do not intend to give me a horse, Mr. Osborne," said Haines.

"As my guest, I can do no less," replied Mr. Osborne. "If Lieutenant Pennington had not taken his, I should have let him have one to continue on his way to Kentucky. So you see, after all, I am out nothing."

Just then they were aroused by the sound of horses' feet, and looking up they saw Sergeant Latham accompanied by two soldiers coming on a gallop. Riding up, the Sergeant saluted, and casting his sharp eyes around, said, "Lieutenant, excuse me, but you were so long in joining us that I feared something—an accident—had befallen you, so I came back to see. Where in the world is your horse, Lieutenant?"

[pg 47]

"Coming," answered his superior, briskly, for he had no notion of explaining just then what had happened.

When the colored boy came leading an entirely strange horse with citizen saddle and bridle on, the Sergeant exchanged meaning glances with his companions, but said nothing.

Mounting, Lieutenant Haines bade the family good day, and rode moodily away. No sooner were they out of hearing than the Sergeant, forgetting military discipline, exclaimed, "What in blazes is up, Lieutenant? I suspected something was wrong all the time."

"That is what made you come back, is it?" asked the Lieutenant.

"Yes; I did not march the command far before I halted and waited for you. Pretty soon we heard the sound of a galloping horse, and thought you were coming. But when you didn't appear, I became alarmed and concluded to ride back and see what was the matter."

"Thank you, Sergeant, for your watchfulness. I shall remember it."

Then as they rode along, the Lieutenant told Latham his story.

"And that pesky Reb was concealed in the house all the time, was he?" asked Latham.

"Yes; the girl worked it fine."

The Sergeant laughed long and loud. "And she coaxed the letters from you too. Oh, my! Oh, my!" And he nearly bent double.

[pg 48]

"Shut up, you fool you!" growled Haines. "Say, you must help me out of this scrape."

"Trust me, Lieutenant; I will tell how brave you were, and how you run the Rebel down, and how you would have captured him if he hadn't shot your horse. But look out after this how you let Southern girls fool you."

The Lieutenant sighed. "She is the most beautiful creature I ever saw," he murmured. "Gods! I shall never forget how she looked when she sprang in between me and that Pennington when he had his revolver levelled at my head."

"Forget her," was the sage advice of the Sergeant; but the Lieutenant did not take it.

CHAPTER III.

RECRUITING IN KENTUCKY.

It did not take Calhoun long after he had plunged into the wood to ascertain that he was not pursued; so he slackened his headlong pace, then stopped that he might catch his breath.

"Whew!" he panted, "here is a go. Horse gone—arms, except this small revolver, gone—baggage gone—letters gone. Thank God the dispatches are safe," and he tapped his breast, where they lay hidden. "That is about as tight a place as I care to be in," he continued, as he began to work his way through the woods. "I call this blamed tough luck. Here I am nearly three hundred miles from my destination. A horse I must and will have, and that quickly. Surely the planters in this section are too loyal to the South not to let me have a horse when they know the predicament I am in. I will try my luck at the very first opportunity. If worse come to worst, I will steal one; that is, I will confiscate one."

With this resolve he pushed rapidly on, and after going a half mile or more, he came out of the woods, and beyond lay a fine plantation. "I wonder if those pesky Yankees will trouble me if I try to make that house," he thought. "I will risk it anyway, for if I can reach it, it means a horse."

[pg 50]

Making his way cautiously he soon reached the road in safety. He listened intently, but could hear nothing of the enemy; but from the opposite direction there came the measured beat of a horse's hoofs. Looking up he saw, not a Yankee, but a lady approaching, at a swift gallop. Calhoun's heart gave a great bound, for he knew that no Southern woman would betray him, and he stepped out from his place of concealment and stood in plain view by the side of the road.

When the rider saw him she gave a start of surprise, and then reined in her horse with such ease and grace as to charm him. He saw at a glance she was young and exceedingly beautiful.

"Pardon me," he exclaimed, reaching for his hat, and then he remembered he had none, having lost it when his horse fell. "Excuse my appearance," he laughed. "I find I have no hat to take off. Probably some Yankee has it as a trophy by this time. I am a Confederate officer in distress, and as a daughter of the South, I know I can appeal to you, and not in vain."

"You can," she replied, quickly. "I thought I heard firing and I rode down to see what it meant, as I knew of no party of Confederates in the vicinity."

"A company of Federal cavalry were firing at me," answered Calhoun. "My horse fell, and I had to run, or be captured."

"Were you all alone?" she queried.

"Yes, all alone."

"Then I forgive you for running," she answered, [pg 51]with a ringing laugh, "otherwise I should not. But how came you here, and all alone?"

In a few words Calhoun told her who he was and his business.

"Come with me," she cried, quickly. "Let us gain the house before the Yankees come, as no doubt they will. Father will let you have a horse. If no other be forthcoming, I will give you my Firefly here, although it would almost break my heart to part with him," and she lovingly patted the neck of her gallant steed.

"I sincerely hope such a sacrifice will never be called for," replied Calhoun.

"No sacrifice is too great to aid our beloved cause," she answered; "but come, we are losing time, the Yankees may be here any moment."

If Lieutenant Haines had not stopped to read the captured letters, Calhoun and his fair guide would not have reached the house undiscovered. As it was, they had hardly entered it when the Federals hove in sight.

"There is that Yankee officer riding my horse!" exclaimed Calhoun. "How I should like to meet him alone."

"They are going to stop," gasped the girl. "They may search the house, but they will not if I can outwit them. Mother," she said, to an elderly lady who had just entered and was gazing at Calhoun in surprise, "take this officer upstairs and conceal him. There is now no time for explanations. The Yankees are in the yard."

[pg 52]

The mother, without a word, motioned Calhoun to follow her, and led him upstairs. Hardly had they disappeared when her father entered.

"There is that Lieutenant Haines and his company visiting us again," he said, with some anxiety. "I wonder what they want."

"Father," said the girl, "go and meet Lieutenant Haines, use him nicely. Invite him to dinner."

Mr. Osborne looked at his daughter in surprise. "I never expected to see the time you would want me to invite a Yankee officer to dinner," he said.

"Never mind now, I will explain afterwards. Go quick, for I see he is throwing a guard around the house," was her answer.

Mr. Osborne went, wondering what had come over his daughter, and was entirely successful in carrying out her scheme, although it was unknown to him. Before his return, Mrs. Osborne came downstairs, her face denoting her anxiety.

"Mother," said the girl, "do not let father know we have any one concealed. It will enable him to say truly he knows of no Confederate around. And, mother, I have told him to invite the Federal commander—it's that odious Lieutenant Haines—to dinner. Be nice to him. Use him like a welcome, honored guest. We must disarm all suspicion, and keep them from searching the house, if possible."

We have seen how well her plan worked, and how completely Lieutenant Haines was thrown off his guard. Little did he think that while he was [pg 53]enjoying his dinner downstairs, the Confederate officer who had escaped him was feasting like a king upstairs.

It soon became evident to Calhoun that there was no danger of the house being searched, and from a window he observed all that was passing without. When he saw the troop ride away, and his own horse led up to the house for the Federal commander, that spirit of recklessness for which he was noted came over him, and without thinking of what the effect might be on those who had, at great risk, so kindly befriended him, he resolved to try to capture his own. With satisfaction he saw the last Yankee depart, leaving the commander behind.

"Now is my time!" he exclaimed, exultingly, and looking to see that his revolver was in perfect condition, he crept softly downstairs, and as has been noted, was perfectly successful. So sudden was his appearance, so swift were his movements, that the little company could only gaze after him in astonishment until he had disappeared.

For a few minutes Calhoun was hilarious over the success of his bold dash; then came to him the thought that he had cruelly wronged the Osbornes in what he had done. He suddenly checked his horse, and then turned as if he would ride back, hesitated, then turned once more, and rode on his way, but more slowly.

"It is too late now," he sighed, to himself, "to undo the wrong I may have done. To think I may [pg 54]have brought trouble on the head of that glorious girl, who even would give me her own horse! It's the meanest trick you ever did, Calhoun Pennington, and it would serve you right if the Yankees captured you."

It was in no enviable frame of mind that Calhoun continued his journey. It was not long before he noticed that his horse was lame. The fall that he had had, had evidently strained his shoulder. Calhoun more bitterly than ever regretted that he had not restrained himself. If he had, he might now have been riding a good fresh horse, given him by Mr. Osborne.

"Serves me right," he groaned. "Oh, what a fool, and not only a fool, but a brute, I have been. That girl! I can't help thinking that I may have got her into serious trouble."

A few miles more and his horse became so lame that Calhoun had to come down to a walk. He dismounted with a ruthful face.

"It's no use," he said; "I shall have to leave him. Where can I get another horse?"

The opportunity came sooner than he expected. He had dismounted in a wood, a thick growth of cedars screening him from the observation of any one passing along the road. Hearing the sound of an approaching horseman, he crept to the side of the road, and to his surprise saw a Federal officer approaching unattended. He was riding leisurely along unsuspicious of danger, and whistling merrily. With Calhoun to think was to act.

[pg 55]

"Halt! Surrender!" were the words which saluted the startled officer, as Calhoun sprang into the road by his side, and levelled a revolver at his breast.

The officer was a brave man, and he reached for his revolver.

"Touch that weapon, and you are a dead man," said Calhoun, in a low, firm voice. "Fool, don't you see I have the drop on you?"

The set features of the Federal relaxed, he even smiled as he replied: "I guess you are right. No use kicking. What is your pleasure?"

"Dismount. No, on this side."

The officer did as he was bidden. Calhoun took hold of the horse's bridle, still keeping the man covered with his revolver.

"Now," continued Calhoun, "your name, rank, and regiment."

"Mark Crawford, Captain Company B, —th Ohio Cavalry," was the answer.

"Captain Crawford, I am very happy to have met you. As it may be a little inconvenient for you and me to travel together, I ask you to give me your parole of honor that you will not bear arms against the Southern Confederacy until regularly exchanged."

"May I be permitted to ask," replied the Captain, with a peculiar smile, "who it is that makes this demand?"

"Lieutenant Calhoun Pennington of Morgan's cavalry."

[pg 56]

"Well, Lieutenant Calhoun Pennington of Morgan's cavalry, you may go to the devil, before I will give you my parole."

Calhoun was astounded at the reply. "I am afraid I shall have to shoot you," he said.

"Shoot an unarmed prisoner if you will," was the fearless reply; "it would be an act worthy of a Rebel and traitor. Lieutenant Pennington, I am well aware you are alone, that you cannot take me with you. It would be an act of cowardice in me to give you my parole."

As Captain Crawford said this, he folded his arms across his breast and looked Calhoun in the face without the quiver of a muscle.

Calhoun was filled with admiration at the bravery of the man. "Captain, you are too brave a man to die a dog's death, neither would I think of shooting a defenceless man. I shall let you go, but shall be under the necessity of borrowing your horse. You will find mine in the bushes there badly crippled. Good-bye. May we meet again." Thus saying, Calhoun sprang on the Captain's horse, and dashed away.

Captain Crawford stood looking after him until he was out of sight. "May you have your wish, my fine fellow!" he exclaimed; "I would ask nothing better than that we should meet again."

Both had their wish; they met again, not once, but several times.

"A brave fellow, that," said Calhoun to himself, as he galloped away. "I would as soon have [pg 57]thought of shooting my brother. He didn't bluff worth a cent."

The horse which Calhoun had captured was a good one, and he rode him for many a day. We will not follow Calhoun in all his adventures in his journey toward his destination in Kentucky. Suffice it to say, he met with numerous perils and made some narrow escapes, but at last found himself near Danville. There resided a few miles from Danville a rich planter named Ormsby. Calhoun knew him as an ardent friend of the South, one well versed in all secret attempts to take Kentucky out of the Union, and one who kept well posted in everything which pertained to the welfare of the Confederacy; and at Ormsby's he resolved to stop and lay his plans for the future.

He was received with open arms. "So you are from John Morgan," said Mr.

Ormsby, "and wish to recruit for his command. You have come at an opportune time. To-morrow there is a secret meeting of prominent Confederates near Harrodsburg. I am to attend. You will meet a number there for whom you have letters. Of course you will go with me?"

Tired as he was, Calhoun rode that night with Mr. Ormsby to be present at the meeting. If he was to meet Morgan at Glasgow during the first days of May, his time was short, very short, and what he should do had to be done quickly.

When he was introduced to those present as from Morgan, and just from Corinth, their enthusi[pg 58]asm knew no bounds. He had to tell the story of Shiloh, of the tragic death of Governor Johnson, of the retreat, but how the spirit of the Southern army was unbroken, and that the South would not, and could not, be conquered.

To his delight, Calhoun found that two companies of cavalry were nearly ready to take the field, and it was unanimously agreed that they should cast their fortune with Morgan.

"I believe that Morgan with a thousand men can ride clear to the Ohio River," declared Calhoun. "It only remains for Kentuckians to rally to his standard, and give him the support that he desires."

It was agreed that the companies should be filled as soon as possible, and should go whenever Calhoun said the word.

Calhoun returned with Mr. Ormsby, as he wished to enter Danville to visit his parents. Disguised as a country boy with produce to sell, he had no trouble in passing the pickets into town. With a basket of eggs on his arm, he knocked at the back door of his father's residence. It was opened by Chloe, the cook.

"Want eny good fresh eggs?" asked Calhoun.

"No; go way wid ye, yo' po' white trash," snapped the old negro woman, as she attempted to shut the door in his face.

"Chloe!"

The dish which she held in her hand went clattering to the floor. "Fo' de land's sake!" she [pg 59]cried, "if it isn't Massa Calhoun. De Lawd bress yo', chile! De Lawd bress you!" And she seized him and fairly dragged him into the house.

"Hush, Chloe, not so loud. Don't tell father I am here yet. And, Chloe, don't whisper I am here to a soul. If the Yankees found out I was here, they might hang me."

"Oh, Lawd! Oh, Lawd! hang youn' Massa?" she cried. "Ole Chloe tell no one."

"That's right, Aunt Chloe. Now bake those biscuits I see you are making, in a hurry. And make my favorite pie. I want to eat one more meal of your cooking. No one can cook like Aunt Chloe."

"Yo' shell hev a meal fit fo' de king!" cried the old negress, her face all aglow.

"You must hurry, Chloe, for I can't stay long. Now I will go and surprise father." And surprise him he did. The old Judge could hardly believe the seeming country boy was his son.

"Where in the world did you come from?" he asked.

"From Corinth," answered Calhoun. "I am now back to recruit for Morgan."

"So you have joined Morgan, have you?"

"Yes. Now that Governor Johnson is killed, I know of no service I would like as well as to ride with Morgan."

"You could have come home, my son."

"Father! what do you mean? Come home while the South is bleeding at every pore? Come [pg 60]home like a craven while the contest is yet undecided?"

"I am wrong, my son; but it is so hard for you, my only child, to be in the army. Oh! that dreadful battle of Shiloh! The agony, the sleepless nights it has caused me! Thank God you are yet safe."

"Yes, father, and I trust that the hand of a kind Providence will still protect me. But here is a letter from Morgan."

The Judge adjusted his spectacles, and read the letter with much interest. "My son," he said, after he had finished it, "it is well you were not captured with such letters on your person. It might have cost you your life. Even now I tremble for your safety. Does any one know you are in Danville?"

"Only Aunt Chloe, and she is as true as steel."

"Yet there is danger. I know the house is under the closest surveillance. The Federal authorities know I am an ardent friend of the South, and they watch me continually. Morgan says in his letter that he hopes it will not be long before he will be in Kentucky."

"And mark my word," cried Calhoun, "it will not be! Before many weeks the name of Morgan will be on every tongue. He will be the scourge of the Yankee army. But, father, what of Uncle Dick and Fred?"

"Colonel Shackelford is at home minus a leg. The Federal authorities have paroled him. Fred is [pg 61]at home nursing him. Your uncle won imperishable honors on the field of Shiloh. What a pity he has such a son as

Fred!"

Calhoun's face clouded. The remembrance of his last meeting with Fred still rankled in his breast. "I never want to see him again," he said.

The Judge sighed, "Oh, this war! this war!" he exclaimed; "how it disrupts families! You and Fred used to be the same as brothers. I thought nothing could come in between you and him. Calhoun, he is a noble boy, notwithstanding he is a traitor to his state and the South. They say he is going to resign from the army for the sake of his father. Won't you go and see him?"

"No," brusquely answered Calhoun, yet he felt in his heart he was wronging his cousin by his action.

Dinner was now announced by Aunt Chloe, and it did her honest old heart good to see the way that Calhoun ate.

"I jes' believe dat air chile hab had nuthin' to eat fo' a week," she declared.

"I reckon I shall have to go now," said Calhoun, rising reluctantly from the table. "I have already made too long a visit for a country boy with eggs to sell. I declare, Aunt Chloe, I do believe I should kill myself eating if I stayed any longer."

"No danger of dat, chile," replied Aunt Chloe, grinning.

The words of parting were few. "Do be careful, my son," said Judge Pennington, his voice [pg 62]trembling with emotion. "God only knows whether I shall ever see you again or not."

As Calhoun started to leave, a pair of sharp eyes was watching him. Those eyes belonged to a pretty girl named Jennie Freeman. The Freemans were Judge Pennington's nearest neighbors, but Mr. Freeman was as strong a Union man as the Judge was a Secessionist. Once the best of friends, a coldness had sprung up between them since the opening of the war.

Jennie was two years older than Calhoun, but they had been playmates from babyhood, and were great friends. Jennie called him her knight-errant. More than once he had carried a pair of black eyes in fighting her battles when some of the larger boys had teased her.

Jennie had seen the supposed country boy enter the kitchen of Judge Pennington, and there was something in his walk and manner which attracted her attention. "If that isn't Cal Pennington I am a sinner!" she exclaimed to herself.

She was on the watch for him, and when he remained so long she became more than ever convinced that her suspicions were correct. At length the boy came out with his basket on his arm.

"Hi, there, boy! come here," she called. "What have you to sell?"

Calhoun paid no attention to her call, but hurried on the faster.

"I tell you, boy, you had better come here if [pg 63]you know when you are well off!" she called, in a threatening voice, "Oh, I know you!"

Calhoun saw that he was discovered, and that his best way was to try to make peace with her. "What do yer want?" he growled, as he walked toward her. "I hev nuthin' to sell; all sold out."

"Well, I never!" said the girl as Calhoun came up. "Do you think I don't know you, Cal Pennington? A pretty figure you cut in those old clothes, and with that basket. What in the world are you doing here?"

"Hush, Jennie, not so loud. If discovered, I might be hanged," said Calhoun, in a low voice.

"Yankees don't hang traitors; they ought to," replied the girl, with a toss of her head.

"But don't you see I am in disguise? I might be taken as a spy."

"What are you but one? I ought to inform on you at once."

"Jennie, you wouldn't do that. I am only here to see father and mother. I had to come in disguise, or I might be taken prisoner by the Yankees."

"And you are not here to spy? You know there are many rumors afloat?" asked the girl.

"Just here to visit father and mother. Can you blame me, Jennie?" As Calhoun said this his heart smote him, for while it was true he was in Danville for the purpose of visiting his parents, his mission to Kentucky was for an entirely different object.

[pg 64]

"Now, Jennie, you won't tell on me, will you?" he continued, in a coaxing tone.

"No, if you behave yourself; but don't let me hear of any of your capers," answered the girl.

"You won't, Jennie. Good-bye. I may be able to do you a good turn one of these days."

Jennie stood looking after him until he disappeared, then shaking her head, she went into the house, saying: "I couldn't inform on him, if he is a Rebel."

The next few days were busy ones for Calhoun. He visited Nicholasville,

34

Lexington, Harrodsburg; had interviews with a large number of prominent Secessionists; found out, as near as possible, the number of Federal troops garrisoning the different towns; in fact, gathered information of the utmost value to Morgan if he should ever raid Kentucky.

But all these things could not be done without rumors reaching the Federal authorities. It was known that the Southern element was extremely active; that recruiting for the Confederate army was going on; and at last, the name of Calhoun Pennington was mentioned. Some one who knew him well declared that he had seen him, and it was common report he was back recruiting for Morgan's command. The Federal commander at Danville was ordered to keep a close watch on the house of Judge Pennington to see if it was not visited by his son.

It was on the evening of May 2d, and Calhoun [pg 65]was in Lexington when he was startled by hearing the news-boys crying, "Pulaski, Tennessee, captured by John Morgan!" "He is headed north, closely pursued by the Federal forces!"

Then Morgan had commenced his raid. There was no time to be lost. That night, the next day, and the next night horsemen could be seen galloping furiously along unfrequented roads, throughout central Kentucky. The word was, "Meet at the rendezvous near Harrodsburg." Three days afterwards, two hundred of the best, the bravest, and the noblest youths of Kentucky were ready to march to join Morgan. Each one of them had provided his own outfit. They asked no pay to fight for their beloved South.

Before going, Calhoun determined to pay his father one more visit, although he knew it was dangerous to do so. Concealing his horse in a thicket outside the limits of the city, he waited until dark, then stole across fields, and through alleys home.

No sooner did the Judge see him than he cried, "Calhoun! Calhoun! what have you done! Do you know they are on the watch for you?"

"I had to see you once more before I went," answered Calhoun. "I was careful, and I do not think any one saw me come. I have some things of importance to tell you."

Father and son talked together for some five minutes in low, confidential tones, when they were interrupted by Jennie Freeman bursting unan[pg 66]nounced into the room and crying, "Run, Cal, run! the soldiers are coming! They are most here!" And before either could say a word, she was out again like a flash.

"Who would have thought it, of that Abolitionist Freeman's daughter," gasped the Judge. "Fly, my boy, fly! and may God protect you."

Calhoun knew his danger. Grasping his trusty revolver, he cried, "Good-bye, all," and ran through the house to pass out by the back way. Just as he reached the door, it was opened, and he fairly rushed into the arms of a soldier who was entering. So surprised were both that they could only stare at each other for a brief second; but Calhoun recovered himself first, and dealt the soldier a terrific blow over the head with the butt of his revolver. The soldier sank down with a moan, and Calhoun sprang out over his prostrate body, only to meet and overturn another soldier who was just ascending the steps. The force of the collision threw him headlong, but he was up again in a twinkling, and disappeared in the darkness, followed by a few ineffectual shots by the baffled Federals.

Judge Pennington heard the firing and groaned, "My son, oh, my son!"

The firing had alarmed the neighborhood, and there were many pale faces, for the people knew not what it meant.

A short time afterwards a Federal officer arrested [pg 67]Judge Pennington, and he was dragged off to jail. But he did not think of himself. "My son," he asked, "was he captured? was he hurt?"

"I think the devil protected his own," roughly replied the officer, "but we will attend to you for harboring Rebels."

Judge Pennington lay in jail among criminals, not only that night, but for nearly a week. There was talk of sending him to a Northern prison as a dangerous man. But Fred Shackelford heard of his arrest and his probable fate, and came in and had a stormy interview with the Federal commander. He showed that Judge Pennington had committed no overt act; that his son, who was a Confederate soldier, had simply come to visit him, and had resisted capture, as any soldier had a right to do. As Fred threatened to report the case to the commander of the Department, the Judge was released.

Jennie Freeman had many qualms of conscience over what she had done. But Judge Pennington kept her secret well, telling only Fred; and when he congratulated Jennie over her act, she felt relieved; for young Shackelford was not only known as a favorite of General Nelson, but as one of the most daring and successful of Union scouts.

Calhoun met with no more adventures. He had no trouble in finding his way to his horse, and he lost no time in joining his comrades.

"Boys, John Morgan told me to meet him at [pg 68]Glasgow," he cried, and two hundred voices answered with a loud "Hurrah! we will do it!"

Little did Calhoun or they think that at that very time John Morgan, his forces defeated and scattered, was fleeing before the enemy. But like them, he had set his face toward Glasgow.

[pg 69]

CHAPTER IV.

MORGAN'S FIRST RAID.

All through the month of April General Halleck had been concentrating the mighty armies of almost the entire West for the purpose of crushing Beauregard at Corinth. For a month the two armies lay but a few miles apart, almost daily skirmishes taking place between the outposts.

During the month General O. M. Mitchell had overrun Middle Tennessee, and was holding the Memphis and Charleston railroad from Decatur to Bridgeport, Alabama. Two railroads led south from Nashville, Tennessee, both connecting with the Memphis and Charleston Railroad, one at Decatur, and the other at Stevenson, Alabama. Both of these roads were of vital importance to General Mitchell, for on them he depended for transportation for the sustenance of his army.

These roads had been badly damaged by the Confederate army when it retreated from Nashville, and General Mitchell was busily engaged in repairing them. If repaired and held, it meant that Chattanooga must fall, and the Confederate army be driven still farther south.

John H. Morgan, now promoted to a colonelcy, believed that with a small force the rear of the [pg 70]Federal army could be raided, the railroads cut, bridges burned, and their communications so destroyed that they would be forced to fall back. General Beauregard was not so sanguine. While great damage might be done, and the Federal army subjected to much inconvenience, the contest, after all, would have to be decided by the great armies. Then he needed every man, as Halleck was about to move.

At last he gave Morgan permission to make his raid, but with a force not to exceed five hundred.

It was in the last days of April that Morgan started with his little force, on what seemed to many certain destruction. But every man in the command was full of enthusiasm. They had unlimited faith in their leader, and where he went they would follow.

Following almost the exact route taken by Calhoun, Morgan's first blow fell on Pulaski, Tennessee. So swift and unexpected had been his movements that the Federals were taken completely by surprise. The place was surrendered without a struggle.

Moving rapidly north, the command attacked and, without any loss, captured a wagon-train en route from Columbia to Athens. Thus at the very commencement of his raid, Morgan captured Pulaski, with all its military stores, a wagon-train, and some two hundred and seventy prisoners, and this without the loss of a man. Among the prisoners captured were a son of General O. M. [pg 71]Mitchell, and our old acquaintance, Lieutenant Haines.

The prisoners were all paroled, and were astonished at the kind treatment they received. Both Captain Jumper, who was in charge of the wagon-train, and the son of General Mitchell were loud in their praise of the way they were used by Morgan.

After destroying all the Federal property captured, and damaging the railroad as much as possible, the command continued on their raid, their route taking them by the plantation of Mr. Osborne. The welcome they received there was a royal one. Colonel Morgan stopped and took dinner with the family.

Here he heard of the adventure of Calhoun, and he laughed long and heartily over the way Calhoun had recovered his horse.

"Tell him," said Miss Osborne, "that I forgive him his abrupt leaving, as no harm came to father. By the way, Lieutenant Haines has become quite friendly, coming out to see us two or three times."

"No one can blame him, even if you give him but a moment of your company," replied Morgan, gallantly. "But Miss Osborne, I am sorry to say we took your friend prisoner. He was paroled, and no doubt is now on his way North."

Miss Osborne blushed, and then said, "A good riddance; I trust I shall never see him again. But he was kind to papa. He even returned the horse; would not keep him."

[pg 72]

"That is lucky," responded Morgan, "for if he hadn't been returned, one of my men would be riding him now, and your chance of getting him would be small."

From Pulaski Morgan pushed northeast, avoiding Shelbyville and Murfreesboro, both of these places being too strongly garrisoned for him to attack with his small force. He crossed the Nashville and Chattanooga railroad ten miles north of Murfreesboro, burned the depot, and destroyed as much of the track as his limited time would admit. From there he rode straight for Lebanon, Tennessee, which place he reached just at nightfall. The inhabitants received him with the wildest demonstration of joy. But trouble was in store for him. His men, wearied with their long ride, and elated over their continued success, became careless. They knew they were among friends, and thought that no harm could come to them, so they slept without fear.

The Federal authorities had become thoroughly alarmed over his progress. Strong bodies of troops were in swift pursuit, from Shelbyville, from Murfreesboro, and from Nashville.

Just before daylight the Federals charged into the little city with whoop and hurrah. Taken entirely by surprise, Morgan's men thought only of flight. Two companies under the command of Colonel Robert C. Wood being cut off from their horses, threw themselves into a college building in the outskirts of the city, and for three hours [pg 73]defended themselves with desperation. At last being out of ammunition they were forced to surrender.

In this unfortunate affair Morgan lost nearly two hundred of his best troops. The rest were more or less scattered. He himself was chased for eighteen miles, and the pursuit ceased only when he, with the remnant of his troops, had crossed the Cumberland.

The Federals thought they had thoroughly whipped Morgan, and he would give them no more trouble. But they did not know the man. He had started for Kentucky, and to Kentucky he would go. After crossing the Cumberland, he halted, gathered his scattered command together, and then with less than three hundred men, started for Glasgow.

"Lieutenant Pennington will meet us at Glasgow with reinforcements," he told his men.

But there were some of his officers who had misgivings. Chief among these was Captain Conway. Speaking to another officer, a Captain Mathews, Conway said: "It's strange that the Colonel has such confidence in that young upstart. As for me, I look for no reinforcements. The best thing we can do is to get back as soon as possible."

"Captain, what is the matter?" asked Mathews. "What has that young fellow done that you have taken such a dislike to him?"

"Nothing; but the idea of sending a mere boy [pg 74]on such an important mission! Why did he not send some one back with influence?"

"Pennington is well connected; you know his father is Judge Pennington of Danville."

"That makes little difference. His mission will be a failure; see if it isn't. We shall see no reinforcements at Glasgow."

Just then Morgan came riding along, and seeing Conway said, "Captain, I want to thank you for the gallant manner in which you held back the enemy while the command crossed the Cumberland. You did nobly."

This praise so pleased Conway that for a time he forgot his supposed grievance.

Without further trouble from the Federals, the little command reached Glasgow, where they were received with open arms by the inhabitants. Houses were thrown open to them and food provided in abundance. But nothing had been heard of any reinforcements.

"What did I tell you?" said Conway to Mathews.

"Wait," was the answer.

The night was an anxious one. Morning came, but still nothing was heard of any reinforcements.

"We will wait another day," said Morgan.

About noon cheering was heard, and Morgan's men nearly went wild with enthusiasm, as nearly two hundred splendidly mounted men came galloping into camp.

When the captain in command reported, Morgan [pg 75]thanked him in the warmest terms, and then looking eagerly around, said: "Where is Lieutenant Pennington? I do not see him."

"Lieutenant Pennington," answered the Captain, "asked leave to take twenty men and scout toward Cave City. I gave him permission to do so. He has an idea that the railroad might be reached and broken at that point."

"Ah! I have thought so myself," replied Morgan. "I shall wait for his report with interest."

The arrival of the two fresh companies had raised the command to as large, or larger, than it was when it started from Corinth, and every man was eager to go on. It was nearly night when Calhoun reported with his little company. He was jubilant over what he had discovered.

"Colonel," he said, "we can easily capture Cave City, and thus sever the connection between Louisville and Nashville. The place is lightly guarded."

"Oh! If we could only take the place, and capture the train on which my gallant men taken prisoners at Lebanon are being taken North, I should be supremely happy," said Morgan, with much feeling.

"Perhaps we can," replied Calhoun, with enthusiasm.

"How about going farther north than Cave City?" asked Morgan.

Calhoun shook his head. "It will not do," he replied; "all the towns are too strongly held for your small force to cope with."

[pg 76]

"At least we can try Cave City," answered Morgan, and orders were given for the command to be ready to march at sundown. The vicinity of Cave City was reached about two o'clock in the morning. The column was halted and the men were ordered to rest until daylight.

As soon as it was light, Calhoun, with a soldier named Emory, was sent in advance to the place. They were disguised as countrymen, and were to linger around the depot, and when the charge came they were to prevent the telegraph operator from sending warning of the raid.

Dressed in homespun clothes, and riding sorry steeds, Calhoun and Emory played their part to perfection. Their entrance into the little place caused no comment, and excited no suspicion. Sauntering into the depot, they gazed curiously around.

SAUNTERING INTO THE DEPOT THEY GAZED CURIOUSLY AROUND.

"What's that?" asked Calhoun, pointing at the clicking telegraph instrument.

"That, my boy," said the operator, patronizingly, "is a telegraphic instrument. Did you never see one before?"

"No. What makes it tick?"

"Lightning, my son, lightning; that's a lightning-catcher."

Calhoun opened his eyes in wonder. "Jes' heah that," he said to Emory. "What is it fer?" he continued, turning his attention to the operator once more.

"To send messages," replied the operator, [pg 77]amused at the ignorance displayed. "With this little instrument, I can talk with any one at Louisville or Nashville."

"What's yo-uns givin' we-uns," drawled Calhoun. "Do yo' take we-uns fo' a fule?"

A guard who stood idly by laughed long and loud. "A fine specimen of Southern chivalry," he chuckled.

Just then there came the sound of cheering, pistol shots, and the clatter of horses' hoofs, mingled with affrighted cries.

"By heavens! the town is being raided," shouted the operator, as he sprang to his instrument.

"Stop!" thundered Calhoun. "Touch that instrument and you are a dead man."

The operator looked up amazed, only to find himself covered with a revolver.

The guard at the same time was looking into the muzzle of a weapon held by Emory.

"Drop that gun," said Emory to the trembling man.

The gun went clanging to the floor.

"You two stand there in the corner with your hands above your heads," commanded Calhoun.

The operator and the guard obeyed with alacrity. "Keep them covered with your revolver, Emory," continued Calhoun, "while I see what I can find. Think I will pocket these dispatches first; they may be of use."

Just then he glanced out of the window and saw four or five soldiers running toward the depot. [pg 78]There might be more following. Giving the telegraphic instrument a kick which sent it flying, he started to leave in a hurry. Then noticing the blanched faces of the soldiers, as they came rushing into the depot, he called out, "No use running, Emory, we can take the whole crowd prisoners, green as we look."

And they did. There was no fight in the frightened men.

When the excitement was over Calhoun looked over the dispatches which he had captured, and found that a passenger train was due from the south in half an hour, and that it had orders to wait at Cave City for a freight train to pass, coming from the north. This was good news, and Morgan's men waited, in glee, for the approaching trains.

At the appointed time the passenger train came rolling in. The reception it received astonished every one on board. To Colonel Morgan's great disappointment his men captured at Lebanon were not on the train; but there were a great many Federal soldiers, principally officers, aboard on their way North. A few of these at first made some show of resistance; but when they saw how hopeless their case was, they sullenly submitted to their fate.

It was not long before the freight train came slowly puffing in. It was an immense train of forty-five cars, heavily loaded with rations, clothing, and munitions of war for Buell's army. Morgan's [pg 79]men freely helped themselves from the rich stores to everything that they needed and could carry, and then the work of destruction began.

The torch was applied, and soon the two trains were wrapped in flames. The prisoners, who had gloomily watched the work of destruction, were now lined up, and told that they would be released upon their giving their parole. This they gladly consented to do.

It fell to Calhoun to take a list of their names, with rank and regiment.

"Don't see why I should be asked to give another parole," growled a lieutenant. "I gave you fellows one at Pulaski, a short time since, and was on my way home now, to stay until I am exchanged. How often do you want to take a fellow prisoner, anyway?"

Calhoun glanced up much amused. The officer started, stared at him a moment, and then abruptly asked, "Is your name Pennington?"

"It is, Lieutenant Pennington, if you please."

"You and I have met before."

"Ah! I know you now. I wish to thank you, for I am told you did not visit your wrath on the Osbornes on account of my abrupt leave-taking."

"No, the girl had concealed you in the house unbeknown to the old gentleman, and as he had assured me there were no Confederates about, he felt real cut up about it. He actually proffered me another horse in the place of the one you took. Said I was his guest, and should not suffer."

[pg 80]

"Just like an old-fashioned Southern gentleman, the very personification of honesty," replied Calhoun. "It may interest you, Lieutenant, to know that recovering my horse did me little good, for he went so lame I had to leave him."

"And took mine in his place," spoke up a fine-looking Federal officer who stood near, and whose name Calhoun had not yet taken.

"Captain Crawford, as I live," exclaimed Calhoun, extending his hand.

"Captain, I want to give you my sincere thanks. That was a fine horse you loaned me. Must have Kentucky blood in him. I am riding him yet. How about your parole, Captain? You know you absolutely refused to give it to me."

"I have changed my mind."

"Ah! that is good. If you refused this time we might be obliged to take you along with us, and that might not be agreeable to you."

As the Captain gave his parole, he said, "This is the second time we have met. There may be a third meeting, and it may be my time."

"*Au revoir*," gayly replied Calhoun.

Little did he think then of their next meeting, and what it would mean to him.

The prisoners all being paroled, and the work of destruction complete, Morgan's command returned to Glasgow, loaded with booty.

The capture of the trains and the breaking of the railroad at Cave City caused the greatest excitement throughout the Federal army. It showed the [pg 81]Federal authorities how weak their line of communication was. Although so much depended on Morgan's capture, he was left for some days almost unmolested. He made a demonstration toward Lebanon, captured a number of prisoners, and then, when the combination against him grew too strong to be resisted, he withdrew at his leisure and at length found rest for his command at Chattanooga.

CHAPTER V.
MORGAN'S FIRST GREAT RAID.

The struggle for the possession of Corinth was ended. General Halleck, with his immense army of one hundred and twenty-five thousand men, had thought to reduce the place by regular siege, and force General Beauregard to capitulate, surrendering himself with his whole army.

But Beauregard was too able a general to be caught in a trap. For a month he held the Federal army at bay, and then, when Halleck was about to spring his trap, Beauregard silently withdrew, leaving to him but a barren victory.

The Confederate army was saved, and to the Federal forces the occupation of Corinth proved as demoralizing as a defeat. The result showed that John Morgan was right when he said that the hope of the South rested, not on the occupancy of any single place, but on the safety of its armies.

The fall of Corinth at once changed the theatre of war. The Federal army was divided, the Army of the Tennessee, under Grant, remaining in Mississippi and Western Tennessee, and the Army of the Ohio, under Buell, being ordered to march east and capture Chattanooga.

If Buell had acted promptly and swiftly, he might have been successful, and the death-blow [pg 83]would have been given to the Confederacy long before it was. But he moved slowly and haltingly, and the golden opportunity was lost. It gave the Confederacy time to transfer to Chattanooga the larger part of the army which had been at Corinth. The command of this army was given to General Braxton Bragg, a brave man, and by many thought to be one of the ablest generals of the South.

It at once became the dream of General Bragg to gather as large an army as possible, then march northward clear to the Ohio River, sweeping everything before him. This dream came near being realized. It was made possible by the efforts and deeds of two men, General John H. Morgan and General N. B. Forrest. These two great raiders and leaders of cavalry nearly turned the scale in favor of the Confederacy. They raided the rear of the Federal army, tore up railroads, destroyed millions of dollars' worth of property, and captured thousands of prisoners. They ran General Buell nearly distracted, and caused him not to know which way to turn. They made it possible for General Bragg to reach Kentucky unopposed; and if, after reaching Kentucky, General Bragg had proved as able a leader of infantry as Morgan was of cavalry, Buell's army would have been destroyed. While Bragg was organizing his army at Chattanooga, another Confederate army was being organized at Knoxville under General E. Kirby Smith; this army was to invade Kentucky by way of

East Tennessee, while General Bragg was to invade by [pg 84]way of Middle Tennessee. Once in Kentucky, the two armies were to unite.

This programme was successfully carried out, and yet the whole movement was a failure, as far as the occupancy of Kentucky was concerned.

After the fall of Corinth, Colonel Morgan rendezvoused his little force at Chattanooga. From Chattanooga he proceeded to Knoxville, where he at once began the preparations for another raid. As Cumberland Gap was held by the Federals, Colonel Morgan decided to cross over into Middle Tennessee before invading Kentucky. His command consisted of about nine hundred men, made up of two regiments and two independent companies. His own regiment was commanded by Lieutenant-Colonel Basil Duke. All through Morgan's career Colonel Duke was his chief adviser, so much so that many claim that Morgan's success was mainly due to Colonel Duke.

"Why don't some one shoot Basil Duke through the head, and blow out John Morgan's brains?" exclaimed a disgusted Federal officer, after a fruitless effort to catch Morgan.

But the officer was mistaken; both had brains. Like Grant and Sherman they worked hand in hand, and one needed the other. Together they were invincible.

Before leaving Knoxville Morgan picked out twenty-five men, mounted on the best and fleetest horses, and placed them in the command of Calhoun Pennington. They were to be the scouts of the [pg 85]command, and well did they do their duty. More than once did they save Morgan from heavy loss by ascertaining the movements of the enemy.

Morgan left Knoxville July 4th. His route lay directly west over the Cumberland Mountains to Sparta, a distance of one hundred and four miles. This, in spite of the rough roads, he made in three days. Many of the mountaineers of East Tennessee clung to the Union, and much of the way he had to ride through almost as hostile a country as if raiding through the North. The utmost vigilance had to be used, and Calhoun, with his scouts, was kept well in front to see that the road was clear.

On the second day's march there was the crack of a rifle from a mountainside, and one of the scouts tumbled from his horse dead. A little cloud of smoke up the mountain showed from where the shot was fired. With a cry of rage the scouts sent a volley where the little cloud was seen, then springing from their horses, clambered up the mountain to hunt down the murderer; but their search was fruitless.

About a mile beyond where the shooting took place they came to a rough log cabin, surrounded by a few acres of comparatively smooth ground. A small patch of corn and potatoes was growing near the cabin, and an old man with tangled gray hair and beard was hoeing in the field. An old woman sat in the door calmly smoking a corn-cob pipe. Neither seemed to notice the soldiers as they came riding up.

[pg 86]

"You, man, come here!" sternly called Calhoun.

The mountaineer deliberately laid down his hoe, and slowly came to where Calhoun was. He seemed to be in no hurry, nor did he appear to be disturbed.

"What is your name?" demanded Calhoun.

"Nichols—Jim Nichols," drawled the man.

"Are you well acquainted around here?" demanded Calhoun.

"Hev lived heah goin' on twenty years," was the answer.

"We have just had a man shot, by one of you skulking mountaineers. Do you know of any one likely to do such a deed? Tell the truth, or it will be the worse for you."

The old man shook his head. "The men be all gone in one army or de other," he answered.

"Are you Union or Confederate?" asked Calhoun.

"The wah is nuthin' to we-uns," he drawled; "we-uns own no niggers."

"That's no answer," fiercely replied Calhoun, "I have a mind to hang you up like a dog. A little stretching of the neck might loosen your tongue."

At the word "hang" a strange look came into the old man's eyes, a look as of mortal hatred, but it was gone in a moment, and the drawling answer came, "We-uns knows nuthin'; thar may be strange men hidin' in the mountin. We-uns don't know."

"Have you a family?"

[pg 87]

"A gal."

"Where is she?"

"Done gone over the mountin to see the Jimson gals."

"You have no son?"

At the word "son," again that deadly glint came in the old man's eye. Again it

49

was gone in a moment, and the answer came, "No."

The cabin was searched—the mountaineer and his wife apparently perfectly unconcerned as to what was going on—but nothing suspicious was found, and Calhoun had to confess himself baffled. But after Morgan's column had passed, a tall, lank girl with unkempt hair might have been seen coming down the mountainside, carrying a long rifle in her hand. Swiftly and surely as a deer she leaped from rock to rock, and soon neared the cabin. Carefully concealing her rifle beneath a huge rock, she came slowly up to the door of the cabin, where the old man sat smoking. He looked up at her, inquiringly, but did not say a word.

"We-uns got one, dad," she said, as she passed in. Not another word was spoken, but the old man sat and smoked and watched the sun as it slowly sunk to rest behind the mountain.

If Calhoun had known that Nichol's only son had been hanged the winter before by the Confederate authorities for bridge-burning, and that his sister had sworn revenge, he would not have been at a loss as to who had fired the deadly shot, for every mountain girl can use a rifle.

[pg 88]

From Sparta Morgan made a rapid march to Selina, where he forded the Cumberland River. At Selina he learned that there was a Federal force at Tompkinsville, which is just over the line in Kentucky. By a swift advance he hoped to surprise and capture this force. As the command crossed the line from Tennessee into Kentucky, the enthusiasm of the men knew no bounds. They sang "My Old Kentucky Home," and cheered again and again.

Tompkinsville was reached at five o'clock on the morning of the 9th of July. The Federals, under the command of Major Thomas J. Jordan, of the Ninth Pennsylvania Cavalry, though surprised, made a stand, and the battle at once opened. But a few shots from Morgan's mountain howitzers utterly demoralized the Federals, and they fled in confusion.

Major Jordan, after retreating about a mile, succeeded in rallying about seventy-five of his men, and made a stand to cover the retreat of his force. Calhoun, with some fifteen of his scouts far in advance of the main column, charged down on them without hesitating a moment. The Federals, although they outnumbered the scouts five to one, were ridden down, and throwing down their arms they cried for mercy.

In this fight the gallant Colonel Hunt was mortally wounded. He was one of Morgan's best officers, and his loss was deeply mourned.

From Tompkinsville Morgan moved to Glasgow, arriving there at one o'clock in the morning.

[pg 89]

The Federal garrison had heard of his approach, and had fled, leaving everything behind them. A large quantity of military stores fell into Morgan's hands, and was destroyed.

Although it was in the middle of the night, the glad news spread through the town, and the citizens were hailing each other with the glad shout, "Morgan has come again! Morgan has come again!" Soon from every house lights were flashing, and every woman was engaged in cooking. When morning came, not only a steaming hot breakfast of the best that the place afforded was set before the men, but three days' cooked rations were given each man.

At Glasgow Morgan gave out that he was again to raid the Louisville and Nashville Railroad. In order to carry out the deception, when he left Glasgow he followed the road which would lead him to strike the railroad in between Woodsonville and Mumfordsville; but when he was within a few miles of the road, he halted his command, and taking only Calhoun and his scouts, he struck the road at a lonely place a short distance from Horse Cove. Here he had his telegraph operator, a sharp young fellow named Ellsworth, attach his private instrument to the telegraph wire, and for two hours Ellsworth, in the midst of a driving storm and standing in water up to his knees, took every message that passed over the wire. It was rare fun to hear the Federal officers telling all their secrets, and revealing the terror they were in over Morgan's [pg 90]raid. After listening to their plans of how they would try to capture him, Morgan had Ellsworth send the following dispatch to the provost marshal at Louisville:

Nashville, Tenn., July 10, 1862.

General Forrest, commanding brigade, attacked Murfreesboro, routing our forces, and is now moving on Nashville. Morgan is reported to be between Scottsville and Gallatin, and will act in concert with Forrest, it is believed. Inform general commanding.

STANLEY MATHEWS,

Provost Marshal.

Morgan sent this dispatch to lead the Federal authorities to believe that he was returning from Kentucky. But the strange part of it is that Forrest did on that very day attack and capture Murfreesboro, and of this fact Morgan was entirely ignorant.

Leaving the telegraph and railroad intact, so as to have the Federals remain in ignorance of what he had done and where he was, Morgan rejoined his command and set out for Lebanon, a ride of over forty miles. The place fell, almost without struggle. Dashing in at the head of his scouts, Calhoun took possession of the telegraph office. This was at three o'clock in the morning. Unsuspicious of danger the regular telegraph operator was at home asleep, and Ellsworth was once more installed at the instrument.

It seemed that the day before Colonel Johnson, commanding the place, had telegraphed for reinforcements, saying he feared an attack. The first dispatch that Ellsworth received was:

[pg 91]

"What news? Any more skirmishing?"

To which Ellsworth answered: "No, we drove what few cavalry there were away."

The next was: "Has the train arrived yet?"

"No. How many troops on train?" asked Ellsworth.

"About five hundred," was the answer.

This was what Morgan wanted to know, and he at once dispatched a column to intercept the train. But the train scented danger, and backed with all speed toward Louisville.

At Lebanon immense stores fell into Morgan's hands. Two large warehouses filled to overflowing with clothing, rations, and the munitions of war were given to the flames. Five thousand stand of arms were among the trophies; Morgan picked out the best of these to arm his men.

The destruction of Federal property being complete, Morgan started north, going through Springfield and Mackville to Harrodsburg. Here he met with a most enthusiastic reception. Nothing was too good for Morgan's men.

While at Harrodsburg Calhoun greatly wished that Morgan would make a detour and visit Danville, but this Morgan refused to do, as it would take him too far out of his route and give the Federals time to concentrate against him. Thus Calhoun was prevented from entering his native town in triumph.

Morgan had caused the report to be circulated far and near that he had a force of five thousand [pg 92]and that his object was the capture of Frankfort. From Harrodsburg he moved to Midway on the line of the Louisville and Lexington Railroad. The place was about equidistant from Frankfort and Lexington, and from it either place could be equally threatened.

Here he once more took possession of the telegraph office, and Ellsworth was once more busy in sending telegrams. In the names of the different Federal officers Morgan telegraphed right and left, ordering the Federal troops here and there, everywhere but to the right place, and causing the utmost confusion. The poor Federals were at their wits' end; they knew not what to do, or which way to turn. The whole state was in terror. The name of Morgan was on every tongue; his force was magnified fivefold. General Boyle, in command of the Department of Kentucky, was deluged with telegrams imploring assistance. He in turn deluged General Halleck, General Buell, and even President Lincoln. "Send me troops, or Kentucky is lost. John Morgan will have it," he said.

Lincoln telegraphed to Halleck at Corinth: "They are having a stampede in Kentucky. Please look to it."

Buell telegraphed: "I can do nothing. Have no men I can send." Thus Kentucky was left to her fears. Never did a thousand men create a greater panic.

From Midway Colonel Morgan made a strong demonstration toward Frankfort, strengthening the [pg 93]belief that he was to attack that place, but his real object was the capture of Lexington.

Calhoun, with his men, scouted clear up to the outskirts of the place, driving in the Federal outposts; but he learned that the city was garrisoned by at least five times the number of Morgan's men. This fact he reported to his chief, who saw that it would be madness to attempt to capture it. Morgan therefore resolved to swing clear around Lexington, thoroughly breaking the railroad which led from that place to Cincinnati, so he gave orders to start for Paris. But he was unexpectedly delayed for a day at Midway by an unfortunate incident, the capture of Calhoun and one of his men by the Home Guards.

[pg 94]

CHAPTER VI.
CAPTURED BY HOME GUARDS.

All through Kentucky during the war there were companies of troops known as Home Guards. They were in reality the militia of the state. They in many instances rendered valuable services, and did much to keep Kentucky in the Union. If it had not been for them, the Federal government would have been obliged to keep twice as many troops in the state as it did. Not being under as strict discipline as the United States troops, they were more dreaded by the Southern element than the regular army.

These Home Guards were very bitter, and lost no opportunity of harassing those who clung to the cause of the South. Now and then there were bands of these Guards that were nothing but bands of guerrillas who lived by plundering, and they were frequently guilty of the most cold-blooded murders. It was by such a band that Calhoun was captured. He had been scouting toward Frankfort to see if the Federals were moving any considerable body of troops from that place to attack Morgan. He found them so frightened that they were not thinking of attacking Morgan; they were bending every nerve to defend the city from an expected attack by him. He was on his way back with the news that [pg 95]there was no danger from the direction of Frankfort, when he was told that a band of Home Guards, that were in fact a set of robbers, had their haunts in the rough, hilly country to the south of him, and he determined to try to effect their capture. After riding several miles, and hearing nothing of them, he ordered a return to Midway.

The day was very hot, and coming to a cross-road, where several trees cast their grateful shade and a little brook ran babbling by, he ordered his men to halt and rest. The shade and the water were very acceptable to both man and beast; dismounting, the men lay sprawling around in the shade. Seeing a house standing on an eminence up the cross-road, Calhoun decided to take one of his soldiers named Nevels, and ride up to it to see if he could learn anything.

"Better let us all go, there is no telling what one may run into in this country," said a sergeant named Graham, who in the absence of Calhoun would be in command of the little company.

"No, Graham," answered Calhoun, "both men and horses are tired, and need the little rest they are getting. I do not think there is any danger. If I see anything suspicious, I will signal to you." With these words Calhoun with his companion rode away.

"There he goes as careless as if there was not an enemy within forty miles," said Graham, looking after them, and shaking his head. "I tell you the Lieutenant will get into trouble some of these [pg 96]days. He is altogether too rash; never thinks of danger."

"Don't worry about the Lieutenant," lazily replied one of the men; "he never gets into a scrape without getting out of it. He is a good one, he is."

The Sergeant did not answer, but stood earnestly gazing after his chief, who by this time was about a quarter of a mile away. Here Calhoun and Nevels descended into a depression, which for a moment would hide them from the watchful eyes of the Sergeant.

As Calhoun entered this depression, he noticed that a thick growth of underbrush came up close to the side of the road, affording a splendid place for concealment. For a moment a feeling as of unseen danger came over him, but nothing suspicious could be seen or heard, and dismissing the thought, he rode forward. Suddenly Calhoun's horse stopped and pricked up his ears.

"What's the matter, Selim? What do you see?" exclaimed Calhoun, as he gently touched him with the spur.

The horse sprang forward, but had gone but a few yards, when as suddenly as if they had arisen out of the ground, a dozen men, with levelled guns, arose by the side of the road, and demanded their surrender. Desperate as the chance was, Calhoun wheeled his horse to flee, when before him stood a dozen more men; his retreat was cut off.

[pg 97]

"Surrender, or you are dead men," cried the leader. Calhoun saw they were surrounded by at least twenty-five men, and a most villainous-looking set they were. There was no help for it. To refuse to surrender meant instant death, and Calhoun and Nevels yielded as gracefully as possible.

The Sergeant stood still looking up the road waiting for them to appear, when he caught sight of the head of a man, then of another, and another.

"Boys," he shouted, excitedly, "something is wrong; the Lieutenant is in trouble."

The little squad sprang to their horses, and without thinking of danger, or what force they would meet, rode to the rescue, the Sergeant in the lead. But when they neared the place, they were met with a volley which brought three of the horses down and seriously wounded two of the men.

"Forward!" shouted the Sergeant, staggering to his feet, and holding his wounded arm, from which the blood was streaming.

But another volley brought down two more of the horses, and the Sergeant seeing they were outnumbered more than two to one, ordered a halt, and made preparations to resist a charge, which he thought would surely come. No charge came, and all was silent in front. The Sergeant ordered an advance, but no enemy was found. They had silently decamped and left no trace behind, and had taken Calhoun and Nevels with them.

Crippled as they were, and the Sergeant suffering [pg 98]terribly from his wound, it was decided it would be madness to pursue with their small force. So one of the men on a swift horse was sent to carry the news to Morgan, while the others followed more leisurely.

When the news reached camp, the greatest excitement prevailed, and every man in the command clamored to be sent to the rescue. Colonel Morgan chose Captain Huffman, who, with thirty of his famous Texan rangers, was soon galloping to the scene of the encounter, under the guidance of the courier who had brought the news. On the way they met Calhoun's little squad sorrowfully returning. Not a man but begged to be allowed to go with the rescuing party, but this, on account of the tired condition of their horses, and on account of the two wounded men, had to be refused.

It was well along in the afternoon when the theatre of the encounter was reached. Captain Huffman had with him three or four men who for years had been accustomed to Indian fighting in Texas; these men took up the trail and followed it like bloodhounds. After going three or four miles, the advance ran into two men, who sought safety by running into the woods; but a shot in the leg brought one of them down, and he was captured. At first he denied knowing anything of the affair, saying he had heard nothing of a fight. But when Captain Huffman ordered a rope to be brought and it was placed around his neck, he begged pite[pg 99]ously, saying that if they would spare his life he would tell them all he knew. And this is what he told them:

He belonged to a band led by a man known as "Red Bill" from his florid complexion. It was this band that had captured Calhoun and Nevels. It seemed that the officer whom they had captured had known Red Bill in Danville, and taunted him with being a chicken-thief. This so angered Red Bill that he determined to hang the officer. This resulted in a quarrel among the members of the band, many of whom had become tired of the leadership of Red Bill, being fearful that his crimes would bring retribution on their heads. At last it was agreed that the band would disperse, Red Bill, on the promise that he might have the two horses captured, agreeing to deliver the two prisoners to the Federal commander at Frankfort.

"But," added the prisoner, whose name was Evans, "I doubt if they ever reach Frankfort. I reckon Red Bill will find some means of getting rid of them before he gets there."

Captain Huffman listened to this story with horror. "If this miscreant makes way with Lieutenant Pennington and Nevels, I will hunt him to his death, if it takes ten years," he declared. Then turning to Evans, he asked: "Did any of the gang side with Red Bill?"

"Yes, five of them did, and stayed with him," was the answer.

"And you men, at least twenty of you, by your [pg 100]own story, coolly left our men to be foully murdered?" furiously demanded Captain Huffman.

The prisoner hung his head, but did not answer.

"Answer!" thundered Huffman.

"Red Bill promised to take them to Frankfort," he at length managed to say.

"And you have just admitted that his promise was worth nothing. Where did this thing occur? Where did you leave Red Bill and his prisoners?" demanded Huffman.

"About three miles from here," answered Evans.

"Lead us to the place at once."

"I dare not," he whimpered; "Red Bill will kill me if I give away the place of rendezvous. We are under a terrible oath not to reveal it."

"You need not fear Red Bill," answered Captain Huffman, in ominous tones, "for I am going to hang you. Boys, bring the rope."

"Mercy! Mercy!" gasped the shivering wretch.

"Then lead us to the place where you left Red Bill, and that quickly."

"My wound," he whined, pointing to his leg.

"Bind up his leg," said Huffman to one of his men.

The wound was rudely dressed, and then Evans was placed on a horse in front of a sturdy trooper.

"Now take us to the place where you left Red Bill, by the shortest and quickest route; you say it is three miles. If we don't reach it in half an hour, I will hang you like a dog. And," continued Huffman, to the trooper in front of whom Evans [pg 101]was riding, "blow out his brains at the first sign of treachery."

For answer the trooper touched his revolver significantly.

After riding swiftly for about two miles, Evans bade them turn into a path which led into the woods. The way became rough and rocky, and their progress was necessarily slower. Evans was in mortal terror lest the half-hour would be up before they could reach the place.

"It is right down thar," he at length said, pointing down a ravine which led to a stream.

The place was admirably adapted for concealment. On a small level place surrounded by high cliffs stood a tumble-down house. It was shut in from view from every point except the single one on which they stood.

"Leave the horses here," whispered Huffman, "I think I caught sight of some one down there. We will creep up on them unawares."

Leaving the horses in charge of ten men, Captain Huffman, with the rest of his force, silently crept down the gorge.

THEY SILENTLY CREPT DOWN THE GORGE.

We will now turn to Calhoun. After he was captured and heard his men cheering as they made the charge, his heart stood still, for he expected they would all be killed. He was, therefore, greatly surprised when the firing ceased, and his captors came running back, and hurried him through the woods at a break-neck speed. The rapid pace was kept up for about three miles, when [pg 102]finding they were not pursued, they adopted a more leisurely gait. Of this Calhoun was glad, for he was entirely out of breath. The leader of the gang, and another, probably the second in command, had appropriated the horses, and Calhoun and Nevels had been forced to walk, or rather run.

Once Calhoun ventured to ask the result of the fight, and was told that all of his men had been killed. This he knew to be a lie, as his captors would not have retreated so hastily if they had achieved so sweeping a victory. He asked another question, but was roughly told to shut up.

When the rendezvous was reached Red Bill for the first time noticed his prisoners closely. He started when he saw Calhoun, and then turning to his gang, said, "I reckon we had better string these fellows up, and get them out of the way."

"String us up," boldly answered Calhoun, "and I would not give a cent for your worthless lives; Morgan would never rest, as long as one of you encumbered the earth."

"Who is afraid of Morgan!" exclaimed Red Bill, with an oath. "He and the rest of you are nuthin' but hoss-thieves an' yo' will all hang one of these days. I know yo', my young rooster, you air the son of that ole Rebil, Judge Pennington of Danville. I hev it in fur him."

"And I know you now," hotly replied Calhoun, forgetting the danger he was in. "You used to live in Danville, and went by the name of Red Bill. Your popularity consisted in the fact that [pg 103]you were known as an adept chicken-thief. My father once sent you to jail for petit larceny."

Bill's face grew still redder. "Yo' lie, yo' dog!" he hissed. "Yo' father did send me to jail, but I war innocent, an' he knowed it. But he thought I war only po' white trash, while he is an aristocrat. I swore to hev my revenge, an' I will hev it. Boys, what do we-uns do with hoss-thieves in ole Kentuck?"

"Hang 'em," exclaimed four or five voices.

"An' we-uns will hang this crowin' bantam. I will learn him to call me a chicken-thief, classin' me with niggers!" exclaimed Red Bill, with fury.

"What will we-uns do with the other feller?" asked one of the men.

"Hang him too. Dead men don't talk."

But some of the gang began to demur over this summary proceeding, saying that the Federal authorities would deal severely with them if it became known they murdered prisoners in cold blood. Not only this, but Morgan had captured hundreds of Home Guards and paroled them. But if they should execute one of his prominent officers, he would show no mercy.

The discussion became so hot, they came nearly fighting among themselves. At last one of them said, "I am tired of the hull business. I am goin' home."

"An' I!" "An' I!" cried a dozen voices.

It was finally agreed that the gang should disband, only five agreeing to remain with Red Bill. [pg 104]Being allowed to keep the plunder and horses they had captured, these men, with Red Bill, promised to deliver Calhoun and Nevels to the Federal authorities at Frankfort, unharmed.

Calhoun and Nevels had watched this quarrel among their captors with the utmost anxiety, knowing that upon the result depended their lives. It was with the deepest concern that they beheld the members of the party depart, leaving them with Red Bill and his five boon companions.

No sooner were they alone than the six, with oaths and jeers, tied their prisoners securely to trees, drawing the cords so closely that they cut into the flesh. Although the pain was terrible, neither Calhoun nor Nevels uttered a moan. After the prisoners were thus securely tied, Red Bill produced a bottle of whisky, and the six commenced drinking, apparently taking no notice of their captives. The whole six were soon fiendishly drunk.

Staggering up to Calhoun, Red Bill growled: "Think we-uns goin' to take you to Frankfort, I reckin'."

"That is what you promised," replied Calhoun, calmly.

"Well, we-uns ain't. We-uns goin' to hang ye!"

Calhoun turned pale, then controlling himself by a powerful effort, he replied: "Do the Home Guards of Kentucky violate every principle of honorable warfare?"

"Damn honorable warfare! Yo-uns called me [pg 105]a chicken-thief; I call you a hoss-thief. Hoss-thieves air hanged. Ha! ha! the son of Judge Pennington strung up fo' stealin' hosses! Won't that sound nice?" and he burst into a devilish laugh, in which he was joined by the others.

Calhoun saw there was no hope. It was hard to die such an ignominious death. "Oh!" he thought, "if I had only been permitted to die amid the flame and smoke of battle. Such a death is glorious; but this——" A great lump arose in his throat, and came near choking him.

Gulping it back, he whispered to Nevels: "Don't show the white feather. Let them see how Morgan's men can die."

The brave fellow nodded; he could not speak. He had a wife and child at home.

They were unbound from the tree, but their arms and limbs were kept tightly pinioned. Ropes were brought and tied around their necks, and the free ends thrown over a limb of the tree.

"Can ye tie a true hangman's knot, Jack?" asked Red of the villain who was adjusting the rope around Calhoun's neck.

"That I can, Red," he answered, with a chuckling laugh. "It's as neat a job as eny sheriff can do."

The sun had just sunk to rest; the gloom of night was settling over the forest. Calhoun saw the shadows thicken among the trees. The darkness of death would soon be upon him.

"String 'em up!" shouted Red.

[pg 106]

Just then the solemn hoot of a distant owl was heard. One of the men holding the rope dropped it, and shivered from head to foot.

"Boys," he whispered, "let's don't do it. That's a note of warning. I never knew it to fail."

"Cuss ye fo' a white-livered coward!" yelled Red Bill. "String them up, I tell ye!"

For answer there came the sharp crack of rifles, the rush of armed men, and the infuriated Texans were on them. No mercy was shown; in a moment it was all over.

Quickly the cords which bound Calhoun and Nevels were cut, and the terrible nooses removed from their necks. "Thank God, we were in time!" cried Captain Huffman, wringing Calhoun's hand.

But Calhoun stood as one in a trance. So sudden had been his deliverance, he could not realize it. He had nerved himself to die, and now that he was safe, he felt sick and faint, and would have fallen if he had not been supported. Both he and Nevels soon rallied, and poured out their thanks to the brave men who had come to their rescue.

"We would never have found you," said Huffman, "if we had not run on one of the gang who under the threat of death piloted us here."

"Where is he?" asked Calhoun.

"With the boys up with the horses."

"Let him go," pleaded Calhoun; "but for him I would now have been food for the buzzards."

"To which we will leave these carrion," answered Huffman, pointing to the dead Home [pg 107]Guards. "But we must be going; Morgan is impatient to be on the road."

Great was the rejoicing in Morgan's command when Captain Huffman returned bringing Calhoun and Nevels safe; and much satisfaction was expressed over the fate of their captors. In half an hour after the return of Captain Huffman's command, Morgan's men were en route for Paris.

[

CHAPTER VII.
CALHOUN TAKES FRED PRISONER.

After leaving Midway, Morgan did not march directly to Paris, but halted at Georgetown, a little city twelve miles north of Lexington. The citizens of Georgetown gave Morgan's command the same joyous welcome which they had received at almost every place visited; for Morgan came to them not as an enemy, but as a liberator.

From Georgetown Morgan resolved to attack Cynthiana, which lies north of Paris, having heard there was a considerable body of Federal troops stationed there. Sending a small force toward Lexington to keep up the fiction of an attack upon that place, Morgan moved with the main body of his force upon Cynthiana.

Here was fought the fiercest battle that Morgan was engaged in during his raid. Cynthiana was held by Colonel John J. Landram of the Eighteenth Kentucky. He had under him about four hundred men, mostly Home Guards and raw recruits. Landram put up a most gallant defence, and the battle raged for an hour and a half with the greatest fury. It was at last decided by a furious charge made by Major Evans at the head of his Texas rangers. The entire force of Colonel Landram was killed, wounded, and taken prisoners. Colonel [pg 109]Morgan lamented the loss of some forty of his bravest men. Calhoun was not in this fight, having been sent with his scouts toward Lexington to watch the movements of the enemy.

From Cynthiana, Morgan moved on Paris, and the place surrendered without a shot being fired. Some twenty-five miles of the Cincinnati and Lexington railroad was now in Morgan's possession, and he proceeded to destroy it as thoroughly as his limited time admitted. But he was being encompassed by his enemies. A large force was moving on him from Frankfort; another from Lexington. Calhoun with his faithful scouts kept him fully informed of these movements.

Just in time to elude General Green Clay Smith's forces from Lexington, he marched for Winchester. His next move was to Richmond. This left all the pursuing forces in the rear. The celerity of Morgan's movements, the marvellous endurance of his men, astonished and confounded his enemies.

At Richmond, Morgan decided to make a stand and give battle to his pursuers; but Calhoun brought word that at least five thousand Federals were closing in on him. To give battle to such a number would have been madness, so he marched for Crab Orchard. On the march Calhoun made a detour toward Danville so as to visit the plantation of his uncle, Colonel Richard Shackelford. He was also in hopes of meeting his cousin Fred. He had heard how Fred had interceded for his father, keeping him from being sent to a Northern prison, and [pg 110]he wished to thank him. He was ashamed of the hatred he had felt toward him, and resolved to make amends for it.

His arrival was a genuine surprise, but to his consternation Fred presented himself in the uniform of a captain of the Federal army. His men clamored to take Fred prisoner, but just as Calhoun had succeeded in quieting them, to his dismay Captain Conway came galloping upon the scene at the head of his company. He had obtained permission from Morgan to scout toward Danville. His real object was to capture Fred, who he knew was at home. Once in his hands, he hoped to convict him as a spy. His plan was frustrated by the bold stand taken by Colonel Shackelford, who delivered Fred as a prisoner to Calhoun with instructions to take him to Morgan. This Calhoun did, and Morgan at once paroled him, although Conway tried his best to have him held as a spy. Morgan not only paroled Fred, but let him return with the horse he had ridden, although many of the men looked on the splendid animal with envious eyes. But Morgan would not hear of their taking a horse which belonged to his old friend, Colonel Shackelford.

"Why didn't you ride that horse of yours?" asked Captain Mathews of Fred, alluding to Fred's famous horse, Prince.

"Afraid you might keep him," laughed Fred; "you are a good judge of a horse, Captain."

"Right you are," responded Mathews; "I am sorry I didn't think of that horse when we were at [pg 111]Richmond. I would have visited you with my friend Conway, and taken the horse. Think I will have to return for him yet."

Fred thought little of what Mathews said, but that very night Mathews dispatched two of his men back in disguise to steal Fred's horse.

From Crab Orchard Morgan marched to Somerset, surprising the place, and capturing a large wagon-train. It was also a depot for army supplies, all of which Morgan gave to the torch. Here he again took possession of the telegraph office, and enlightened the Federals as to his movements.

At Somerset Morgan's raid was practically at an end. There were no Federal troops in front of him; his pursuers were a day behind. After he had completed the destruction of all the United States property in the place, and was ready to leave, he caused the following dispatches to be sent:

Somerset, Ky., July 22, 1862.

George D. Prentice, Louisville, Ky.

Good morning, George D. I am quietly watching the complete destruction of all of Uncle Sam's property in this little burg. I regret exceedingly that this is the last that comes under my supervision on this route. I expect in a short time to pay you a visit, and wish to know if you will be at home. All well in Dixie.

JOHN H. MORGAN,

Commanding Brigade.

Somerset, Ky., July 22, 1862.

GENERAL J. T. BOYLE, Louisville, Ky.

Good morning, Jerry! This telegraph is a great institution. You should destroy it, as it keeps me too well posted. My friend Ellsworth has all of your dispatches since July 10 on file. Do you wish copies?

JOHN H. MORGAN,

Commanding Brigade.

[pg 112]

Somerset, Ky., July 22, 1862.

HON. GEORGE DUNLAP, Washington, D. C.

Just completed my tour through Kentucky. Captured sixteen cities, destroyed millions of dollars of United States property. Passed through your county, but regret not seeing you. We paroled fifteen hundred Federal prisoners. Your old friend,

JOHN H. MORGAN,

Commanding Brigade.

The feelings of the above gentlemen as they received these telegrams can better be imagined than described. The one to General Boyle must have cut him to the quick as he read it. To know how completely Morgan had outwitted him was like gall and wormwood to him.

From Somerset Morgan halted his command at Livingston, Tennessee, to take a much-needed rest. Never did men need it more. They had accomplished one of the most astonishing feats in the annals of American warfare. No wonder the name of Morgan struck terror to the hearts of the Federals. Morgan in his report of his raid sums it up as follows:

"I left Knoxville on the 4th day of this month with about nine hundred men, and returned to Livingston on the 28th instant with nearly twelve hundred, having been absent just twenty-four days, during which time I travelled over one thousand miles, captured seventeen towns, destroyed all the government

66

property and arms in them, dispersed about fifteen hundred Home Guards, and paroled nearly twelve hundred regular troops. I lost in killed, wounded, and missing of the number I carried into Kentucky, about ninety."

[pg 113]

CHAPTER VIII.
THE CAPTURE OF GALLATIN.

Morgan's command had not been encamped at Livingston more than two or three days when, to every one's astonishment, a couple of soldiers belonging to Captain Mathews's company came riding into camp, one on Fred Shackelford's famous horse, Prince, and the other on a well-known horse of Colonel Shackelford's, called Blenheim.

Calhoun, hearing the cheering and laughter which greeted the soldiers as they galloped in waving their hats and shouting, ran out of his quarters to see what was occasioning the excitement. He could hardly believe his eyes when he saw the well-known horse of Fred. Then his heart gave a great jump, for the thought came to him that his cousin had been waylaid and killed. But if so, how did the soldiers come to have Blenheim too? To his relief he soon learned the truth of the story, how from Crab Orchard Captain Mathews had sent back two of his company to capture Prince, and they had returned not only with Prince, but with Blenheim. Mathews was in high spirits as he appropriated Prince. Jumping on his back he galloped him through camp, showing off his fine points, and declaring he could outrun any horse in the brigade. [pg 114]A match was soon arranged, but Prince so easily outstripped every competitor that soon no officer was found who had the hardihood to enter his horse in the lists against him.

Blenheim was awarded to Conway, much to his satisfaction. He could not forego the opportunity of crowing over Calhoun, thinking he would be vexed over the capture of his cousin's horse.

"Why do you come blowing around me?" asked Calhoun, nettled by his manner, "I am neither the keeper of my cousin nor the keeper of his horse."

"Oh, you were so careful of his precious person when I took him prisoner, I did not know but your carefulness might extend to his horse," replied Conway, with a sneer.

Calhoun felt his blood boil, but controlling himself, he replied: "You did not take Captain Shackelford, and I am surprised that you should make such a statement. You forget that I was there before you."

"You would have let the fellow go," snapped Conway.

"Just as Colonel Morgan did, on his parole," answered Calhoun.

"It was your fault that he slipped through my fingers," exclaimed Conway, angrily, "but my time will come. I have swore to see him hanged before this war is over, and I shall."

"Catch your rabbit before you skin him, Captain," replied Calhoun, with provoking coolness; [pg 115]and the laugh was on Conway, who turned away with a muttered oath.

Conway had entertained a secret dislike to Calhoun ever since their first meeting, partly because he had been chosen by Morgan, instead of Conway himself, to go back to Kentucky, and partly on account of his being Fred's cousin. But after the affair at Colonel Shackelford's house, he took little pains to conceal his dislike. Many of the officers of the brigade noticed this, and predicted that sooner or later there would be trouble between the two.

But Calhoun was not through with being bantered over the capture of Prince. Captain Mathews came riding up and with a flourish said: "Ah! Lieutenant, I reckon you have seen this hoss before; what do you think of him?" Now, Mathews was a rough, rollicking fellow, and quite a favorite in the command. He and Calhoun were good friends, and so Calhoun answered pleasantly: "He is the best horse in Kentucky. I know it, for I was once beaten by him in a race. But," continued Calhoun, with a laugh, "my advice is to guard him very carefully, or Captain Shackelford will get him back, sure. That horse has more tricks than you dream of."

"I am not worrying," replied Mathews. "One of your scouts has just had to fork over five dollars to one of my men, on a bet they made at Crab Orchard that I could not get the hoss. Perhaps you would like to bet I can't keep him?"

[pg 116]

"Yes, I will go you twenty-five that Captain Shackelford will have his horse back in less than two months," answered Calhoun, dryly.

"Done!" exclaimed the Captain, gleefully, and the stakes were placed in the hands of Captain Huffman. The bet afforded much amusement to the officers, but all of them looked upon it as a very foolish bet on the part of Calhoun.

"That twenty-five is gone," said Huffman to Calhoun, as he pocketed the stakes, "but I am sure of having fifty dollars for at least two months."

"I reckon I shall lose," said Calhoun, "but Mathews had better not let Shackelford get sight of his horse."

"Why?" asked a dozen voices in concert.

"Because that horse is up to more antics than a trick horse in a circus. You will see, if we ever run across my cousin in our raids."

"I don't know what you mean," said one of the officers, "but your cousin will have a fine time getting that horse away from Jim Mathews."

"Wait and see," was Calhoun's answer.

It was not many days before they knew what Calhoun meant. A few days sufficed to rest Morgan's command, and it was not the nature of Morgan to remain long idle. He had to be doing something. It was known that the Confederate armies were about ready to make the long-talked-of forward movement into Kentucky. In fact, General Kirby Smith had already set out from Knoxville to invade Eastern Kentucky, and General Bragg [pg 117]was nearly ready to take the initiative from Chattanooga.

The Federal army in Tennessee was scattered, and owing to the raids of Morgan and Forrest, the men were on short rations. General Buell was at his wits' end. He knew that General Bragg was preparing to advance, but thought he would not attempt the invasion of Kentucky before attacking him. He therefore looked for a great battle somewhere in Middle Tennessee, and concentrated his forces for that event.

Before Bragg moved, Morgan decided to strike another blow at the Louisville and Nashville Railroad, and this time right under the noses of the Federal army. Gallatin is only twenty-six miles from Nashville, and Morgan decided to attempt its capture. In order to spy out the land, Calhoun entered the place as a country lad. He found that it was garrisoned by a Federal force of about four hundred, under the command of Colonel Boone. The discipline was lax. In the daytime no pickets were out, and Calhoun found no difficulty in entering the place. He made himself known to a few of the citizens, and they gave him all the information possible. To them the coming of Morgan meant deliverance from a hateful foe.

It did not take Calhoun long to find out the station of every picket at night. The camp of the Federals was on the fair-ground, half a mile from the city. Colonel Boone was accustomed to sleep at a hotel in the city; in fact, his wife was sick at [pg 118]the hotel. Colonel Boone knew that Morgan was near, and was fearful of an attack. He telegraphed both to Nashville and to General Buell at MacMinnville for reinforcements, but no attention was paid to his demand. Instead, he was ordered to send nearly half of his force away to intercept a drove of beef cattle which it was reported the Confederates were driving down from Kentucky.

That the citizens might not know that his numbers were depleted, Colonel Boone did not send this force away until midnight, thinking no one would see them depart. But sharp eyes were watching. Nothing was going on in Gallatin without Calhoun's knowledge. He lost no time in reporting to Morgan, and the attack came swiftly.

Knowing the location of every picket post, Calhoun was able to effect their capture without the firing of a gun, and Morgan rode into Gallatin without the knowledge of the Federal force, which was only half a mile away. Colonel Boone was captured at the hotel. The first intimation he had that Morgan was in the city was when he was commanded by Calhoun to surrender. A demand was now made on the camp that it should surrender, which it did. Thus without firing a gun Gallatin, with the entire Federal garrison and all the military stores which it contained, was captured.

Losing no time, Morgan ordered the companies of Captain Mathews and Captain Conway, together with Calhoun's scouts, to take the stockade which guarded the tunnel six miles north of town. The [pg 119]attack was successful, the stockade surrendering after a slight resistance. The tunnel was now in the possession of the Confederates.

A long train of cars which had been captured was piled with wood, rails, and other combustibles, set on fire, and run into the tunnel. The sides and roof of the tunnel were supported by heavy woodwork, and the whole tunnel was soon a roaring mass of flame. The wood being burned away the tunnel caved in, and it was months before a train ran through from Louisville to Nashville. Morgan had effectually blocked the road. Highly elated with their success, the command returned to Gallatin, Mathews and Conway riding at the head of the column. To Calhoun was committed the care of the prisoners, and he brought up the rear.

When about half-way to Gallatin, Calhoun heard the report of a single pistol shot in front, then a rapid succession of rifle shots. The head of the column seemed to be thrown into confusion, and the whole command came to a halt.

Fearful that an attack had been made by a Federal force coming from Nashville, Calhoun gave orders to shoot down the first prisoner who attempted to escape, and prepared to resist any attack that might come. But no more firing was heard, and the column began to move again. Soon an officer came riding back and told Calhoun a story that interested him greatly.

Mathews and Conway were riding at the head of the column, when, as it reached a cross-road, a [pg 120]peculiar sharp whistle suddenly pierced the air. Mathews's horse gave a prodigious bound, unseated his rider, and dashed up the cross-road. Conway's horse bolted, and in spite of Conway's efforts, followed.

A boy sprang out of the bushes into the road, and Mathews's horse stopped by his side. He fired at Conway, hitting him in the shoulder. To save himself from being shot again, Conway flung himself from his horse. The boy sprang onto Mathews's horse and rode away at full speed, followed by the other horse. An ineffectual volley was fired at the boy. Captain Mathews's arm was broken by the fall.

HE FIRED AT CONWAY.

"So Captain Mathews has lost his horse?" asked Calhoun, with a faint smile.

"Yes, he will quit blowing now."

"And I have won twenty-five dollars; but I am sorry Mathews had his arm broken."

When Calhoun reached Gallatin, Captain Conway had had his wound dressed, and Mathews's arm was in splints. Conway was in a towering passion. He blamed Calhoun for his ill-luck, saying if it had not been for him, Fred Shackelford would have been hanged as a spy. From this time he did not try to conceal his hatred of Calhoun.

Captain Mathews took his misfortune more philosophically. "It was a blamed sharp trick on the part of young Shackelford!" he exclaimed. Then turning to Captain Huffman, he said: "Give that money to Lieutenant Pennington; he has won it. [pg 121]But I give you all fair warning I shall get that hoss back. My reputation depends upon it. Then to think that I, who prided myself on being one of the best hossmen in Morgan's troop, should be thrown. Bah! it makes me sick," and his face took on a look of disgust.

"I warned you," said Calhoun, "that that horse was up to tricks. When Fred gives that whistle he will unhorse any rider who is on his back. I have seen Fred try it time and time again with his father's nigger boys as riders, and Prince never failed of unhorsing them. When Fred gave that whistle his horse would have gone to him, or died in the attempt."

"I am sorry you didn't let Conway hang him," replied Mathews, gently rubbing his broken arm, "but I will get even with him, see if I don't. I want that hoss worse than ever."

A few days after the capture of Gallatin, a Federal force moved up from Nashville, reoccupied the city, committed many depredations, and began arresting the citizens right and left, accusing them of complicity with Morgan. When Morgan heard of this he at once moved to the relief of the distressed city. Attacking the rear guard of the enemy as it was leaving the place, he not only defeated them, but drove them to within seven miles of Nashville, capturing the force at Pilot Knob, and burning the high railroad trestle at that place. He also captured a train of cars and liberated forty of the citizens of Gallatin who were being [pg 122]taken to Nashville as prisoners. They had been used with the greatest cruelty by their captors.

In this raid Morgan captured nearly two hundred prisoners. Notwithstanding the provocation was great, considering the way the citizens of Gallatin had been used, Morgan treated his prisoners kindly and paroled them.

The Federal authorities, now being thoroughly alarmed, resolved to crush Morgan. To this end a brigade of cavalry was organized at MacMinnville, placed under the command of General R. W. Johnson, and sent against him. Johnson thought that Morgan was at Hartsville, and marched against that place. But when he reached Hartsville and learned that Morgan was at Gallatin, he at once marched to attack him there, confident of easy victory.

Up to this time the Federals had boasted that Morgan would not fight anything like an equal force; that he always attacked isolated posts with overwhelming numbers. They were now to learn something different. Morgan had been kept well posted by Calhoun and his scouts with regard to every movement of Johnson. Although he knew that he was greatly outnumbered, Morgan resolved to give battle and teach the boasting Yankees a lesson.

Early on the morning of August 21 Calhoun came galloping into Gallatin with the information that Johnson was close at hand. To avoid fighting a battle in the city Morgan moved out on the Hartsville pike, meeting the enemy about two miles from Gallatin. The engagement opened at [pg 123]once with fury. Up to that time it was the greatest engagement fought in the West in which cavalry only was engaged.

For a time the Federals fought bravely, and for an hour the issue of the battle was doubtful; then a charge stampeded a portion of the Federal forces. Thoroughly panic-stricken they threw away guns, accoutrements, everything that impeded their progress, thinking only of safety in flight. Plunging into the Cumberland River, they forded it and did not stop running until they reached Nashville.

The remaining Federal force under General Johnson retreated about two miles, and then made a brave stand. But nothing could withstand the fury of Colonel Basil Duke's attack, whose command had the advance. General Johnson and many of his men were taken prisoners, and the remainder were scattered.

In this engagement the Federals lost two hundred men, killed, wounded, and missing. Their general himself was a prisoner. Thus, to their cost, they found that when the occasion demanded it Morgan would fight. Morgan's loss in the battle was only five killed and twenty wounded; but among the latter was the brave Captain Huffman, who had an arm shattered.

Colonel Basil Duke, in this fight, won the highest praise from Morgan for the masterly manner in which he handled his regiment. It was greatly owing to the efforts of Colonel Duke that the victory was won.

[pg 124]

In this battle Calhoun bore a conspicuous part. Single-handed he engaged a Federal officer who was trying to rally his men, and forced him to surrender. When he delivered up his sword Calhoun saw to his surprise that it was his old acquaintance, Lieutenant Haines.

"Ah, Lieutenant," said Calhoun, "I am glad to have met you again. When the battle is over I will come and see you."

"Pennington again, as I am alive!" gasped the astonished Lieutenant.

After all was over Calhoun sought him out, and found him sitting dejected and crestfallen among the prisoners.

"Cheer up, Lieutenant," said Calhoun, pleasantly; "we are going to parole you. You will soon be at liberty."

"How often do you want to parole a fellow? This will be the third time," growled Haines. "Curse the luck. I thought we would wipe you off the face of the earth sure this time. We would, too, if it hadn't been for that cowardly regiment which broke."

"An 'if' has stood in between many a man and success," answered Calhoun. "How long ago were you exchanged?"

"About two months," replied Haines, "and here I am in for it again. I expected to win a captaincy to-day. If this is the way it goes, I shall die a lieutenant."

"Oh, you may wear the star of a general yet, [pg 125]who knows? To change the subject, have you met the charming Miss Osborne since your return to the army?"

A change came over the face of Haines—one that transformed his rather handsome features into those of a malignant spirit. Calhoun saw it and wondered. The Lieutenant quickly recovered himself, and answered:

"Yes, but trouble has come upon the family. Mr. Osborne refused to take the oath of allegiance, and as he was looked upon as a dangerous character, he has been sent North as a prisoner."

"To wear his life away in some Northern bastile!" exclaimed Calhoun, in a fury. "Monstrous!"

"That is not all," returned Haines. "By some means the house took fire and burned with all its contents. I did all I could for them—tried to save Mr. Osborne, but could not; but I will not relax my efforts to have him released. I have some powerful friends in the North."

Calhoun thanked him, and went his way. But that look which came over Haines's face, what did it mean? It was months before Calhoun knew.

[pg 126]

CHAPTER IX.

THE DUEL.

In August, 1862, Cumberland Gap, the gateway between Eastern Kentucky and East Tennessee, was held by a Federal force of over ten thousand, commanded by General George W. Morgan. It was this force which confronted General Kirby Smith as he set out to invade Kentucky.

The place being too strong to carry by assault, General Smith left a force in front of the Gap to menace it, made a flank movement with the rest of his army, passed through Roger's Gap unopposed, and without paying any attention to the force at Cumberland Gap, pushed on with all speed for Central Kentucky.

At the same time General Bragg made his long-expected advance from Chattanooga, completely deceiving Buell, who first concentrated his army at Altamont and then at MacMinnville. Bragg marched unopposed up the Sequatchie Valley to Sparta. General George H. Thomas had advised Buell to occupy Sparta, but the advice was rejected. Buell could not, or would not, see that Kentucky was Bragg's objective point. He now believed that Nashville or Murfreesboro was the point of danger, and he concentrated his army at the latter place.

From Sparta General Bragg had marched to [pg 127]Carthage, crossed the Cumberland River, and was well on his way to Kentucky before Buell waked up. Bragg was then three days ahead of him. If Bragg had marched straight for Louisville, there would have been no troops to oppose him until he reached that place, and Louisville would have fallen. But he stopped to take Mumfordsville, and the delay was fatal. It gave Buell the opportunity to overtake him.

When the forward movement began, Colonel John H. Morgan was ordered to Eastern Kentucky to watch the force at Cumberland Gap and prevent it from falling on the rear of the army of General Smith. Smith moved rapidly, and on August 29 fought the battle of Richmond, where a Federal force of seven thousand was almost annihilated, only about eight hundred escaping.

By the movements of Smith and Bragg the Federal force at Cumberland Gap was cut off. For that army the situation was a grave one. In their front was General Stevenson with a force too small to attack, but large enough to keep them from advancing. In their rear were the Confederate armies. They were short of food; starvation stared them in the face. It was either surrender or a retreat through the mountains of Eastern Kentucky.

General George W. Morgan called a council of his officers, and it was decided to evacuate the Gap and attempt the retreat. The Gap was evacuated on the night of the 17th of September. All government property which could not be carried away [pg 128]was given to the flames. The rough mountain road had been mined, and the mines were exploded to prevent Stevenson from following. But as Stevenson's force was infantry, it would be of little avail in following the retreating Federals.

A toilsome march of two hundred and twenty miles over rough mountainous roads lay between the Federals and the Ohio River. To the credit of General G. W. Morgan be it said, he conducted the retreat with consummate skill. It was expected that a Confederate force in Eastern Kentucky under General Humphrey Marshall would try to cut the Federals off; but Marshall never appeared, and it was left to the brigade of John H. Morgan to do what they could to oppose the retreat. One cavalry brigade could not stop the progress of ten thousand well-disciplined troops. Day after day Morgan hung on the Federal flanks and rear, taking advantage of every opening, and making their way a weary one. After a toilsome march of sixteen days, the Federal force, footsore and completely exhausted, reached the Ohio at Greenupsburg on the Ohio River, and was safe.

During these sixteen days, Calhoun was almost continually in the saddle, the foremost to strike, the last to retreat. When the pursuit was ended, his little band of scouts had seventy-five prisoners to their credit.

When Morgan saw that it was useless to follow the retreating army any longer, without taking any rest he turned the head of his column toward [pg 129]Central Kentucky, for he knew he would be needed there.

Calhoun could hardly believe his eyes when he saw the change a few weeks had effected. All Central Kentucky had been swept clear of the Federals. Panic-stricken they had fled back to Louisville and Cincinnati, and were cowering in their trenches. Indiana and Ohio were in an agony of fear. The governors were frantically calling on the people to arise *en masse* and save their states from invasion.

When the command reached Danville, Calhoun was nearly beside himself with joy. Over the courthouse floated the Stars and Bars of the South. It was the first time Calhoun had ever seen there the flag he loved so well. With a proud hurrah he dashed up to the door of his father's residence; there was no one to molest him or make him afraid. From the house of every friend of the South hung a Confederate flag.

"Redeemed! Kentucky redeemed at last!" shouted Calhoun, as he dismounted.

But he was disappointed in not finding his father at home. The Judge was in

Frankfort, helping to form a provisional government for the state. Many of the more sanguine of the Southern element of the state already considered it safe in the Confederacy.

Although his father was not at home, Calhoun received a most joyful welcome. "Bress de chile, if he isn't bac' again," cried Aunt Chloe.

[pg 130]

"Yes, Chloe," said Calhoun, as he shook her honest black hand, "and now be sure and get up one of your best dinners, I can eat it in peace this time. And, Chloe, cook enough for a dozen; Colonel Morgan, with his staff, will be here to dine."

But what Morgan's command learned was anything but satisfactory. Kirby Smith had advanced to within six miles of Covington, there halted, and at last fallen back. Bragg, instead of marching direct to Louisville, had turned aside to Bardstown, allowing Buell's army to enter the city of Louisville unopposed. There Buell had been joined by twenty thousand fresh troops. Clothing and refitting his men, he had turned, and was now marching on Bardstown. A great battle might be fought any day. In fact, it was reported that Bragg had already abandoned Bardstown and was marching in the direction of Danville or Harrodsburg.

"I don't like it at all," said Morgan. "Our generals have already let the golden opportunity pass. But there is still hope. With the armies of Bragg and Smith united, they should be strong enough to give battle and crush Buell."

So good was the dinner and so animated the discussion, that it was late in the afternoon when they arose from the table. As they came out Morgan suddenly stopped and said, "Hark!"

Away in the northwest, in the direction of Perryville, the dull heavy booming of cannon was heard. They listened and the dull roar, like distant thunder, was continuous.

[pg 131]

"A battle is being fought," they said, in low tones; "May God favor the right!"

At Perryville the forces of Buell and Bragg had met, and were engaged in deadly strife. Until nightfall the heavy dull roar was heard, and then it died away. Which army had been victorious? They could not tell.

After the battle of Perryville, Buell, fully expecting that Bragg would fight a decisive battle for the possession of the state, remained inactive for three days for the purpose of concentrating his army. It was fatal to all his hopes, for Bragg had already decided to leave the state, and he utilized the three days in getting away with his immense trains. He had been grievously disappointed in the hope that his army would be largely recruited, and that at least twenty thousand Kentuckians would flock to his standard. But Kentucky had already been well drained of men, furnishing troops by thousands for both sides.

From one point of view, the invasion of Kentucky by the Confederates had been a magnificent success. A loss of at least twenty thousand had been inflicted on the Federal armies, while the loss of the Confederate army had not been over one-third of that number. In addition to that, the immense stores gathered and taken South were of inestimable value to the army. But in the chagrin and disappointment over Bragg's retreat these things were lost sight of and the Confederate general was most bitterly denounced.

[pg 132]

Calhoun went wild when he heard that the state was to be given up without a decisive battle, that all that had been gained was to go for naught; and his feelings were shared by all Morgan's men.

"It won't prevent us from visiting the state once in a while," said Morgan, with a grim smile.

As for Judge Pennington, he was so disgusted that although his whole heart was with the South, he gave up all idea of forming a state government loyal to the Confederacy, and remained quiet during the rest of the war. "The armies will have to settle it," he would say; "we can do nothing here."

One of the first things that Calhoun did after he reached Danville was to see Jennie Freeman and thank her for her timely warning. "It was kind of you, Jennie," he said, "for I know that you hate the cause for which I am fighting."

"My conscience has hurt me awfully ever since," replied Jennie, with a toss of her head; "and then I believe you told me an awful fib."

"Why, how is that, Jennie?" asked Calhoun.

"You worked on my sympathy, and said if you were caught you would be hanged. The Union forces don't hang prisoners. They would only have shut you up, and that is what you deserve."

"But, Jennie, I was in disguise; they would have hanged me as a spy."

"Don't believe it, but I sometimes think half of you Rebels ought to be hanged."

"Oh, Jennie, Jennie! what a bloodthirsty [pg 133]creature you have grown! But where is your father?"

"Thank the Lord, where the old flag yet floats—in Louisville. He will stay there until that rag comes down," and she pointed to the Confederate flag floating over the courthouse.

"Poor girl, never to see her father again," exclaimed Calhoun, in tones of compassion.

"What do you mean?" she asked, turning pale. A sudden fear had come over her; had anything befallen her father?

Calhoun saw her mistake. Laughing, he said, "I only meant that flag would never come down."

"Is that all?" she replied, saucily; "you all will be scurrying south like so many rabbits in less than a week."

"Give us ten days."

"No, not an hour more than a week. And mind, if you get caught, you needn't call on me for help."

"Well, Jennie, don't let's quarrel. Perhaps I can return the favor you did me, by helping you some day."

The opportunity came sooner than he expected. The next day Jennie ventured out to visit a sick friend. On her return she had to pass a couple of Confederate officers, one of whom was intoxicated. The other appeared to be reasoning with him, and trying to get him to go to his quarters.

As Jennie was hurrying past them, the one who was intoxicated staggered toward her, and leering [pg 134]at her, exclaimed, "How—how do, pretty one? Give me a—a kiss!"

Jennie turned to flee, but he caught her roughly by the arm. Just as he did so, he was struck a terrific blow in the face, which sent him rolling in the gutter.

"Take my arm, Jennie," said Calhoun, for it was he who struck the blow, "I will see you safe home."

The trembling girl took his arm, saying: "Oh, Calhoun, how glad I am you came! How can I thank you enough! Do you know that dreadful man?"

"Yes, I am sorry to say he is a captain in Morgan's command. His name is Conway. We left him back in Tennessee wounded. But he was able to follow Bragg's army, and he joined us only yesterday. By the way, it was Fred Shackelford who shot him. He shot him when he got Prince back. Conway was riding Blenheim."

"Oh, Fred told me all about that. Wasn't that just splendid in him, getting his horse back!"

"Where is Fred now?" asked Calhoun.

"I don't know. Did you know General Nelson was shot?"

"Shot? Nelson shot?" cried Calhoun. "Where? How?"

Jennie had to tell him what little she knew about it. All that she had heard had come from Confederate sources.

"Well, Jennie, here you are at home. I feel [pg 135]ashamed. It is the first time I ever knew one of Morgan's men to insult a woman."

"I hope that miserable Conway will give you no trouble," said Jennie, as they parted.

"No fears on that score," lightly replied Calhoun, as he bade her good-bye.

But Calhoun well knew there would be trouble. No Kentucky officer would forgive a blow, no matter what the provocation was under which it was given.

The blow which Conway received had the effect of sobering him, but he presented a pitiable sight. His face was covered with blood, and one eye was nearly closed. When he knew it was Calhoun that had struck him, his rage was fearful. Nothing but blood would wipe out the insult. For a Kentucky gentleman not to resent a blow meant disgrace and dishonor; he would be looked upon as a contemptible coward. But Conway was no coward. He knew he was in fault, but that would not wipe out the disgrace of the blow. There was but one thing for him to do, and that was to challenge Calhoun.

That night Calhoun was waited upon by Captain Mathews, who in the name of Conway demanded an abject apology. This, of course, was refused, and a formal challenge was delivered. Calhoun at once accepted it, and referred Mathews to his friend Lieutenant Matson.

"Look here, Pennington," said Mathews, "I do not want you to think I uphold Conway in what he did. I am no saint, but I never insulted a woman. [pg 136]Conway would not have done it if he had not been drunk. I was just going to the lady's rescue when you struck the blow. There was no need of knocking Conway down. I understand the girl is a Lincolnite, but that makes no difference, Conway is right in demanding satisfaction."

"And I am willing to give it to him," answered Calhoun. "The only thing I ask is that the affair be arranged quickly. Let it be to-morrow morning at sunrise. And, Captain, understand that I bear you no grudge. I consider your action perfectly honorable."

Mathews bowed and withdrew. He and Matson quickly arranged the preliminaries. The meeting was to take place at sunrise, in a secluded spot near Danville; the weapons were pistols, the distance fifteen paces. Only one shot was to be allowed. The affair had to be managed with the utmost secrecy;

above all things, it had to be kept from the ears of Morgan. But it was whispered from one to another until half the officers knew of it. None blamed Calhoun, yet none could see how Conway could avoid giving the challenge.

"Both are dead men," said an officer, with a grave shake of the head. "Morgan ought to be told; he would stop it."

"Tell Morgan if you dare!" cried half a dozen voices.

"Oh, I am not going to tell; if they wish to kill each other it's none of my business," replied the officer, turning away.

[pg 137]

Calhoun was known as the best pistol shot in the brigade, and Conway was no mean marksman. Everyone thought it would be a bloody affair. Many were aware of the enmity which Conway held toward Calhoun, and knew he would kill him if he could. Meanwhile Jennie slept unconscious of the danger Calhoun was in for her sake.

It was a beautiful autumn morning when they met. The sun was just rising, touching woods, and fields, and the spires of the distant town with its golden light. The meeting was in a place which Calhoun well knew. How often he had played there when a boy! It was an open glade in the midst of a grove of mighty forest trees. The trees had taken on the beautiful hues of autumn, and they flamed with red and gold and orange.

At least twenty had assembled to witness the duel. A surgeon stood near with an open case of instruments at his feet. Many glanced at it, but turned their eyes away quickly. It was too suggestive.

The principals were placed in position. A hush came over the little group of spectators. Even the breeze seemed no longer to whisper lovingly among the trees, but took upon itself the wail of a dirge, and a shower of leaves, red as blood, fell around the contestants.

"Are you ready, gentlemen?" asked Mathews.

"Ready!" answered Calhoun.

"Ready!" said Conway.

"One—two—three—fire!"

[pg 138]

Conway's pistol blazed, and Calhoun felt a slight twinge of pain. The ball had grazed his left side, near the heart, and drawn a few drops of blood. For a moment Calhoun stood, then coolly raised his pistol and fired in the air.

The spectators raised a shout of applause; but Conway was white with rage. "I demand another shot," he shouted, "Pennington's action has made a farce of this meeting."

"It was the condition that but one shot should be allowed," remonstrated Mathews.

"The condition has not been fulfilled," angrily replied Conway; "I demand another shot."

In the mean time Matson had gone up to Calhoun, and seeing the hole through his clothing, exclaimed. "My God! are you shot, Lieutenant?"

"A mere scratch; it's nothing," answered Calhoun.

An examination showed it to be so, but blood had been drawn. This should have satisfied Conway, but it did not; he still insisted on a second shot. This the seconds were about to refuse absolutely, when Calhoun asked to be heard.

"Although Captain Conway richly deserved the blow I gave him," he said, "yet as a gentleman and an officer I felt he could do no less than challenge me. I have given him the satisfaction he demanded. If he insists on continuing the duel, I shall conclude it is his desire to kill me through personal malice, not on account of his injured honor, which according to the code has been satisfied. [pg 139]This time there will be no firing in the air. Give him the second shot, if he desires it."

"No! No!" cried a dozen voices.

Mathews went up to Conway, and speaking in a low tone, said: "You fool, do you want to be killed? Pennington will kill you as sure as fate, if you insist on the second shot. Now you are out of it honorably."

Conway mumbled something, and Mathews turning around, said: "Gentlemen, my principal acknowledges himself satisfied. It is with pleasure that I compliment both of the principals in this affair. They have conducted themselves like true Kentucky gentlemen, and I trust they will part as such."

"Shake hands, gentlemen, shake hands," cried their friends, crowding around them.

Calhoun gave his freely, but Conway extended his coldly. There was a look in his eye which foreboded future trouble.

Such a meeting could not be kept secret, and it soon came to the ears of Morgan. Both of the principals, as well as the seconds were summoned into his presence. He listened to all the details in silence, and then said:

"It is well that this affair resulted as it did. If either one of the principals had fallen, the other would have been summarily dealt with. Both of you," looking at Conway and Calhoun, "were to blame. Lieutenant Pennington should not have struck the blow: no gentleman will tamely submit [pg 140]to the indignity of a blow. As for you, Captain Conway, I am surprised that you, one of my officers, should insult a lady. If this offence is ever repeated, intoxication will be no plea in its extenuation. Heretofore it has been our proud boast that where Morgan's men are there any lady, be she for North or South, is as safe as in her own home. Let us see that it will always be so."

The men who heard burst into a wild cheer. Each of them was a knight to uphold the honor of woman.

As Captain Conway listened to the reprimand, his red face became redder. His heart was full of anger, but he was diplomat enough to listen with becoming humility. To his fellow-officers his plea was intoxication, and in the stirring times which followed, his offence was forgotten.

Scouts came dashing into the city with the startling intelligence that a large Federal force was advancing on the place. It was not long before a battle was being waged through the streets. Before an overwhelming force of infantry Morgan had to fall back.

Bragg was in full retreat, and to Morgan fell the lot of guarding the rear. As they were falling back from Camp Dick Robinson, Calhoun met a Major Hockoday, who to him was the bearer of sad news. The Major said that that morning his men pursued a Federal scout who had ventured inside their lines. In his effort to escape he had fallen over the cliff [pg 141]of Dick River, and been killed. "And I am sorry to say," added the Major, "that that scout was your cousin, Captain Fred Shackelford."

"Are you sure?" asked Calhoun, in a trembling voice.

"Perfectly sure. I knew him too well to be mistaken. For the sake of his father, I sent word to the overseer of the General's plantation so that the body could be found, and given Christian burial."

"Thank you," replied Calhoun, as he turned away with swimming eyes. All his old love for his cousin had returned. There was little heart in Calhoun for battle that day. It was weeks before he learned that Fred was not dead.

CHAPTER X.
HARTSVILLE.

W<small>HEN</small> Bragg evacuated Kentucky his weary army found rest at Murfreesboro. This little city is thirty-two miles southeast of Nashville, situated on the railroad leading from Nashville to Chattanooga. It had already become famous by the capture of a Federal brigade there in August, by General N. B. Forrest, and was destined to become the theatre of one of the greatest battles of the war.

In the Federal army a great change had taken place. General Buell had been relieved from command, and General W. Rosecrans, the hero of the battle of Corinth, appointed in his place. This general assembled his army at Nashville. Thus the two great armies were only thirty-two miles apart, with their outposts almost touching.

Bragg, believing that it would be impossible for Rosecrans to advance before spring, established his army in winter quarters, and the soldiers looked forward to two or three months of comparative quiet.

Rosecrans's first duty was to reopen the Louisville and Nashville Railroad, which had been so thoroughly destroyed by Morgan. An army of men did the work—a work which took them weeks to [pg 143]accomplish. But it was not in the nature of Morgan to be quiet. Not only he, but his men, fretted in camp life. Its daily routine with its drills did not suit them. Their home was the saddle, and they wanted no other. Therefore Morgan began to look around in search of a weak point in the Federal lines. For this purpose Calhoun and his scouts were kept busy. They seemed to be omnipresent, now here, now there. They would ride in between the Federal posts, learn of the citizens where the enemy were posted, and whether their camps were guarded with vigilance or not. Many a prisoner was picked up, and much valuable information obtained. In this way Morgan soon knew, as well as the Federal commander himself, how his troops were posted, and the number at each post.

Taking everything into consideration, Calhoun reported that Hartsville offered the best opening for an attack. "It is the extreme eastern outpost of the Federals," he said. "The nearest troops to them are at Castalian Springs, nine miles away. The country from here to Hartsville is entirely free of Federal troops, and we can approach the place unobserved. The Cumberland River is low and can be forded. But if you wish, I will go and make a thorough reconnaissance of the place."

"Go, and be back as soon as possible," replied Morgan, "but be careful; do not take too many risks."

With a dozen of his trusty scouts, Calhoun had no trouble in reaching the bank of the Cumberland [pg 144]River opposite Hartsville. Here, concealed in the woods, through his glass he noted the position of every regiment, and drew a map of the camp. But he was not satisfied with this. Under the cover of darkness he crossed the river, determined to learn more. Above all, he wished to learn where the enemy's pickets were posted at night, their exact force, as nearly as possible, and the discipline which they were under. He wanted to do all this without alarming them.

After crossing the river he concluded to call at a commodious farm-house, situated some three miles from Hartsville. He was almost certain of a hearty welcome; there were few disloyal to the South in that section. At first he was taken for a Federal soldier in disguise, and admittance was refused; but once the inmates were convinced that he was one of Morgan's men, the heartiness of his welcome made up for the coldness of his first reception.

The planter was well posted. There was one brigade at Hartsville. Until a few days before, the brigade had been commanded by a Colonel Scott, but he had been relieved by a Colonel Moore. This Moore was the colonel of one of the regiments at Hartsville, and had been in the service but a short time. Most of the troops were raw and inexperienced. Calhoun was glad to hear all this.

In the morning, dressed as a rough country boy, he made a circuit of the entire place. This he did by going on foot, and keeping to the fields and woods. The location of every picket post was [pg 145]carefully noted, and the best way to approach each one. In two or three instances he did not hesitate to approach soldiers who were foraging outside of the lines, and in a whining tone, enter into conversation with them, informing them he was looking for some of his father's pigs.

"Mighty 'fraid sum ov yo-uns Yanks got 'em," he said, with a sigh.

"No doubt, sonny, no doubt," replied a soldier with a hearty laugh. "You see, if a pig comes up and grunts at the flag, we have a right to kill him for the insult offered. Probably your pigs were guilty of this heinous crime, and were sacrificed for the good of the country."

"Do yo-uns mean the Yanks hev 'em?" asked Calhoun.

"Undoubtedly, sonny. What are you going to do about it?"

"Goin' to tell dad," replied Calhoun, as he limped off, for he pretended to be lame.

Calhoun found that the post was picketed much more strongly to the east than the west, for Castalian Springs lay to the west, and the Federals had no idea that an attack would come from that direction. If attacked, the Confederates would try to force the ford, or they would come from the east. For this reason Calhoun decided that Morgan should cross the river in between Hartsville and Castalian Springs, and assault from the west.

There was a ferry two miles below Hartsville where the infantry could cross the river, but the [pg 146]cavalry would have to go to a ford seven miles or within two miles of Castalian Springs. To his surprise, but great gratification, he found neither the ferry nor the ford guarded.

Calhoun recrossed the river in safety, and joining his scouts, whom he had left on the southern side of the river, he lost no time in making his way back to Murfreesboro. Morgan heard his report with evident satisfaction.

"Our only danger," said Calhoun, as he finished his report, "is from the force at Castalian Springs. From what I could learn there are at least five thousand Federals there. To be successful we must surprise the camp at Hartsville, capture the place, and re-cross the river before the force from the Springs can reach us. A hard thing to do, but I believe it can be done."

"So do I," said Morgan; "with General Bragg's consent, I will start at once."

General Bragg not only gave his consent, but owing to the importance of the expedition, added to Morgan's cavalry brigade two regiments of infantry and a battery.

The force marched to within five miles of Hartsville, and halted until night. The night proved very dark, and the way was rough. There was but one small ferry-boat in which to cross the infantry, and it was 5:30 in the morning before the infantry were all across, and in position two miles from Hartsville.

The cavalry had had even a rougher time than [pg 147]the infantry, and one large regiment had not yet reported. But Morgan determined not to wait, for it would soon be light, and they would be discovered. So with thirteen hundred men Morgan moved to capture a Federal brigade of over two thousand, and in a position of their own choosing.

To Calhoun and his scouts was assigned the difficult but important task of capturing the outposts without alarming the camp. The success of the whole movement might depend upon this.

So adroitly did Calhoun manage it, that the surprised pickets were captured without firing a gun. Nor was the Confederate force discovered until they were within four hundred yards of the Federal camp, and advancing in line of battle. It was now getting light, and a negro camp-follower discovered them and gave the alarm.

The Federals having been taken by surprise and most of the officers and men being raw and inexperienced, consternation reigned in the camp. But they formed their lines, and for a few moments put up a brave fight. Then their lines broke. Colonel Moore did not seem to have his brigade well in hand, and each regiment fought more or less independently. In a short time only the One Hundred and Fourth Illinois regiment was left on the site of the camp to continue the battle. Although this regiment had been only three months in the service and had never been in an engagement before, under the command of their brave Lieutenant Colonel, Douglass Hapeman, they did not surrender until [pg 148]they were entirely surrounded and nearly two hundred of their number had been shot down.

Morgan warmly complimented this regiment on its bravery, saying if all the regiments had been like it, the result of the contest would have been doubtful. In one hour and a quarter after the battle opened, all was over. A whole brigade had laid down their arms to the prowess of Morgan.

But now a new danger arose. Calhoun had been sent toward Castalian Springs to watch the enemy in that direction. One of his scouts came dashing in with the intelligence that five thousand Federals were hurrying to the relief of Hartsville. They must be stopped, and time given to get the prisoners and munitions of war across the Cumberland.

Morgan hurried two regiments to where Calhoun and his little band of scouts were resisting the advance of the enemy. The show of strength made halted the Federals, and a precious hour and a half was gained. In this time, by almost superhuman efforts, Morgan had succeeded in crossing the prisoners and his men to the south side of the Cumberland. They were now safe from pursuit.

It was during the fight with the approaching reinforcements that an incident happened which caused Calhoun many hours of uneasiness. During the hottest of the engagement a ball, evidently fired from the rear, grazed his cheek. He thought little of it, supposing some one had fired in his rear, not seeing him. But in a moment a ball passed through his hat. Wheeling suddenly, to his [pg 149]surprise he saw Captain Conway with a smoking revolver in his hand.

"You are shooting carelessly, Captain!" exclaimed Calhoun, angrily, riding up to him.

For a moment the Captain cowered, then recovering himself, he said: "You are mistaken, Lieutenant; it was some one in the rear. The same balls came close to me." Just then the order was given to fall back, and Conway rode hastily away. There was no direct proof, but Calhoun was certain Conway had tried to kill him. More than one man has been disposed of in time of battle by a personal enemy. Many an obnoxious officer has bitten the dust in this manner. Calhoun could only bide his time and watch. But he now firmly believed his life was in more danger from Conway than it was in battle with the Federals.

Hartsville, considering everything, was one of the greatest victories Morgan ever won, as he captured a whole brigade with a vastly inferior force. The Federals lost in killed, wounded, and captured two thousand one hundred men. Of these nearly three hundred were killed and wounded. Morgan's actual force engaged was only thirteen hundred, and of these he lost one hundred and forty, a small loss considering he was the assaulting party.

The capture of Hartsville caused the utmost chagrin in the Federal army, and not only in the army but throughout the North. Even President Lincoln telegraphed asking for full particulars. General Halleck ordered the dishonorable dis[pg 150]missal of Colonel Moore, but the order was never carried into effect. Of his bravery there was no question.

This victory caused the name of Morgan to be more feared than ever. "Morgan is coming!" was a cry which caused fear and trembling in many a Yankee's heart.

President Davis of the Confederate States, shortly after the capture of Hartsville, visited Murfreesboro, and as a reward for his services, presented Morgan with a commission as Brigadier-General in the Confederate army. General Hardie asked that he be made a Major-General. Hardie knew Morgan, and appreciated his worth, but for some reason President Davis refused the request.

[pg 151]

89

CHAPTER XI.
MORGAN'S SECOND GREAT RAID.

General Morgan was allowed but ten days' rest after his return from his great victory at Hartsville. General Rosecrans had finished repairing the Louisville and Nashville Railroad, and trains were running again between the two cities. Reports had been brought to General Bragg that the Federal troops at Nashville were suffering greatly for want of food; that military stores of all kinds were short; and he thought if the road were again broken, Rosecrans would be forced to fall back on account of supplies. Who so willing and able to break it as General Morgan?

But there was little use of trying to raid the road south of Bowling Green, for it was guarded by thousands of men. To cripple the road effectually meant another raid clear through the state of Kentucky. To this General Morgan was not averse.

When his men heard that another raid was to be made into Kentucky, their enthusiasm knew no bounds. What cared they for the dangers to be encountered, for long rides, for sleepless nights, and the tremendous fatigue they would be called upon to endure? They were to stir up the Yankees once more; that was enough.

"Kentucky! Ho, for Kentucky!" was their cry, [pg 152]and they shouted and sang until they could shout and sing no longer for want of breath.

Bragg was fully alive to the importance of the expedition, and was willing to give Morgan all the troops he could possibly spare. Morgan was soon at the head of the most formidable force he had ever commanded. It consisted of over three thousand cavalry, with a full battery, besides his own light battery.

The task which had been assigned him was indeed a perilous one. It was to ride almost to the very gates of Louisville, and to destroy the immense trestle works at Muldraugh Hill. This done, the Louisville and Nashville Railroad would again be effectually crippled for weeks.

He set out from Alexandria, on December 22, and in two days he was in Glasgow, Kentucky. The citizens of Glasgow had come to look upon Morgan as a monthly visitor by this time; therefore they were not surprised at his coming. Here he met with the first Federal force, which was quickly scattered.

Remaining in Glasgow only long enough to rest his horses, he pushed on for Mumfordsville, where the great bridge spans the Green River. But learning that the place was held by so strong a force that it would be madness for him to attack it, he passed a few miles to the right, and struck the railroad at Bacon

Creek. Here a stout block-house, defended by ninety soldiers, guarded the bridge. They put up a stout defence in hopes of being reinforced [pg 153]from Mumfordsville, but at last were compelled to surrender, the block-house being knocked to pieces by Morgan's artillery.

Burning the bridge and destroying four miles of road, the command moved on to Nolan, where another block-house was captured and a bridge burned. This was the third time that these bridges had been destroyed by Morgan.

Elizabethtown was the next goal to be reached. As they approached the place, Calhoun, who was in advance with his scouts, was met by an officer bearing a flag of truce, who handed him a dirty envelope, on which was scrawled:

ELIZABETHTOWN, KY., December 27, 1862.

To the Commander of the Confederate Force.

Sir: I demand an unconditional surrender of all of your forces. I have you surrounded, and will compel you to surrender.

I am, sir, your obedient servant,

H. S. SMITH,

Commanding U. S. Force.

"Well," exclaimed Calhoun, as he glanced at it, "I have often been told that Yankees have cheek, but this is the greatest exhibition of it I have met. Who is H. S. Smith, anyway?"

"One of the numerous Smith family, I reckon," dryly responded one of his men. "He should have signed it John Smith. This would have concealed his identity, and prevented us from knowing what a fool he is."

But the message was taken back to Morgan, and Calhoun never saw him laugh more heartily than when he read it.

[pg 154]

"Go back and tell Mr. Smith," replied Morgan, trying to keep his face straight, "that he has made a little mistake. It is he who is surrounded, and must surrender."

The message was taken back, but Mr. Smith answered pompously that it was the business of United States officer to fight, not to surrender.

"Very good," replied Calhoun, "get back and let us open the ball."

It took only a few shells from Morgan's battery to convince Mr. Smith he had made a mistake, and that it was the business of at least one United States officer to surrender, and not to fight. Six hundred and fifty-two prisoners fell into Morgan's hands, also a large quantity of military stores. The stores were destroyed. At Elizabethtown Morgan was in striking distance of the object of his expedition, the great trestles at Muldraugh Hill. There were two trestles, known as the upper and lower, both defended by stout stockades.

General Morgan divided his forces, Colonel Breckinridge with one brigade attacking the lower stockade, while Morgan with Colonel Duke's brigade attacked the upper. A couple of hours of severe shelling convinced the commanders of these stockades also that it was the duty of a United States officer to surrender, and not to fight. Seven hundred more prisoners and an immense store of military goods were added to Morgan's captures. The goods, as usual, were destroyed.

It was but a few minutes after the surrender of [pg 155]the block-houses when the trestles were a mass of flames. They were immense structures, each nearly fifteen hundred feet long, and from eighty to ninety feet high. Thus the object of the expedition had been gained. Again the Louisville and Nashville Railroad was rendered useless to Rosecrans's army.

But Morgan's danger had just commenced. Thus far he had had his own way. The enraged Federals were moving heaven and earth to compass his capture. A brigade was transported from Gallatin to Mumfordsville by rail, joined to the force at that place, and ordered to move east and cut off his retreat. The forces in Central Kentucky were ordered to concentrate at Lebanon. Thus they hoped to cut off every line of retreat.

"Don't let Morgan escape," was the command flashed to every Federal officer in Kentucky.

From Muldraugh Hill Morgan marched for Bardstown. This led him across the Lebanon Railroad. Before all of his force had crossed the Rolling Fork of Salt River, the pursuing force, under Colonel Harlan, came up and engaged the rear. The rear guard under Colonel Duke gallantly resisted them until all had crossed in safety, but during the action Colonel Duke was severely wounded by a piece of shell. General Boyle, the Federal commander at Louisville, gave out that he had died of his wounds and there was great rejoicing. But the gallant Colonel lived, to the disappointment of his enemies.

[pg 156]

The Federals, in close pursuit, left Morgan little time to destroy the railroad leading to Lebanon, but he captured a stockade, and burned the bridge at Boston. Reaching Bardstown in safety, he pushed rapidly on to Springfield. From that place he could threaten either Danville or Lebanon. His rapid movements puzzled the Federals, and prevented them from concentrating their forces, for they knew not which way he would go next.

From Springfield Morgan turned south, leaving Lebanon a few miles to his left, so as to avoid the large force at that place; he reached New Market a few hours in advance of his pursuers. To avoid the troops which had been concentrating at Hodgensville, he now took the road to Campbellsville.

In going through the Muldraugh range of hills to the south of New Market, his rear guard was struck by the advance of the Federals under Colonel Hoskins, and was only beaten back after a lively fight. There was now more or less skirmishing for some miles.

There now happened to Calhoun one of the most thrilling adventures he experienced during the whole war. As the post of danger was now in the rear, he was there with his scouts doing valiant service in holding back the Federals. There had been no skirmishing for some time, and nothing had been seen or heard of their pursuers. Not thinking of danger, he and a Captain Tribble halted their horses by the side of a bubbling spring and dismounted to get a drink, the rest of the guard [pg 157]passing on. They lingered longer than they thought, and had just remounted their horses when they were suddenly surprised by three horsemen, who came galloping up, yelling to them to surrender. For Calhoun and Tribble to snatch their revolvers and fire was the work of a moment. The Federals returned the fire. A pistol duel now took place, and both sides emptied their revolvers, but strange to say, no one was hurt.

Throwing down their now useless weapons, all drew their swords and furiously spurred their horses on to the combat. It was almost like a mediæval contest, where knight met knight with sword only. While one of the Federals engaged Captain Tribble, two rode straight for Calhoun, the foremost a fine-looking man in the uniform of a Federal colonel. Parrying his blow, Calhoun, by a skilful turn of his horse, avoided the other. They wheeled their horses, and came at Calhoun again. Again did Calhoun parry the fierce blow aimed at him; at the same time he managed to prick the horse of the other, so that for a moment it became unmanageable. This left Calhoun free to engage the Colonel alone, who aimed at him a tremendous blow. This blow Calhoun avoided, and as it met with no resistance, its force threw the Colonel forward on his saddle. As quick as lightning, the point of Calhoun's sword reached his heart, and the combat was over.

THE FORCE OF THE BLOW THREW THE COLONEL FORWARD ON HIS SADDLE.

During this time Tribble had vanquished his antagonist. The remaining Federal, seeing one of [pg 158]his comrades dead and the other a prisoner, threw down his sword and surrendered. The dead officer proved to be Colonel D. J. Halisy of the Sixth Kentucky cavalry.

This conflict was long remembered as one of the most remarkable ever engaged in by any of Morgan's men, and Calhoun was warmly congratulated by the whole command on his prowess.

The death of Colonel Halisy seemed to dampen the enthusiasm of Morgan's pursuers. Although they followed him to Campbellsville, and from Campbellsville to Columbia, the pursuit was a feeble one. In fact, so timid was Colonel Hoskins that he ordered his advance not to engage Morgan if they found him at Columbia, but to wait for the column from Hodgensville to come up. From Columbia all pursuit ceased, and Morgan was left to return to Tennessee at his leisure.

While at Columbia Morgan reports that his men heard distinctly the sound of distant cannonading away to the southwest. To their accustomed ears it told of a battle raging. It was the thunder of Rosecrans's cannon at Stone River. Little did Morgan's men think at that time that that distant thunder meant that hundreds of their brave brothers were being slaughtered in that fatal charge of Breckinridge. Murfreesboro is, as the crow flies, a hundred and eighteen miles from Columbia. In no other battle during the war is it reported that cannonading was heard so far.

[pg 159]

From Columbia Morgan proceeded by easy stages to Smithville, Tennessee, which he reached January 5, just fourteen days after he had started on his raid from Alexandria. During this time his command had travelled fully six hundred miles. This raid was one of the most remarkable Morgan ever made, when we consider what he accomplished, and the number of troops that tried in vain to capture him. Riding within a few miles of thousands of men, he easily eluded all his pursuers and escaped almost scot free.

General Morgan, in summing up the results of this raid, says: "It meant the destruction of the Louisville and Nashville Railroad from Mumfordsville to Shephardsville within eighteen miles of Louisville, rendering it impassable for at least two months; the capture of eighteen hundred and seventy-seven prisoners, including sixty-two commissioned officers; the destruction of over two million dollars' worth of United States property, and a large loss to the enemy in killed and wounded. The loss of my entire command was: killed, 2; wounded, 24; missing, 64."

It seems impossible that so much could be accomplished with so slight a loss. The number of his killed and wounded shows that the Federals touched him very gingerly; that they did not force the fighting. In the capture of the stockades in which he took so many prisoners, Morgan suffered hardly any loss, as he forced the surrender with his [pg 160]artillery. But the joy which Morgan and his men felt over the success of the raid was clouded when they reached Tennessee by the news of the result of the battle of Stone River. Murfreesboro no longer belonged to the South. Bragg had retreated to his new line along Duck River.

[pg 161]

CHAPTER XII.

A SPY! A SPY!

For nearly six months after the battle of Stone River, the Federal army made no general advance. General Rosecrans made his headquarters at Murfreesboro, while Bragg's was at Tullahoma. But these months were not months of idleness. Almost daily skirmishes took place between the lines, and there were a number of contests which arose to the dignity of battles.

Morgan's cavalry protected the right of Bragg's army. His headquarters were nominally at MacMinnville, but it could truly be said they were in the saddle. Morgan did not stay long in any one place. A number of expeditions were made against him, sometimes with a whole division, but he managed to elude them with slight loss.

Only twice during all this time did severe reverse overtake him—once at Milton, when he failed in his efforts to capture a brigade of infantry, and again at Snow Hill, when he was charged by a whole division of cavalry under the leadership of General David Stanley.

His captures of scouting and forage parties were numerous during these months, and he added a long list of prisoners to those he had already captured. But so strongly was every place held, and so numer[pg 162]ous had become the Federal cavalry, it was impossible to make any large capture. The enemy had learned by bitter experience, that eternal vigilance was their only safety in guarding against Morgan, and the troops which held the left of Rosecrans's army were always in fear. No Federal soldier was safe half a mile outside the lines. Bitterly did many sleepy soldiers curse him, for at three o'clock every morning they were forced to get up and stand at arms until broad daylight. The Federal officers wanted no more surprises. But in spite of all their vigilance, Morgan would swoop down and carry off prisoners from under their very noses.

These months were busy ones for Calhoun; he and his scouts were always on the go. At the battle of Milton he greatly distinguished himself, and was the subject of a complimentary order. But during the battle he received a slight flesh wound in the arm and the ball came from the rear. Again was Conway behind him. The thought that he might be slain in this treacherous manner was distracting, but what could he do? He durst not complain; such a monstrous charge against a brother officer would have to be substantiated by the best of proof. He could only avoid Conway as much as possible during battle, and hope for the best. After the battle at Milton, by reason of losses in the regiment, Conway was promoted, being appointed major. It was fortunate for Calhoun that he was chief of scouts, and on Morgan's staff, or Conway would have made his life a burden, [pg 163]for he was a member of the regiment of which Conway was major.

One day Calhoun, being sent on special duty over to the left of Bragg's army, found himself in Columbia. He now remembered what Captain Haines had told him of the misfortunes which had befallen the Osbornes, and he determined to visit them. As he approached the place a sigh escaped him, for the plantation no longer was blooming like a rose, and the splendid mansion house was a charred mass of ruins.

He found the family living in a small house which once had been occupied by the overseer. Their story was soon told. After Lieutenant Haines had been exchanged, he came back and was stationed at Columbia. He visited them frequently, was very attentive to Miss Osborne, and at last asked her to become his wife. He was very politely but firmly refused. He now began a series of petty persecutions, and was forbidden the house as a guest. Then he began to threaten. He reported to the commander that Osborne's house was the headquarters of a gang of guerrillas which gave the Federal authorities in Columbia and Pulaski a great deal of trouble.

About this time the murder of General Robert McCook by guerrillas greatly angered the Federals. A few days after he was killed a couple of foragers from Columbia were found dead. Lieutenant Haines lost no time in reporting that the gang of guerrillas sheltered by Osborne had murdered the [pg 164]men. A party was sent out, who burned the house, took away everything of value in the shape of stock, and arrested Mr. Osborne, who was afterwards sent North as a prisoner.

Calhoun listened to the recital with flashing eyes. "The villain!" he exclaimed; "if I had only known this he would not have escaped so easily when we captured him at Gallatin."

"That is not all," continued Mrs. Osborne, in a broken voice. "After all this had happened, the scoundrel had the effrontery to renew his suit, and say if Emma would marry him he would see that Mr. Osborne was released; that he had powerful political friends who could accomplish this. We spurned his proposition as it deserved. I knew my husband would rather rot in prison than consent to such a monstrous thing."

"Oh! had I known! had I known!" exclaimed Calhoun, pacing up and down the room in his excitement; "but we may meet again."

Little did Calhoun think that before many days they would meet again, and that that meeting would nearly mean for him the ignominious death of a spy. A few days after his return from Columbia, he asked the permission of

Morgan to visit Nashville. "I would like to see," said he, "what our friends, the enemy, are doing in that city."

Morgan shook his head. "I don't want to see you hanged," he replied.

But Calhoun argued so zealously, that at last Morgan's scruples were overcome, and he gave his [pg 165]consent, but added, "If you should be captured and executed, I would never forgive myself."

Calhoun looked upon it as a mere holiday affair; he had passed through too many dangers to be terrified. Taking half a dozen of his trusty scouts with him, he had no trouble in reaching the Cumberland River a few miles above Nashville. The few scouting parties of the enemy they met were easily avoided. He ordered his scouts to remain secreted in a thick wood near by a friendly house, from which they could obtain food for themselves and provender for their horses.

"If I am not back in three days," said he, "return to Morgan, and tell him I have been captured."

His men pleaded with him to let at least one of them accompany him, but this he refused, saying it would but add to his danger.

From the gentleman who resided in the nearby house he secured a skiff which had been kept secreted from the lynx-eyed Federals. In this Calhoun proposed to float down to Nashville.

Night came dark and cloudy. It was just such a night as Calhoun wished. Clad in a suit of citizen's clothes, and with muffled oars, he bade his comrades a cheerful good night, and pushed out into the river, and in a moment the darkness had swallowed him up. He floated down as noiselessly as a drifting stick.

In an hour's time the lights of Nashville came in view; the dangers of his trip had just commenced. [pg 166]He knew that the banks of the river would not only be strongly patrolled, but the lights from the shore and from the steamers moored at the wharfs shone across the stream in places, making it impossible for an object the size of his boat to pass without being noticed.

But Calhoun was prepared for just such an emergency. He was a capital swimmer, and had no fears of the water. He had weighted his skiff with stones, bored a hole in the bottom, and filled it with a plug which could easily be removed. When he had drifted as far as he dared, he removed the plug. The skiff gradually filled and at last sank. If any person had looked after it disappeared, all he would have seen would have been the small branch of a tree, covered with leaves, floating down with the current.

When Calhoun was well down abreast of the city, and coming to a place where shadows covered the river, he turned toward the bank. Fortunately he landed near a dark alley which led down to the water. Listening intently, he heard nothing, and making his way up the alley, he soon came to a street. A violent storm came on, which was of advantage to him, for if he met any one, it would account for his dripping clothes. It also had the effect of driving the patrol guards into shelter.

Calhoun was no stranger in the city. He had visited it frequently when a boy, for he had an uncle residing there, now a colonel in the Confederate army. But his family still resided in the old [pg 167]home, and he knew that there he would find a haven of safety. Carefully making his way, and dodging the few guards that he met, he soon reached the house. The yard was inclosed with a high iron fence, the pickets provided with sharp points. But Calhoun had been in the army too long to be baffled by any such obstacle. He mounted the fence with but little trouble and dropped down into the yard.

Making his way to the rear of the house, he found refuge in a small shed. The night had turned cool and he shivered with the cold. But he durst not arouse the household, for the alarm might be heard outside. The hours passed wearily by, but at last morning came. He looked eagerly for some of the family to appear, but only the colored servants passed in and out. To escape being seen he had hidden behind a large box in the shed.

He heard the call for breakfast, and concluded he had never been so hungry before in his life. After a while his patience was rewarded. A young lady came out of the house, and entering the shed, began looking around, as if searching for something. It was his cousin Kate.

"Kate!" he whispered.

The girl started and looked wildly around.

"Kate!"

She uttered a little scream and turned as if to flee.

"Kate, don't be afraid. It is I, your cousin Calhoun Pennington."

[pg 168]

"Where? Where?" she half-whispered, looking eagerly around and poised as if still for flight.

"Here behind the box. Come close. There, don't ask a question. Get the servants out of the way and smuggle me into the house unseen. I am wet, cold, and hungry."

Kate flew to do his bidding. In a few moments she came out and beckoned to him, and right gladly he followed her into the house. One risen from the dead would hardly have created more surprise than did his appearance. His aunt and Kate persisted in embracing him, wet and dirty as he was.

To their eager questions, he said: "Dry clothes first, Auntie, and breakfast. I am famished. I will then talk with you to your heart's content."

Mrs. Shackelford had had a son about the size of Calhoun killed in the army, and our hero was soon arrayed in a nice dry suit, and seated before a substantial breakfast, upon which he made a furious assault. When his hunger was fully appeased, he informed his aunt and Kate he was ready to talk. And how they did talk! They had a thousand questions to ask, and he had full as many.

To his surprise and joy he learned that his cousin, Fred Shackelford, had not been killed by his fall over the cliff, as Major Hockoday reported. Instead he was alive and well, was with the army at Murfreesboro, and frequently visited them.

"He has been a good friend to us," said Mrs. Shackelford, "but at one time he was nearly the death of Kate."

[pg 169]

"Why, how was that?" asked Calhoun.

Then for the first time he heard of Forrest's plot to capture Nashville, and of Kate's part in it, of her condemnation, and imprisonment as a spy, and how Fred had secured her pardon.[2]

Calhoun listened to the story in wonder. When it was finished, he exclaimed: "Why, Kate, you are a heroine! I am proud of you."

"I am not proud of myself," answered Kate. "I blush every time I think of how—how I lied and deceived."

"Oh! that is a part of war," laughed Calhoun. "If Morgan didn't lie about the number of men he had, the Yanks would gobble him up in no time. We don't call such things lying; it's a righteous deceiving of the enemy."

"But I am ready to sink into the earth with shame every time I think of Ainsworth," sighed Kate.

"That's rich," laughed Calhoun; "crying because you broke the heart of a Yankee! Kate, I have a mind to send you into the enemy's lines. If Cupid's darts were only fatal, your bright eyes would create more havoc than a battle."

"No use sending her away," broke in Mrs. Shackelford; "there are more Federal officers buzzing around her now than I wish there were."

"Mighty useful to worm secrets from," exclaimed Kate; "but I make no promises to any of them."

[pg 170]

"That's right, Kate, get all the secrets from them you can," said Calhoun; "that is what I am in Nashville for. Can any one get around the city without much danger?"

"Oh, yes, in the daytime; but there is always more or less danger to strangers. Business is going on as usual. The city is lively, livelier than before the war; but it is soldiers—soldiers everywhere."

"And you have to have no passes?" asked Calhoun.

"It is best to have one. Most of us have standing permits to come and go in the city as we please."

"Can you get me a permit?" asked Calhoun, eagerly.

"There is Jim Grantham," replied Kate, thoughtfully; "his description will suit Calhoun close enough. I can get Jim to loan you his."

Calhoun was now told that the Southern people in Nashville were thoroughly organized into a secret society. They had their signs and pass-words, so that they could know each other. So far no one had proved a traitor. The Federal authorities suspected that such an organization existed, but their shrewdest detectives never succeeded in finding out anything about it.

Kate, who had gone for the permit of James Grantham, soon returned with it. The description fitted Calhoun almost as well as if made out for himself. He could now walk the streets of Nashville with little fear of arrest.

[pg 171]

He was given a list of those who could most probably give him the information he desired. He marvelled to see how quickly a little sign which he gave was answered, and was amazed at the work this secret organization was doing. Not a regiment entered or left Nashville but they knew its exact strength, and to what point it was ordered.

In two days Calhoun had gathered information which would be of vast value to the Confederate cause, and it was now time for him to see by what means he could leave the city. He was on his way to see three gentlemen who said they could get him outside of the city without trouble or danger, when an incident happened which came near sending him to the gallows. He was walking unconcernedly along the street, when he suddenly came face to face with Haines, now a captain. Although Calhoun was dressed in citizen's clothes, the captain knew him at a glance.

101

"A spy! A spy!" he yelled at the top of his voice, and made a grab at Calhoun. Calhoun struck him a tremendous blow which sent him rolling in the gutter, and fled at the top of his speed.

But a score of voices took up the cry, and a howling mob, mostly of soldiers, were at his heels. He hoped to reach the river, where among the immense piles of stores heaped along the levee, or among the shipping, he might secrete himself, but a patrol guard suddenly appeared a block away, and his retreat was cut off. He gave himself up for lost, and reached for a small pistol which he carried, [pg 172]with the intention of putting a bullet through his own heart; "for," thought he, "they shall never have the pleasure of hanging me before a gaping crowd."

Just then he saw two young ladies standing in the open door of a house. What told him safety lay there he never knew, but hope sprang up within his breast. Dashing up the steps, he thrust the ladies back into the house, slammed the door to, and locked it. So rude was his entrance, one of the ladies fell to the floor.

"Save me! Save me!" he cried, "I am a Confederate spy," and he gave the sign of the secret order.

The young lady who had not fallen was terribly frightened, but she grasped the situation in a moment.

"Upstairs," she gasped, pointing the way; "tell mother, the secret place."

Calhoun lost no time in obeying her. The girl flew to the back door and opened it, then back just as her sister was rising, her face covered with blood, for she had hit her nose in falling.

"Quick, Annette, in the parlor," said her sister; "assent to everything I say."

Annette staggered into the parlor hardly knowing what she did, for she was dazed and terribly frightened. The sister, whose name was Inez, was now at the door, which was giving way before the blows of Calhoun's pursuers. All this happened in less than a minute.

[pg 173]

"Stop!" she cried, "I will unlock the door," and she did so, and when the soldiers rushed in, crying, "Where is he? Where is the spy?" she stood wringing her hands and sobbing, "My sister! Oh, my sister! he has murdered her."

The words brought the soldiers to a halt. "Who murdered your sister?" asked a sergeant who seemed to be the leader.

"The man! the man who ran in here!"

"Where is he? He is the fellow we want."

"He rushed out of the back door. Oh! my sister, my sister!"

"After him, boys; don't let him get away!" yelled the sergeant, and they rushed through the house in hot pursuit.

The house was rapidly filling, when a captain appeared, and learning of the sobbing Inez what the trouble was, said: "Murdered your sister! Horrible! where is she?"

"Here," said Inez, leading the way into the parlor. Annette was reclining on a sofa, her face bloody; she was apparently in a fainting condition.

The captain acted quickly. He ordered the house to be cleared, sent a subordinate for a surgeon, and another to have the whole block surrounded. In the mean time the mother of the girls had appeared, and was adding her sobs to those of her eldest daughter. When the surgeon came and had washed the blood from Annette's face, her only injury was found to be a bruised nose.

Both the captain and the surgeon looked in[pg 174]quiringly. "How is this?" they asked, "you said your sister was murdered."

"I—I thought she was," stammered Inez. "I saw the blood and thought the man had stabbed her."

"Tell us just what happened," said the captain.

Annette, who had by this time so far recovered from her fright as to comprehend what was going on, saw Inez give her the signal of danger. It put her on her guard.

"Why, it was this way," said Inez, in answer to the captain, "sister and I were going out, but just as we opened the door, there was a tumult on the street. We stopped to see what the trouble was, when a man dashed up the steps. We tried to oppose him, but he struck sister a cruel blow, knocking her down, flung me backward, and slamming the door to, locked it; then running through the house, disappeared through the back door. Seeing sister's face covered with blood, I picked her up and carried her into the parlor. By this time the soldiers were breaking down the door, and I went and unlocked it."

Annette only knew that she tried to oppose the entrance of a strange man, who knocked her down. She must have been rendered unconscious, for she remembered nothing more, until she found herself lying on the sofa in the parlor. The mother, Mrs. Lovell, was upstairs, and knew nothing of what had happened until alarmed by the screams of her daughters and the noisy entrance of the soldiers. [pg 175]These stories so accorded with the known facts that the captain did not for a moment doubt them. But when the sergeant returned and reported that no trace of the fugitive could be discovered, he was puzzled.

Orders were given to search every house in the block. This was done, but the search was fruitless. When this fact was reported, the captain bit his lip in vexation. Then turning to Inez, he said: "Pardon me, Miss Lovell, while I do not doubt your story in the least, are you sure the fellow ran out of the house? Was not his opening the back door just a ruse? He opened the door and then dodged into some room, thinking this house the safest place for him. Every house in the block has been searched except this one, and we can find no trace of him. While I regret it, I shall be compelled to have this house searched."

"I am sure he ran out," answered Inez, "but I confess I was very badly frightened. If you think he is in the house, search it. I ask as a favor that you search it, for if he is concealed in the house as you think, he may murder us all."

A thorough search was made, but there was found no trace of Calhoun. The officers and soldiers retired greatly puzzled. A strong guard was maintained around the block for three days; then all hopes of catching Calhoun were given up, and the guard was withdrawn.

The Federal authorities had become aware who the fugitive was through Captain Haines. "I can[pg 176]not be mistaken," he said; "I have met him too many times. He is one of the most daring of all of Morgan's cutthroats"; and then he gave an account of his first meeting with Calhoun.

But where was Calhoun all this time? When he rushed upstairs at the command of Inez, he was met at the top by Mrs. Lovell, who started in affright at the sight of him.

"Your daughter said, 'The secret place!' " he exclaimed, as he gave her the sign of danger. "My pursuers are already at the door."

The lady quickly recovered herself. "Come!" she said, and led Calhoun into a room. Here she began working in a corner. Her hands trembled as she did so, for the soldiers were thundering at the door downstairs, and she could hear it giving way. To Calhoun's intense surprise, a section of the apparently solid wall gave way, leaving an opening large enough for a person to enter by crawling on his hands and knees.

"Quick, go in!" said the lady.

Calhoun needed no second bidding, but crawled in, and the wall slowly came back to place. Calhoun found himself in a narrow place, between the wall of the room and the side of the house. The house had been built with a mansard roof on the sides, thus leaving a space. This space was about three feet wide at the bottom, coming to a point at the top. Close under the eaves, where it would not be noticed, an aperture had been left for the admission of air, and through it a ray of light came.

[pg 177]

Narrow and contracted as his quarters were, to Calhoun they were more welcome than a palace. It was plain that the place had been occupied before, for on the floor there were soft blankets, and in feeling around Calhoun discovered a jug of water and some provisions. It was evident that no one who was put in there hurriedly was to be allowed to suffer from thirst or hunger.

Calhoun could hear every word which was said when the soldiers searched the room. His heart stood still when he heard them sounding the walls, but they gave forth no uncertain sound, and the soldiers departed, much to his relief.

It was not until the next day that Calhoun was allowed to leave his hiding-place, and then he was told he must not leave the room. He had to be ready to seek his refuge at a moment's notice, if found necessary. For three days he was virtually a prisoner, then the guards around the block were withdrawn.

Word was taken to his aunt and Kate where he was. They had been in an agony of fear over his non-return. But they durst not visit him.

To Mrs. Lovell and her daughters Calhoun felt he could never repay what they had done for him. He felt like a brute, when Annette was introduced to him, her pretty features disfigured by a swollen nose, and when he was making his most abject apologies, she interrupted him with a gay laugh.

"I am proud of that nose!" she exclaimed; "as [pg 178]proud as a gallant soldier of his wounds, for does it not show that I have shed my blood for our beloved South?"

We are of the opinion that during his enforced imprisonment, Calhoun would have lost his heart to Annette if he had not learned she was engaged to a gallant officer in Bragg's army.

What troubled Calhoun the most was the thought that his scouts would return to Morgan with the news that he was captured, but there was no help for it.

After the guards had been withdrawn, he at once began to make plans for his escape from the city. The original plan had to be given up, for the vigilance of the Federals had been redoubled, and it was impossible for any one to leave the city without his identity being fully established.

At last Inez clapped her hands. "I have it," she cried. "Get him out to Dr. Caldwell. The doctor lives clear on the outskirts of the city, and on the bank of the river. Lieutenant Pennington can take to the river going as he did coming."

"But he can't float up stream," said Annette, "and as for a boat, that will be impossible."

"He can swim," said Inez, "swim across the river. He will be above the pickets around Edgefield."

"But how can he get to Dr. Caldwell? It is not safe for him to appear on the street. Not a guard but has a description of him," said the careful Annette.

[pg 179]

"Dr. Caldwell is attending Mrs. Robinson (the Robinsons lived next door); it will be easy for the doctor to take him in his buggy; no guard will think of disturbing the doctor, he is too well known."

Calhoun eagerly caught at the idea. When Dr. Caldwell visited Mrs. Robinson during the day, he was seen, and consented to the scheme. "Muffle him up," he said, "he will be taken for one of my patients." Before Calhoun left he wrote a letter, and directed it to Captain Haines — Regt. This Inez promised to mail when Calhoun was well out of the city.

Dr. Caldwell had no trouble in taking Calhoun to his home. Here he stayed until dark, then bidding the hospitable physician good-bye, he plunged into the river and was soon across, and began to make his way slowly up the northern bank. But the night was dark, and after many falls and bruises, he concluded to wait for daylight. Having made himself a bed of leaves beside a log, he was soon sleeping as peacefully as if no dangers were lurking near.

As for Captain Haines, he was bitterly disappointed when Calhoun was not caught. But his leave of absence was out, and he had to return to his regiment near Murfreesboro. A day or two after his return the following letter came with his mail:

NASHVILLE, TENN., April 25, 1863.

To Capt. Chas. Haines,

My Dear Captain: When you receive this I shall be well out of Nashville. We have already met three times, and I trust we [pg 180]may meet once more. If we do, it will be our last, for one or the other of us will die. I know of your damnable treatment of the Osbornes. Be assured it will be avenged.

Sincerely yours,

CALHOUN PENNINGTON,

Lieutenant, Morgan's Command.

Captain Haines was no coward, but his hand trembled like a leaf when he laid the letter down.

CHAPTER XIII.

UNDER ARREST.

Calhoun did not wake until the light of the morning sun was sifting through the branches of the trees. He arose stiff and somewhat chill, but the day promised to be a warm one, and a little exercise put a delightful heat through his body. All he lacked was a good breakfast, and he must not look for that until he had crossed the river; he was yet too close to Nashville to try to cross it. Then he must secure a horse, and where would he be so likely to secure one as at the home of Mr. Edmunds, the gentleman of whom he had obtained the skiff, and who had given him all possible aid? He had no hopes of finding his men, for at the end of three days they would return to Morgan, taking his horse with them.

He slowly made his way up the river, dodging two or three scouting parties, until he thought he must be nearly opposite to where Mr. Edmunds lived. The place seemed favorable, as there were woods on both sides of the river, so he determined to cross. But if he had known it, he had selected a very dangerous place. A road which led down to the river was but a few yards in front of him, and it was one of the places to which the Federal cavalry came as they patrolled the bank of the river.

[pg 182]

Just as he was about to remove some of his clothing, which he would carry over on his head as he swam the stream, he was startled by the sound of horses' hoofs, and he hastily concealed himself in a thicket. Soon a Federal sergeant, accompanied by two soldiers, came down the road, and riding near the edge of the river, dismounted.

"Here is the place," said the sergeant.

"What are we to do here?" asked one of the men.

"Keep watch to see if any Johnny attempts to cross the river," answered the sergeant; "but I doubt if we see anything larger than buzzards, and we can't stop them."

The men made themselves comfortable, and lay in the shade smoking their pipes. Calhoun was considering the proposition whether he could not quietly withdraw, and flank them without being seen, when one of the men said: "Sergeant, let me go to that house we passed and see if I cannot get a canteen of milk. It will go good with our hardtack."

"You can both go," replied the sergeant; "I guess I can stop any one who attempts to cross the river while you are away. But don't be gone long."

The men quickly availed themselves of the opportunity, and mounting their horses rode away. The sergeant stretched himself on the ground, and lazily watched the river. Now was Calhoun's time. He had secured a good revolver when he left Nash[pg 183]ville. This he had kept dry when he swam the river by wrapping it in his outside clothing, which he had made into a bundle, and carried over on his head. Taking the revolver in his hand, ready for instant use, he cautiously crept up on the sergeant.

HE CAUTIOUSLY CREPT UP ON THE SERGEANT.

That individual leaped to his feet as if he had springs when he heard the stern command, "Surrender!"

He reached for his weapon, but suddenly stopped when he saw he was looking into the muzzle of a revolver.

"Hands up! Be quick about it!"

The hands of the sergeant slowly went above his head.

"Pardon me, but I will relieve you of this," said Calhoun, as he took a revolver from the belt of his prisoner, and tossed it into the river.

Up to this time the sergeant had not said a word, but now he exclaimed, with the utmost disgust, "How thundering careless of me! Sergeant Latham, you are no good; you ought to be reduced to the ranks."

"Oh! don't feel too bad about it; better men than you have been caught napping," replied Calhoun, consolingly.

"But no bigger fool. To be gobbled in like this, and by a blamed skulking citizen, too. Now, if—"

"Rest your mind there, if it will make you feel any better," broke in Calhoun, "I am no civilian, I am Lieutenant Calhoun Pennington of Morgan's command."

[pg 184]

"You don't say," replied the sergeant, apparently much relieved. "Lieutenant, allow me to introduce myself. I am Sergeant Silas Latham. We have had the pleasure of meeting before."

"Where?" asked Calhoun, in surprise.

"Down in Tennessee, when you got away with Lieutenant Haines's horse so slick."

Calhoun's face darkened. "Did you have anything to do with the persecution of the Osbornes?" he asked, threateningly.

"Not I. That was the blamedest, meanest trick I ever knew Haines to do. But he was dead gone on the girl. I half believe he would have turned Reb if he could have got her."

"I saw Haines the other day," remarked Calhoun.

"Where?" asked the Sergeant.

"In Nashville. I had the pleasure of knocking him down."

The Sergeant chuckled. "Served him right. He threatened to have me reduced to the ranks because I told him he ought to be ashamed of himself, the way he persecuted that girl."

"Are you in his company now?"

"No; he is the captain of another company. Glad of it."

"Sergeant Latham, I would like to continue this conversation, but time presses. Give me your parole, and I will be going."

"By gum, I won't do it!" exclaimed Latham, with energy. "If you want to take me prisoner, take me. But do you think I am going sneaking [pg 185]back to camp with the story that I let one Johnny gobble me? No, sir, not by a jugful!"

"Latham, you are a character. Can you swim?"

"Never learned when a boy."

"Will your horse carry double?" asked Calhoun.

"No, he is a poor swimmer, he would drown us both."

"Latham, I am afraid I shall have to shoot you. I don't see any other way to get rid of you."

Latham thought a moment, and said: "Let me ride the horse across and you swim."

"A brilliant idea, declined with thanks."

Latham scratched his head as if for an idea. "Perhaps I can hang on by the horse's tail," he remarked, hesitatingly.

"That's better. It's either a parole, the tail, or death. Which shall it be?"

"I will take the tail."

"All right; but you must give me your word of honor that you will hang on."

"Like grim death," answered Latham.

"Come, then, I have fooled away too much time already."

Marching his prisoner up to where his horse was tethered, Calhoun took Latham's sword and carbine which hung to the saddle and pitched them into the river after the revolver.

Mounting the horse, Calhoun said, "Now, no fooling. The slightest attempt on your part to escape, and I shall shoot you without compunction of conscience."

[pg 186]

"I am not fool enough to run when there is a revolver at my head," growled Latham.

"Nevertheless you will bear watching. I am of the opinion you are a slippery customer. You just walk by my side here until we reach deep water."

They entered the river. Latham wading quietly by the side of the horse, until the water became so deep the horse began to plunge.

"Now, grab his tail," commanded Calhoun, and he watched Latham until he had taken a firm hold of the horse's tail and was in water beyond his depth.

"For the Lord's sake, keep his head above water," shouted Latham from behind, as the horse made a fearful plunge.

For the next few minutes Calhoun had enough to do without looking to see what had become of Latham. The horse, as the Sergeant had said, proved a poor swimmer. Twice he came near drowning; but at last managed to struggle through. When he got to where the water was shallow enough for the horse to wade, Calhoun looked around to see how Latham had fared.

To his surprise he saw that worthy leaning against a tree on the bank from which they had started, and apparently he had been watching the struggles of the horse in the water with a great deal of satisfaction.

Calhoun hardly knew whether to laugh or get angry. Riding to the edge of the water, he turned [pg 187]his horse around, and yelled over, "You are a pretty fellow, you are! Like most Yankees, your word of honor is worthless."

"Did just what I said I would!" yelled back Latham.

"You did not. You told me you would hold on that horse's tail like grim death."

"And so I did. I am holding on to it yet," and to Calhoun's surprise Latham shook a large piece of the horse's tail at him. He had neatly severed it.

Calhoun shook with suppressed laughter, but assuming a severe tone, he said: "You lied to me like a Turk, anyway, you miserable Yankee; you told me you could not swim."

"I told you no such thing, you skulking Rebel," yelled back Latham, wrathfully. "Come back here and fight me like a man, and I will wallop you until you can't stand, for calling me a liar. I would have you know I am a member of the church in good standing."

"Didn't you tell me you couldn't swim?"

"No; I told you I had never learned to swim when a boy."

"When did you learn to swim?"

"After I became a man."

Calhoun exploded. "Say, Latham," he cried, "I forgive you. You are the slickest Yankee I ever met. I must be going, for I see your men are coming. Ta! ta!"

Calhoun turned and urged his horse up the bank, [pg 188]but not in time to escape having two balls sing uncomfortably close to his head.

Sergeant Latham had little trouble in recovering his arms from the river, as the water was not deep where Calhoun had thrown them.

The Sergeant made the following report of the affair to his superior officer:

Sir: I have the honor to report that a Rebel scout crossed the Cumberland to-day near the post where I was stationed. I followed him into the river, but my horse being a poor swimmer, I was forced to abandon him in mid-stream to save myself.

SILAS LATHAM, Sergeant.

The capture of Latham's horse and the ludicrous affair with him put Calhoun in the best of humor. He reached the house of Mr. Edmunds without further adventure, and met with a hearty welcome from that gentleman, who informed him that his men had lingered a day longer than he had ordered, in the hope that he would return.

After satisfying his hunger, Calhoun bade his kind host good-bye, and without trouble reached Morgan's camp that night. Here he was received as one snatched from the jaws of death, for they had given him up as lost. The valuable information which he had collected was forwarded to General Bragg, and in due time an acknowledgment was received from that general, warmly congratulating him, and saying he had recommended him for a captaincy.

It was but a few days after his return that Calhoun was with a regiment reconnoitring near Braddyville, when they were suddenly attacked by [pg 189]a whole brigade of Federal cavalry. The engagement was a spirited one, but owing to the superior numbers of the Federals, the Confederates were forced to fall back. During the retreat Calhoun with his scouts was holding back the advance of the enemy. They were furiously charged by two companies of the Federals, and a hand-to-hand conflict took place. During this combat Calhoun became engaged with a Federal captain, and to his surprise he saw that his antagonist was Captain Haines. The recognition was mutual, and it must have unnerved the hand of the Captain, for although but a few feet from Calhoun, he fired and missed him. Before he could fire again, Calhoun dashed his empty revolver into his face. The force of the blow caused him to reel in his saddle, and before he could recover, Calhoun had cut him down.

The bloody repulse of these two companies cooled the ardor of the Federals, and the Confederates withdrew without further molestation.

Major Conway noted Calhoun's growing popularity with the command, and his hatred, if possible, grew more bitter. The sting of the blow he had received still rankled in his heart, and he swore sooner or later to have his revenge. His attempts to assassinate Calhoun in time of battle, so far had failed, and Calhoun's extreme wariness now usually kept them apart during an engagement. The crafty Major was busily thinking of some other scheme by which he could kill Calhoun without bringing suspicion on himself, when an incident [pg 190]happened which he thought would not only cause Calhoun to die a most disgraceful death, but redound greatly to his own credit.

Calhoun was out with his scouts when he fell in with a small party of the enemy. As he outnumbered them, he thought their capture was easy. But he was met with such a rapid and accurate fire that his men were forced to fall back.

"Them Yankees have repeating rifles," growled one of his men, "and they know how to shoot."

This was true, and Calhoun was thinking of withdrawing from the fight entirely, when he caught sight of the leader of the Federals. The horse which he rode he would know among ten thousand. It was Prince, the famous horse of his cousin, and the rider must be Fred. Ordering his men to cease firing, Calhoun tied a white handkerchief to the point of his sword, and rode forward.

Fred, for it was he, rode out to meet him. As soon as he came within hearing distance, he asked, "Do you surrender?"

"Surrender nothing!" answered Calhoun, a little disgusted. "If you only knew how many men I had back there you would think of surrendering yourself. I simply came out to have a little talk with you."

"Cal, as sure as I live!" exclaimed Fred, and in a moment the two cousins had each other by the hand, forgetting they were enemies, remembering only their love for each other.

They had much to say to each other, and talked [pg 191]longer than they thought, but were about to part, mutually agreeing to withdraw their men, when they were startled by the sound of rapid firing. Looking up they saw that Fred's men were being charged by a large force of Confederates. They were in full retreat, firing as they galloped back. Fred was alone in the midst of his enemies.

The Confederates proved to be a full squadron in command of Major Conway. He was accompanied by Captain Mathews. No sooner did they see Fred than they shouted in their delight.

"The hoss is mine again!" cried Mathews.

"And this spy and sneak is in my power at last," exclaimed Conway, pointing at Fred; "and what is better I have you, my fine fellow," said Conway, turning to Calhoun. "I have long known that you were holding treasonable conferences with the enemy, and have only been waiting for indubitable proof. I have it now.

"Lieutenant," turning to one of his officers, "arrest Lieutenant Pennington, and on your life see that he does not escape."

The enormity of the charge dumbfounded Calhoun. He could scarcely believe his ears. He began to protest, but was cut short by Conway, who ordered the Lieutenant to take an escort of ten men and to conduct Calhoun straightway to General Bragg at Tullahoma.

"Tell the General," he said, "that I have positive proof of Lieutenant Pennington's treasonable intercourse with the enemy. The case is so impor[pg 192]tant I thought it best to send the prisoner direct to him. As soon as I see General Morgan I will file formal charges."

The Lieutenant seemed surprised at his orders to take Calhoun direct to Bragg, but he said nothing, and choosing his escort, was soon on the way to Tullahoma with his prisoner.

Major Conway's real object in sending Calhoun to Tullahoma was to bring the case directly to the notice of General Bragg, and thus compel Morgan to take action. He knew that his charge would not be believed in Morgan's command, but he would see that there was plenty of evidence at the right time.

Disarmed, under arrest, charged with the most heinous offence of which an officer could be guilty, it is no wonder that Calhoun's heart sank within him on that dismal journey to Tullahoma.

"Better to have been hanged as a spy by the Federals than to be shot as a traitor by my own men," he muttered to himself. The thought of dying such a disgraceful death was maddening.

When he arrived at Tullahoma, his reception by General Bragg was not exactly such as he had expected. Bragg was noted as a martinet and a great stickler for military forms. When the lieutenant who had Calhoun in charge reported to him, and told him the verbal message which Major Conway had sent, he flew into a furious rage.

"What does Major Conway mean by sending a prisoner to me with such a message as that?" he [pg 193]sputtered. "What is General Morgan about that he has not attended to this, and presented his charges in due form.

"Officer, take the prisoner to General Morgan, and tell Major Conway to read up on army discipline."

If it had endangered his whole army, Bragg would have contended for rigid adherence to military law. When Bragg's order was reported to Calhoun, hope began to revive. Surely Morgan would give him a fair hearing. Every act he had done in the army would disprove the monstrous charges of Major Conway.

It was with a much lighter heart that he set out for MacMinnville. But when he reached that place he was surprised by the astonishing news that Conway had been shot—killed while in the act of murdering his cousin in cold blood.

One of the men who was with Conway at the time was mortally wounded, and confessed the whole thing. Conway was to prepare a paper which they were to swear was found on Fred's person, criminating Calhoun. With such evidence his conviction would have been certain. He thanked God for the death of Conway. It meant a thousand times more to him than life, for it kept his name unsullied.

Morgan made a full report of the whole matter to General Bragg. "The plot was damnable," he wrote, "yet it might have been successful if Major Conway had not met his just deserts. But one [pg 194]might as well accuse me of holding treasonable communications with the enemy as Lieutenant Pennington. He is the officer, as you may remember, that entered Nashville a short time since, and sent you such a valuable report. Moreover, he is the very officer I have chosen to look into that matter which we have discussed so much. I expect to send him North next week."

Thus was Calhoun fully exonerated, and not only that, but he was to be chosen for a most important mission. He also had the satisfaction of seeing Morgan make Captain Mathews return Fred his horse, much to the Captain's disgust. But what was the important duty upon which Calhoun was to be sent North? He had heard nothing of it before.

Some time before the Hon. C. L. Vallandigham, a noted Democratic politician of Ohio, and an ex-member of Congress, had been arrested at his home in Dayton for treason. He was tried by military court-martial, found guilty, and banished South. The excitement was intense. Thousands of his friends rallied to his defence, and at one time it looked as if the streets of Dayton would run red with blood. His friends were in open revolt against the government, and opposed the prosecution of the war.

Before this numerous reports had reached the South of the dissatisfaction of a large number of the Democratic party with Lincoln, especially with his proclamation freeing the slaves. They were [pg 195]sick and tired of the war, and were more than willing to give the South her independence. They were ready to force Lincoln to do this. A secret society, known as the Knights of the Golden Circle, existed throughout the North, and was most numerous in the states of Illinois, Indiana, and Ohio. The purpose of this society was to resist the draft, encourage desertions from the army, embarrass the government in every way possible, and if necessary resort to arms. Already numerous small encounters had taken place between the Knights and the militia of these states.

It was the boast of the Knights that they had a quarter of a million men armed and drilled, ready to take the field. If a Confederate force would only invade the North, their ranks would be augmented by these thousands. It was to investigate these reports and find out the truth that Calhoun was to be sent North.

[pg 196]

CHAPTER XIV.
THE KNIGHTS OF THE GOLDEN CIRCLE.

No one was more surprised than Calhoun when told that he had been selected to go North on a secret and most important mission.

"General Breckinridge and I have selected you," said Morgan, "because we have confidence in your sagacity, bravery, and discretion. We know no one better fitted to intrust this delicate, and perhaps dangerous, mission to than yourself."

"But I am so young," said Calhoun; "while I gladly accept the honor which I feel you have bestowed upon me, would not one older and more experienced than I do better?"

"Your youth is one of the main reasons why we have chosen you," replied Morgan. "A youth like you will not excite suspicion half as quickly as a man."

"Then I am more than willing to go," answered Calhoun, "and trust that the confidence you repose in me will not prove to have been misplaced."

"I have no fears on that score," answered Morgan; "I know that you will succeed, if any one can."

The General then fully explained what was required of him. Calhoun listened in silence.

"I think I fully understand what you want of [pg 197]me, General, but how am I to approach these Knights of the Golden Circle? How am I to find out who are Knights?"

"That has already been provided for," answered Morgan. "We are now ready to initiate you into a camp of the Golden Circle."

"Does the order exist down South, too?" asked Calhoun, in surprise.

"Certainly, to some extent," was the answer. "If not, how could we know the secrets of the order? You are willing, I suppose, to take the oaths required?"

"If there is not anything in them to hinder me from being a true son of the South," replied Calhoun.

"I assure you there is not, for I have taken them," said Morgan; "but you must bear in mind this is a Northern order, its chief purpose to overthrow the Lincoln government; its chief cornerstone is States' Rights. The Hon. C. L. Vallandigham, who was lately sent into our lines for disloyalty, but who has now found a refuge in Canada, is the Supreme Commander of the order. No truer friend of the South exists than Vallandigham. He believes in the doctrine of secession. The North is sick and tired of the war, and wants to put a stop to it and let the South go in peace. This is the purpose of the order."

"All right," said Calhoun; "I am ready to join any order that has that for its purpose."

Calhoun was conducted to a tent where, to his surprise, he met quite a number of the officers of [pg 198]the command. There was one stranger present, a gentleman in civilian dress. Calhoun was told that he was from the North, was a high officer in the order, and that he would conduct the initiatory ceremonies. When Calhoun issued from that tent he was a full-fledged member of the Knights of the Golden Circle. But he had taken only the first degree. The other degrees were to be given to him after he had arrived in the North.

After having fully learned the signs, grips, and passwords of the order, Calhoun was ready for his journey. He now received his final instructions from Morgan and Breckinridge.

It did not take Calhoun long to see that while these gentlemen were willing to use the order, they had the utmost contempt for it. All nations use traitors and despise them at the same time. The Knights of the Golden Circle were traitors to their section. Calhoun felt this, and loathed the men with whom he was to mingle; but if they could help the South to secure her independence, it was all he asked. He, like the noble Major André of Revolutionary fame, was willing to risk his life for the cause he loved. André failed, and suffered an ignominious death; but his fame grows brighter with the centuries, while the traitor Arnold is still abhorred.

"Here is a belt containing ten thousand dollars in United States money," said Morgan, handing him a belt. "You will need it; our money don't go in the North."

[pg 199]

"Whew! you must have had your hand in Lincoln's strong-box," said Calhoun, as he took the money.

Morgan smiled as he answered: "A Yankee paymaster don't come amiss once in a while."

Calhoun was next given an official envelope, which he was to hand to General Forrest, who was then operating in Northern Mississippi and Western Tennessee.

"You will receive full instructions from Forrest," continued Morgan, "what to do, and how to get through the Yankee lines. We have concluded to send you by the way of Western Tennessee, as you will not be so apt to meet with any Federal officer who might know you. Now go, and may success attend you."

Calhoun took his chief's hand. His heart was too full to say a word. A strong grasp, and he was gone. He had no trouble in finding General Forrest, who carefully read the papers that Calhoun handed him. He then scanned Calhoun closely from head to feet. "I reckon you understand the purport of these papers," he said, in rather a harsh voice.

"I suppose they relate to sending me through the lines," answered Calhoun.

"Well, I can send you through, young man, but you are going on a fool's errand. I have had a good deal to do with those Knights of the Golden Circle, as they call themselves. They are all right in giving away everything they know; but when it [pg 200]comes to fighting, bah! one of my companies would lick ten thousand."

"Then you haven't much faith in the fighting qualities of the Knights?" said Calhoun, with a smile.

"Faith? Not I. They are Yankees, mere money-grabbers. Ask one of them for ten dollars and he will shut up as tight as a clam. But they worry the Lincoln government, and keep up a fire in the rear; therefore they should be encouraged. You will find them a scurvy lot to deal with, though."

"How soon can I start North?" asked Calhoun.

"To-night," answered Forrest. "I am the president of an underground railroad, took my cue from the Abolitionists when they were engaged in running our niggers through to Canada. I have a regular mail North. I will send you through with one of the carriers. I reckon I had better send your credentials by a second carrier. It might be awkward if you were captured with them. You must leave here dressed as a citizen, and bear in mind that your name is W. B. Harrison."

"Where shall I find my credentials?" asked Calhoun.

"At Mount Vernon, Illinois, which is the terminus of my railroad at present. Inquire for Judge Worley. Once in his hands, you will be all right. If all the Knights were like him there would be something doing; but he is a Kentuckian, no whining Yankee."

[pg 201]

Calhoun had heard much of General Forrest, and during his interview with him studied him carefully. He put him down as a man of indomitable energy, of great courage, and possessing military genius of a high order. On the other

120

hand, he was illiterate, rough in his language, and lacked the polish of a cultured gentleman, which Morgan possessed. But there was a magnetism about him which drew men to him.

"If I were not riding with Morgan, I should surely want to be with Forrest," thought Calhoun.

Night came, and Calhoun was introduced to the mail-carrier who was to be his guide. He was a thin, wiry man, named Givens. In age, Calhoun put him down at about forty. The few days during which Calhoun was with Givens gave him a very high opinion of the guide's bravery and sagacity. Givens related many of his hairbreadth escapes during their journey, and seemed to treat them as great jokes. During the entire journey through Tennessee and Kentucky, Givens kept to unfrequented roads, and in the darkest night rode as one entirely familiar with the way.

At every place they stopped, they seemed to be expected. A man would take their horses, and in the evening when they started, they would find fresh horses provided. Givens informed Calhoun that these stations were a night ride apart, and that at each a relay of horses was kept concealed in the woods.

"I now understand," said Calhoun, "what an [pg 202]underground railroad means. If the Abolitionists had as complete a one as you, no wonder they were so successful in getting away with our slaves."

Givens chuckled as he answered: "They did, I know all about it; was in the business myself."

"You?" asked Calhoun, in surprise, and he instinctively recoiled from the man.

"A man has to do something for a living," growled Givens; "I got so much for each nigger I ran off." He then refused to discuss the subject further.

One night as they were travelling at a rapid gait, a low, tremulous whistle came from the side of the road. Givens reined in his horse so quickly that he fell back on his haunches. He answered the whistle in the same low, tremulous note. A man stepped from the bushes into the road, and spoke a few words to Givens in a low tone.

Givens turned to Calhoun and said: "Yanks ahead. We will have to go round them."

Under the guidance of the man they turned into a path through the woods. The way was rough, and Givens swore roundly because they were losing time. A good-sized stream was reached, which they had to swim. They emerged from it wet and out of humor, Givens cursing the Yankees to his heart's content. He explained that it eased his mind. When the road was reached their guide bade them good-bye, and disappeared as suddenly as he had appeared.

Givens and Calhoun now urged their horses to [pg 203]their utmost speed, in order to reach their next stopping-place by daylight. But do the best they could, the sun was an hour high before they reached their haven of rest. Luckily they met with no one, and they felt safe.

"One more night and we shall reach the Ohio," said Givens, when they dismounted after a long, wearisome night ride. But it was destined that they should not reach the Ohio the next night, for they had not ridden more than five miles after they had started before they were brought up with the sharp command: "Halt! Who comes there?"

"Citizens without the countersign," answered Givens without a moment's hesitation, and then to Calhoun, "Wheel and run for your life."

They both turned and clapped spurs to their horses, but not before the sentinel had fired. Calhoun heard a sharp exclamation of pain, and turning his head saw Givens tumble from his horse. He had carried his last mail. There was no time to halt, for Calhoun heard the rapid hoof-beats of horses in pursuit. Coming to a cross-road, he sprang from his horse and struck him a vicious blow which sent him galloping wildly down the road. In a moment a squad of Federal cavalry passed in swift pursuit. Calhoun breathed freer after the trampling of their horses died away in the distance. But he was alone, without a horse, and in a strange country. He was now thankful that Forrest had not sent his credentials with Givens.

Calhoun made his way slowly on foot, turning [pg 204]into a road which led in the direction which he wished to go. All through the night he plodded, and when morning came he found he was close to a large plantation. He determined to make himself known. Placing his revolver in his bosom, where he could get it in a moment, he boldly went up to the house. Fortunately he met the owner of the plantation, who saluted him with, "Heah, git off of my place, or I will set the dogs on you. I want no tramps around heah."

Calhoun glanced at himself, and did not wonder he had been mistaken for a disreputable character. His night's walk had made sad havoc with the looks of his clothes. The road was muddy, and he had fallen down several times. Rather in desperation than thinking it would do any good, he made the sign of recognition of the Knights of the Golden Circle. To his surprise it was answered.

"Who are you? and why do you come in such a plight?" asked the gentleman.

Calhoun's story was soon told. "And you are one of Morgan's men," said the gentleman, whose name was Cressey. "I have a son with Morgan," and he gave his name.

"One of my scouts," replied Calhoun, delighted. Calhoun had indeed found a friend, and a place of refuge. The next night, with a good horse and guide, Calhoun was taken to a house but a short distance from the river. The farmer who owned the house was to take a load of produce into Mount [pg 205]Vernon that day. Calhoun could easily go with him without exciting suspicion. This was done, and before noon Calhoun, free and unsuspected, was walking the streets of Mount Vernon.

Shortly after dinner he inquired for the office of Judge Worley, and was shown the most pretentious law office in the little city. Entering, he inquired for the Judge, and was told that he was in his private office.

"Tell him that a gentleman wishes to see him on very important business," said Calhoun.

A clerk bade him be seated, and disappeared. He returned in a moment and said the Judge would see him at once.

When Calhoun entered the private office he saw seated at a desk a dignified-looking gentleman about sixty years of age, who eyed him sharply, and Calhoun was sure a look of disappointment came over his face. This, then, was the gentleman who wished to see him on very important business— hardly more than a boy.

He did not even ask Calhoun to be seated, but said, in a cold voice: "Well, what do you want? Be in a hurry, for I am very busy."

This was not the kind of reception Calhoun was looking for. Gulping down his indignation, he said: "I am just from the South, I was directed to come to you, who would prove a friend."

"Ah! some one must have taken an unwarranted liberty with my name."

While he was saying this, Calhoun was aware a [pg 206]pair of steel-gray eyes were trying to read his very soul.

"Is that all?" at length continued the Judge. "I have no time to give you; as I told you, I am very busy," and he dismissed his visitor with a wave of the hand.

As a last resort Calhoun gave the sign of recognition of the Knights of the Golden Circle. There was no recognition; instead a testy, "Why don't you go?"

Calhoun's face flamed with anger, but controlling himself, he replied: "When you receive some mail from the South, you may find some dispatches from

General Forrest which will cause you to treat me differently. If such dispatches come, be here in your office at nine o'clock to-night."

When Calhoun mentioned "mail from the South," and "General Forrest," the Judge turned pale, and Calhoun fancied he made a motion as if to stop him; but the young man paid no attention to the signal, and strode indignantly from the office.

No sooner was he gone than the Judge turned eagerly to a pile of mail which he had just received, and which the coming of Calhoun had interrupted him in reading. Hurriedly running over the letters, he picked out one, and opened it with nervous fingers. It was written in cipher. Opening a secret drawer in his desk, he took out the key to the cipher, and began the translation of the dispatch. As he did so, he gave vent to his surprise in various exclamations.

[pg 207]

"Lieutenant Calhoun Pennington of Morgan's staff … will go by name of W. B. Harrison … comes North to fully investigate conditions…. If favorable will invade North…. Pennington is member of K. G. C."

The Judge laid down the letter and seemed to be gazing into vacancy. He was thinking—thinking hard. At last he picked up the letter and read it through to the end. Then he made preparations to go out.

"I shall not be back again this afternoon," he said to his clerk, as he passed out. "You can lock up the office when you leave. I shall not need you this evening."

When Calhoun called that evening, he was met at the door by the Judge, and given a reception much different from that he received in the afternoon.

"I am glad to see you, Lieutenant," said the Judge, and he raised his hand as if in military salute, but was careful not to touch his forehead.

"And I am rejoiced to make the acquaintance of Judge Worley," replied Calhoun, raising his hand as if to shade his eyes from the light.

They then advanced and grasped each other by the hand, the fore-finger of each resting on the pulse of the other.

"Nu," said Calhoun.

"Oh," responded the Judge.

"Lac," answered Calhoun.

"Nu-oh-lac," they then both said together.

[pg 208]

Thus were they introduced to each other as members of the Knights of the Golden Circle.

The Judge was now profuse in his apologies for his treatment of Calhoun at their first meeting.

"The fact is," said the Judge, "we are surrounded by Lincoln spies on every hand. Some of them have gained admittance into the order. One cannot be too careful. Then your youth misled me. I am now surprised that one so young should be selected for so important a commission."

"No apology is needed," said Calhoun. "I confess I was indignant at first, but I now see you were right in receiving me as you did. Have you received General Forrest's letter yet?"

"Yes, and it makes all plain. By the way, I see that your name is Calhoun. Have you ever noticed our password particularly?"

"No; you must bear in mind I am a new member."

"Read your name backwards," said the Judge, with a smile.

Calhoun did so, and exclaimed, in surprise: "Nuohlac! Why, it's my name spelled backwards."

"Aye! and it is the name of the greatest American who ever lived," exclaimed the Judge, with enthusiasm. "I trust that you honor the name. Would that John C. Calhoun were alive now. What a glorious day it would be for him. But his spirit lives—lives, and thank God there is no Andrew Jackson in the presidential chair!"

[pg 209]

"Lincoln seems to have more nerve than I wish he had," answered Calhoun.

"Lincoln is an ignoramus, a filthy story-teller, a monster. Seward is the brains of the administration. Without Seward, Lincoln would be nothing."

Calhoun thought it wise not to dispute with the Judge, so he changed the subject by asking the number of Knights of the Golden Circle in the state.

"That, under my oath, I cannot give," answered the Judge. "I see by General Forrest's letter that you have taken only the first degree of the order. That entitles you to very little information. It is the duty of those who take only this degree to obey, not to question. General Forrest advises that the other degrees be given you as soon as possible. I have already made arrangements to have you initiated into the second and third degrees this evening. That is as high as we can go here."

The Judge here looked at his watch, and said it was time to go.

Calhoun accompanied him to a room over a saloon, the Judge explaining that they had selected the place so as not to excite suspicion by so many men passing in and out. Calhoun found at least fifty men assembled, and when he was introduced as one of Morgan's men, he received a perfect ovation.

"Hurrah for John Morgan!" shouted one enthusiastic member, and the cheers were given with a will.

[pg 210]

Three cheers were then given for Jeff Davis, followed by three groans for Abe Lincoln.

Calhoun could scarcely believe his ears. Was this the North? He could well believe he was in the heart of the South.

The object of the meeting was stated, and Calhoun was duly initiated into the second and third degrees. There was no mistaking the nature of the society; its object was the overthrow of the Lincoln government. But resistance to the draft was the main thing discussed. Their hatred of even the name of Lincoln was shown in every word.

Calhoun, now armed with the proper credentials, was told that to obtain the information which he sought, he would have to visit the Grand Commander of the state, who was a Dr. Warrenton, of Springfield. Calhoun marvelled that the head officer of such an order should reside under the very shadow of the state capitol.

The next day found Calhoun in Springfield. It was full of Federal soldiers, and from almost every house a United States flag was flying. It did not look like a very promising place for opposition to the Federal government, but Calhoun afterwards learned that the place was honeycombed with members of the Knights of the Golden Circle.

Calhoun was received by Dr. Warrenton with the greatest caution, and it was only after he was fully satisfied that his visitor was what he represented himself to be that the Doctor consented to talk.

[pg 211]

"Be frank with me," said Calhoun; "John Morgan is contemplating a raid in the North, and he wishes to know whether in that case he can expect any aid from this order, and if so to what number."

The Doctor seemed to be fired with the idea of Morgan making a raid, but said: "If you are to be given the full information you ask for, you must be initiated into the fourth degree of the order. That is a degree which but very few take, and can be given only with the consent of the Supreme Commander.

126

The Grand Commanders of the different states meet the Supreme Commander in Canada next Tuesday. This is Friday. You had better attend that meeting, as your mission is very important."

"Why meet in Canada?" asked Calhoun.

"Because it is safer, and—and we want to meet the Supreme Commander of the order."

"Ah! I understand," said Calhoun. "Mr. —"

"Stop; on your life mention no names! Our oaths forbid it."

"I stand corrected," answered Calhoun, humbly.

It was arranged that Calhoun was to accompany Dr. Warrenton to Canada; but the Doctor warned him that on the cars they must be to each other as strangers.

"When we reach Detroit," said the Doctor, "go to the Russell House, and register as from Chicago. Write Chicago 'Chic.' "

"I think I will go through to Chicago this evening," said Calhoun; "I should like to make some [pg 212]investigations there; you can meet me there Monday."

So it was arranged, the Doctor giving him the names of half a dozen men in that city whom it might be well for him to see. "But mind," said Warrenton, "do not tell any one of Morgan's contemplated raid. That must be a secret."

Calhoun spent two days in Chicago, and what he saw and learned there surprised him more than ever. Opposition to the Lincoln government was everywhere. The leading newspaper boldly demanded that the war be stopped, boastingly proclaimed that there would soon be "a fire in the rear" that would bring Lincoln to his senses. Resistance to the draft was openly talked on the streets. It was even hinted that there was a secret move on foot to liberate the prisoners at Camp Douglas and burn the city.

"This is proving interesting," thought Calhoun; "the whole North seems to be a seething volcano, ready to burst forth into flames, yet something seems to smother the flames."

Calhoun had an inkling of what smothered the flames when, representing himself as a young Englishman, he asked a Federal officer why the government permitted such open talk of treason.

The officer smiled as he answered: "It is better for them to talk than act. The government has its eye on them. As long as they only talk it lets them alone. The first overt act will be crushed with a heavy hand."

[pg 213]

Then Calhoun remembered what both Worley and Warrenton had told him; that government spies were in the order, and that they knew not whom to trust. Would the spies of the government find out who he was, and his mission? It was not a very comforting thought.

CHAPTER XV.
OHO NE! OHO NE! OHO NE!

Monday Calhoun left for Detroit. Dr. Warrenton was on the train, but they met as strangers. When he reached the city and went to register at the Russell House, a gentleman was carelessly leaning against the desk talking with the clerk. He did not appear to notice Calhoun, but he had caught the word "Chic." after his name.

After a few moments the gentleman approached Calhoun and said: "Pardon me, but is not this Mr. Harrison of Kentucky?"

"My name is Harrison," answered Calhoun, "but if you would examine the register you would see I am from Chicago."

"Ah, yes, I understand," and he gave the secret sign of the order. "Come," he continued, "and let me introduce you to some friends."

He led the way to a room where there were several gentlemen seated smoking and talking, among them Dr. Warrenton, who gave him a warm greeting.

"I have been telling them about you," said Warrenton, "and they are all anxious to meet you."

The Doctor then introduced Calhoun to each member of the party. There was Wrightman of [pg 215]New York, Bowman of Indiana, Hartman of Missouri, Bullock of Kentucky, and others.

"You don't tell me you are the son of my old friend, Judge Pennington, of Danville," asked Mr. Bullock, as he shook Calhoun warmly by the hand.

"The very same," answered Calhoun.

"Gentlemen, we need have no fears of Lieutenant Pennington," exclaimed Mr. Bullock, addressing those present. "I will vouch for him with my life. Let's see, your name is now—"

"Harrison for the present," answered Calhoun, with a smile.

The party had no trouble in getting across the river, and that night there was a meeting in Windsor which boded ill for the Federal government.

The Supreme Commander of the order was a gentleman in the full vigor of manhood. He was polished in his manner, rather reserved, but every action showed that he was accustomed to command. Behind it all Calhoun thought that he detected the signs of an inordinate ambition—an ambition which would stop for nothing.

"Isn't he grand," whispered Dr. Warrenton to Calhoun. "A fit representative to wear the mantle of your great namesake."

"Better say the mantle of Aaron Burr," thought Calhoun, but he wisely did not give expression to his thought. The object of Calhoun's coming was fully explained, and it was decided by a unanimous vote, that he should receive the fourth degree, [pg 216]and thus be entitled to all the information which he wished.

The degree was duly conferred on him. Calhoun was now certain he was among a band of conspirators who would stop at nothing to achieve their ends.

"Is this the highest of the degrees?" asked Calhoun, when he was through.

The party exchanged meaning glances, and then the Supreme Commander said: "There is one more degree, but it is given only to the highest officers in the order, and would not be of the least advantage to you."

Calhoun was certain there was something which those present did not wish him to know—some object which they wished to keep secret.

The number of members in the order was now given to Calhoun. The figures astounded him. In Iowa there were twenty thousand members, in Missouri fifty thousand, in Illinois one hundred and twenty thousand, in Indiana one hundred thousand, in Ohio eighty thousand. Throughout the East the order was not so numerous. This seemed strange to Calhoun, for he thought that New York especially would be fertile ground for it.

"How many of these men are armed?" asked Calhoun.

The answer was: "In Missouri nearly all, in Illinois fifty thousand, in Indiana forty thousand, in Ohio the same, in Kentucky nearly all."

"Gentlemen," exclaimed Calhoun, with consid[pg 217]erable warmth, "if these figures are correct, why have you not arisen before this, and hurled the Lincoln government from power? Pardon me, but it looks like timidity. The North is denuded of men, those loyal to Lincoln are in the army."

"That is what I have insisted on," cried Mr. Bowman, of Indiana, jumping to his feet in his excitement. "I say strike, strike now! We of Indiana are ready. Liberate the Confederate prisoners in Northern prison pens! We have arms for them. If necessary, give every Northern city over to the flames."

"Brother Bowman forgets," answered the Supreme Commander, "that our forces are scattered; that if we attempt to concentrate, the government will take alarm and crush us. At present we have to work in secret."

"But what if Indiana and Ohio should be invaded?" asked Calhoun.

"That would be different," was the answer.

"What if you should be successful in your plans?" asked Calhoun.

"Let the South go free. We firmly believe in the doctrine of States' Rights," was the answer.

"Would your states cast their lot with the South?" asked Calhoun, eagerly.

Again there were meaning glances among the leaders. "It is yet too early to answer that question," slowly replied the Supreme Commander, "or even to discuss it. The overthrow of the pres[pg 218]ent Abolition government and the independence of the South is now our object."

But had the leaders a further object? Calhoun resolved to find out, and he did.

The conference at Windsor was over. It was resolved that the order should everywhere be strengthened, and that it should strike at the first favorable opportunity. That opportunity would come at once, should the North be invaded.

From Detroit Calhoun went to Columbus, Ohio, from there to Dayton, the home of Vallandigham. He found that that gentleman was the idol of that section. They wanted him to come home. They swore they would defend him with their lives. The whole country reeked with disloyalty to the Federal government.

Calhoun availed himself of the opportunity of talking with all classes of citizens. He especially tried to get at the feelings of the humbler members of the Knights of the Golden Circle, why they joined the order, and what they proposed doing. All the information he gleaned he treasured up.

From Dayton Calhoun proceeded to Indianapolis, where he was to meet Mr. Bowman. He found Indiana much better organized than any of the other states. Bowman was enthusiastic, and he seemed to hate the Lincoln government with his whole soul. He would stop at nothing to achieve his ends. But the especial object of his hatred was Governor Morton.

"I want to live long enough," he said, "to see [pg 219]that tyrant hanged for trampling on the constitution of the state."

Calhoun found that the Knights stood in great dread of Morton. They declared he had a way of finding out every secret of the order. If he had not been thoroughly guarded, his life would not have been worth a farthing.

Calhoun was taken into the country, where he witnessed the drilling of two or three companies of Knights. These meetings always took place at night, in some secret place, and sentinels were posted to guard against surprise. Calhoun talked with many of the members to get their ideas and to find out what they wished to accomplish.

"What do you think?" asked Bowman of Calhoun, after they had returned to Indianapolis. "I have forty thousand of those fellows."

"Will they fight?" asked Calhoun.

"Fight? Of course they will fight," was the answer. "Let Morgan get into the state, and you will see."

At Indianapolis Calhoun met with a wealthy farmer named Jones, who lived near Corydon. He had no words too severe to say of Lincoln, and boasted of the number of Knights in his part of the state.

"We are going to sweep the Black Abolitionists from the earth," he exclaimed, boastingly, "and hang Old Abe, and Morton too."

"What would you do if Morgan came?" asked Calhoun.

[pg 220]

"Do? I would throw my hat in the air and yell until I was hoarse," was the answer.

"What if Morgan should want some of your horses?" asked Calhoun.

Mr. Jones's countenance fell. At length he mumbled, "Of course he would pay me for them?"

"Of course," replied Calhoun, in a tone which the old gentleman did not quite understand.

Just before Calhoun was ready to leave Indianapolis Bowman told him Morton was to hold a reception, and asked him if he would not like to attend and see the great War Governor.

Nothing would suit Calhoun better. He had a desire to see the man of whom he had heard so much—a man who had the majority of his legislature against him, yet held the state as in the hollow of his hand—a man who borrowed hundreds of thousands of dollars in his own name, that the soldiers of his state might be thoroughly equipped. He had overcome every difficulty, and held his state firmly for the Union. Now, with thousands of the citizens of the state secretly plotting against him, he moved serenely along the path he had marked out. Urged to adopt the most severe measures, he knew when, and when not, to make an arrest. He avoided angering his enemies except when the public safety demanded it. His very name caused every member of the Knights of the Golden Circle to tremble. Little did Calhoun think that when he promised to attend the governor's reception that Morton's detectives were already [pg 221]looking for him. The renewed activity of the Knights had aroused the Governor's suspicions, and he was not long in finding out the cause. To locate and arrest the Southern officer who was causing the ferment, was his order to his detectives.

A large crowd attended the reception, and in such a gathering Calhoun felt in no danger. He saw in Morton a thickset, heavy man with a massive head and brain. He looked every inch the intellectual giant that he was.

"The grandest figure," thought Calhoun, "that I have seen in the North. He is a man to beware of. No wonder the Knights stand in fear of him."

When Calhoun, passing along in the throng, took the Governor's hand, Morton bent his piercing look upon him, and the question came as if shot out of his mouth, "Where from, young man?"

The suddenness of the question threw Calhoun off his guard, and almost involuntarily he answered, "From Kentucky."

"From Kentucky, eh! And how goes it down there?"

Calhoun was himself again. "Of course," he answered, "we are greatly divided in that state, but all the powers of Jeff Davis cannot tear it from the Union."

"Good, pass on," and the Governor turned to the next in line.

But a feeling as of impending danger took possession of Calhoun. Why that question to him? He had heard it asked of no other. Could it be he [pg 222]was suspected? Forcing his way through the throng, he got out of the building as soon as possible.

It was well that he did so, for hardly had the Governor let go Calhoun's hand, when he motioned to General Carrington, and whispered to him: "Arrest that young man. Do it as quietly as possible, but see he does not get away. He is the Southern officer we have been looking for, I am sure. I have a full description of him."

General Carrington in turn whispered to a couple of quiet-looking men, dressed in citizen's clothes who stood near the Governor. They nodded, and started after Calhoun, who was now nearly lost to view in the crowd.

Once out of the building Calhoun found that hundreds of spectators had gathered out of curiosity. They were hurrahing for Lincoln and Morton, and shouting for the Union, and some were singing, "We'll hang Jeff Davis on a sour-apple tree."

Rapidly pushing his way through this mob, he reached the outer edge of the circle. Here groups of men were standing, but they were not hurrahing. Instead, their looks were dark and surly, and it was plain they were not enjoying the proceedings. Just as Calhoun reached these groups, a heavy hand was laid on his shoulder, and a stern low voice said: "You are our prisoner; better come quietly and make no disturbance." And in a trice Calhoun felt each of his arms grasped by strong hands. He [pg 223]was powerless in the iron grip by which he was held; if help there was, it must come from the outside.

"Oho ne! Oho ne! Oho ne!"

The despairing cry cleft the night air like a knife. It fell on the astonished ears of hundreds who did not understand it. But to those groups of silent, sullen-browed men it came as the call of a trumpet, summoning them to duty.

"Oho ne! Oho ne!" they answered, and before the surprised officers could draw a weapon, could raise a hand to defend themselves, they were beaten down, and their prisoner snatched from them.

The alarm was raised, and a company of soldiers came on the run, with fixed bayonets, scattering the crowd right and left. But when they reached the spot they found only a couple of half-dazed and bleeding officers. They could only say they had been set upon, knocked down, and their prisoner taken from them. By whom they did not know, for it was dark, and the crowd had dispersed.

When the onset came, Calhoun felt himself grasped by the arm, and a voice whispered, "Follow me, quick!"

Into the darkness Calhoun dashed, following his guide. In the shadow of buildings, through dark alleys, they ran. At last they came to a part of the city where only a lamp gleamed here and there. They stopped running, both exhausted, their breath coming in quick gasps.

INTO THE DARKNESS CALHOUN DASHED, FOLLOWING HIS GUIDE.

"We are safe now," said the guide, "but it was [pg 224]a close shave for you. What did they arrest you for?"

"To hang me," answered Calhoun, with a shudder. "I am a Confederate officer."

"I thought you must be some big gun, or old Morton wouldn't have tried to arrest you in that crowd; but don't worry, you are all right now."

His guide, whose name proved to be Randall, soon came to a house which he said was his home, "and," he exclaimed, "none of Abe Lincoln's minions will ever find you here. I have sheltered more than one escaped Confederate prisoner from that infernal pen out there called Camp Morton. It should be called Camp Hades."

Calhoun was ushered into the house, and shown a room. "Sleep soundly, and without fear," said Mr. Randall.

Calhoun took his advice, but before he went to sleep he did not forget to return thanks for his escape, and he also had a great deal more respect for the Knights of the Golden Circle than he had had before. The next morning the papers came out with a full description of Calhoun, telling of his escape, and saying he was a famous spy. The article ended with the announcement that so important did the government consider his person that a reward of one thousand dollars would be paid for his recapture. Calhoun now knew that his work was done in the North. The only thing that remained for him was to get out of it as secretly as possible.

[pg 225]

Two days afterwards he was conveyed out of the city concealed in a farmer's wagon. He was passed on from the hands of one true Knight to another, and at the end of three days he found himself on the banks of the Ohio, a few miles above Madison. In the darkness of the night he was rowed over, and his feet once more pressed the soil of his native state. In his ecstasy he felt like kissing the ground, for was it not the soil of Kentucky?

At the house of a true Southerner he found refuge. His measure was taken into Carrolton, where a tailor made him a fine uniform. Purchasing a horse of the gentleman with whom he stayed, he bade him good-bye, and sprang into the saddle. The sun had just set, and the whole west glowed with the beauty which we ascribe to the Golden City. In the midst of the gold hung the new moon like a silver bow.

"See! see!" cried Calhoun, "the new moon, I saw it over my right shoulder. It means good luck."

And while the happy omen still gleamed in the west, he galloped away.

[pg 226]

CHAPTER XVI.

CALHOUN MAKES HIS REPORT.

By keeping off the main roads and avoiding the towns, Calhoun had no trouble in making his way back into Tennessee. He had been gone nearly a month, and was glad to see his old command, who gave him a royal welcome. He was showered with questions as to where he had been, but to each and every one he would laugh and say, "Be glad to tell you, boys, but can't."

"Thought you had deserted us," said his scouts.

"Not till death," replied Calhoun. "I was on a secret mission. The General knows where I was."

"It's all right then, but mark my word, there will be some deviltry going on shortly," one of them remarked, sagely.

As General Breckinridge was greatly interested, Calhoun did not make his report until that General could meet with Morgan. Then Calhoun gave a detailed account of all he had seen and heard. He was listened to with breathless attention.

"His report agrees perfectly with all I have heard," remarked Breckinridge, much pleased. "I have had a dozen different agents in the North, and they all agree."

"But you have not given us your own conclusions, Lieutenant," said Morgan.

[pg 227]

"It might seem presumptuous in me," answered Calhoun.

"By no means; let us hear it," replied both generals.

Calhoun, thus entreated, gave the conclusions he had formed, not from what had been told him by the leaders of the Knights of the Golden Circle, but from his own observations. He was listened to with evident interest.

"Your conclusions seem to be at utter variance with all that was told you, and every fact given," said Breckinridge. "You admit that dissatisfaction in the Democratic party is almost universal over the way the war is being conducted; you say that we have not been deceived regarding the numbers of the Knights of the Golden Circle, that there are eighty thousand of the order in Indiana alone, of whom forty thousand are armed; as you know, every member of that order has taken an oath not to take up arms against the South; that they believe in states' rights; that they will resist by force the tyranny of the Federal government; and yet you say it is your belief that if General

Morgan should invade the state, not a hand would be raised to help him. I cannot understand it."

"I will try to make myself plain," said Calhoun. "The Democratic party is sick and tired of the war, and want it stopped. They believe we can never be whipped, and in that they are right. But they love the Union, revere the old flag. They indulge the vain hope that if the war were stopped, [pg 228]the Union might be restored. We know how foolish that hope is. I speak of the rank and file. Many of their leaders are notoriously disloyal, but they deceive the people with fine words. They make the party believe that if the Republican party were only defeated, things would be as they were.

"As to the Knights of the Golden Circle, the great mass who join it are told it is only a secret political society. They scarcely comprehend its oaths; they are kept in ignorance of the real motives of the order. These Knights hate the party in power with a bitter hatred. They are friendly to the South, believe we are right; but mark my word, they will not fight for us. They are armed, but their idea is to resist the draft. Go among them to-day, and not one in a thousand would enlist to fight in the Southern army. Fighting is the last thing they want to do for either side. For these reasons I conclude that if General Morgan invaded Indiana he would receive no direct aid from the Knights of the Golden Circle. I confess these conclusions are entirely different from what the leaders told me.

"As for the leaders, they are heart and soul with us. They want us to succeed. If they dared they would rise in revolt to-morrow. They are doing all they can, without open resort to arms, to have us succeed. But they are a band of conspirators. They want us to succeed, because they want utterly to destroy the Federal Union. They want to break loose and form a Northwest Confederacy. [pg 229]They dare not tell their followers this, but it is what they are working for."

When Calhoun had stated his opinion, both Breckinridge and Morgan asked him many questions. He was then dismissed. Unknown to Calhoun there were three or four other Southern officers present, who had also been in the North. They were called in, and questioned on the points raised by Calhoun. Every one differed with him. They believed that if an opportunity were presented the Knights would rise almost to a man at the call of their leaders.

Breckinridge and Morgan held an earnest consultation. Morgan was greatly disappointed over Calhoun's report, for he had set his heart on making a raid into Indiana and Ohio. He believed it would be the greatest triumph of his life, and with the Northwest in open revolt, the independence of the South would be assured.

"Lieutenant Pennington must be mistaken," said Breckinridge. "My acquaintance in the North is extensive, and I believe my friends there will do just as they say they will."

Before Morgan and Breckinridge parted, it was fully agreed that Morgan should make the raid. But when the subject was broached to Bragg, that general absolutely refused to sanction it. He gave Morgan permission to make a raid into Kentucky and capture Louisville if possible. That was as far as he would go, and even with that object in view, he limited Morgan's force to two thousand.

[pg 230]

Morgan apparently acquiesced in this decision of his commander; but in his heart he resolved to disobey if, when he neared Louisville, he found conditions at all favorable for the invasion of Indiana.

Some time had passed since Morgan had made a raid, and the news that they were again to ride north, probably clear to Louisville, was welcomed by the rough riders. To them a raid was but a holiday. It did not take Morgan long to prepare. His men were always ready to move. "To Louisville," was the cry, "we want to call on George D.," meaning George D. Prentice, the editor of the Louisville *Journal*.

In all probability few men in the Confederate army knew that Morgan was on another raid, until he was well on his way. This time he entered Kentucky farther east than was his custom, and the first intimation the Federals had that he was in the state, he was crossing the Cumberland River at Burkesville. This was on the second day of July. The alarm was given. The frenzied Federals telegraphed right and left for troops to head off Morgan. It was thought that he intended to strike the Louisville and Nashville Railroad again at his favorite place—Bacon Creek. General Judah hurried from Tompkinsville with a brigade to head him off, but his advance under General Hobson was struck at Marrowbone, and hurled back. This left Morgan an open road to Columbia, and that place fell an easy prey on the 3d.

[pg 231]

Leaving General Hobson to pursue Morgan, General Judah hurried back to Glasgow to bring up another brigade. But General Judah never overtook Morgan until days afterwards, and then he caught him at Buffington Island.

As for Hobson, he stuck to Morgan's trail as an Indian sticks to the trail of his enemy. He followed him all through Kentucky, all through Indiana, all through Ohio, never but a few hours behind, yet never in striking distance until Buffington Island was reached.

After leaving the forces of Judah and Hobson in the rear, Morgan had nearly an open road to Louisville. The 4th found him at the crossing of Green River on the road between Columbia and Campbellsville. Here a portion of the Twenty-fifth Michigan, under Colonel Moore, was strongly fortified, and a charge made by Morgan was bloodily repulsed. As both Judah and Hobson were close in his rear, it would take too much time to bring these determined men to terms, and so Morgan, much to his regret, was forced to leave them, and pass on. The 5th of July found him at Lebanon. The garrison under Colonel Hanson fought desperately, but was forced to capitulate, and Lebanon with all its stores and three hundred and fifty prisoners was again in Morgan's hands.

The next day found him at Bardstown, where twenty-five men of the Fourth Regular Cavalry, under the command of Lieutenant Thomas Sullivan, threw themselves into a livery stable, strongly [pg 232]fortified it, and refused to surrender. Here Morgan made a mistake. He should have left them and passed on; but angered that he should be defied by so few men, he determined to capture them and it delayed him twenty-four precious hours. So enraged were his men over what they considered the obstinacy of the brave little band, that they began to misuse the prisoners, but Morgan stopped them, saying: "The damned Yankees ought to be complimented on their pluck."

Never, in any of his raids, had Morgan met with so fierce resistance as on this one. Cut to the quick by the numerous criticisms which had been published in Northern papers, that cowardice prompted nearly every one of the surrenders to Morgan, these troops fought long after prudence should have caused them to surrender.

From Bardstown Morgan moved to Shepherdsville. He was now within striking distance of Louisville. Here it was that he fully decided, if he had not done so before, upon the invasion of Indiana, instead of attempting the capture of Louisville. At Shepherdsville he was on the Louisville and Nashville Railroad, where a long bridge spans the Salt River. But he did not stop to capture the garrison which guarded the bridge, nor did he attempt to burn it; time was too precious. Instead, he rode straight west, and on the 9th was in Brandenburg. Before him rolled the Ohio River, beyond lay the green hills of Indiana. It was the first time he had led his men clear to the Ohio River. The [pg 233]sight of Yankee land aroused them to the utmost enthusiasm. They would have attempted to cross if ten thousand foes had opposed them.

Calhoun had had the advance into Brandenburg with instructions to sweep through the place, stopping for nothing, and to capture any steamboats which might be at the landing. This he did. Far in advance of the main body, he galloped into the town, to the astonishment and dismay of its citizens.

Two small steamboats were lying at the landing, and before the terrorized crews could cut the hawsers and drift out into the stream, Calhoun and his men were on board and the boats were theirs.

The means of crossing the river were now in Morgan's hands. But a fresh danger arose. A gunboat came steaming down the river from Louisville and opened fire. Morgan brought every piece of his artillery into action, and for two hours the battle raged. Then the gunboat, discomfited, withdrew and went back to Louisville, leaving the way open. There was now nothing to prevent Morgan from crossing the river.

[pg 234]

CHAPTER XVII.
THE PASSING OF THE RUBICON.

Who can tell the thoughts of John H. Morgan, as he sat on his horse that July day, and with fixed gaze looked out upon the river. Beyond lay the fair fields of Indiana, the Canaan of his hopes. Should he go in and possess? The waters needed not to be rolled back. He had the means of crossing. Before him all was calm, peaceful. No foe stood on the opposite bank to oppose him; no cannon frowned from the hilltops. Behind him were thousands of angry Federals in swift pursuit. Would it be safer to go ahead than to turn back?

As Cæsar stood on the bank of the Rubicon debating what to do, so did Morgan stand on the bank of the Ohio. Like Cæsar, if he once took the step, he must abide the consequences. But if there was any hesitation in the mind of Morgan, he did not hesitate long. "Cross over," was the order which he gave. "We shall soon know," he said to Calhoun, "whether they are friends or foes over there; whether the forty thousand Knights who were so anxious for me to come will appear or not."

Now, to look upon the invasion of Indiana and Ohio by Morgan seems like sheer madness. He [pg 235]had a force of only a little over three thousand, and the states which he invaded had millions of population. But he had reasons to believe that thousands of that population were friendly to him, would welcome him with gladness. When he so nearly escaped though no hand was raised to help him, what would he have accomplished if only a few thousand had come to his relief? That there were thousands in the two states who would have flocked gladly to his standard if they had dared, there is no doubt. But the hand of the government was too strong for them to resist. The fires of loyalty burned too fiercely to be quenched by them. With all their boasted strength, the Knights of the Golden Circle were powerless when the supreme moment came.

The order to cross the river was hailed with enthusiasm by every man in Morgan's command. Where they were going they knew not, cared not; they would go where their gallant leader led. He had never failed them, he would not fail them now. They knew only that they were to invade the land of their enemies; that was enough. The war was to be brought home to the North as it had been to the South. Calhoun caught the fever which caused the blood of every man to flow more swiftly through his veins. He had been full of doubts; he trembled for the results if that river were once passed. He had been through the North and noted her resources, how terribly in earnest her people were that the Union should be saved. What if there were thou[pg 236]sands of traitors in their midst? There were enough loyal men left to crush them. What if the state of Indiana was honeycombed with camps of the Knights of the Golden Circle? The lodges of the Union League were fully as numerous. He now forgot all these things. Did not the Knights come to his relief in his hour of sore distress? Surely they would not forget their oaths, when Morgan came. So he tossed his hat in the air, and shouted, "Boys, over there is Yankee land! we will cross over and possess it."

The order to cross once given, was obeyed with alacrity. In an incredibly short time the three thousand men and horses were ferried across the river.

"Burn the boats," was Morgan's order.

The torch was applied, and as the flames wrapped them in their fiery embrace, lo! on the other side came the eager troopers of Hobson. Like beasts baffled of their prey, they could only stand and gnash their teeth in their rage. Between them and Morgan rolled the river, and they had no means of crossing.

"Why don't you come across, Yanks?" Morgan's men shouted in derision.

"Got any word you want to send to your mammy? We are going to see her," they mockingly cried.

And thus with taunt and laugh and hurrah, Morgan's men rode away, leaving their enemies standing helpless on the farther bank.

[pg 237]

"Twenty miles to Corydon," said Calhoun, as he galloped with his scouts to the front to take the advance. "I wonder if I shall meet my friend Jones, and whether, when he sees us, he will throw his hat on high, and give us a royal welcome? If he spoke the truth, the bells of Corydon will ring a joyful peal when the people see us coming, and we shall be greeted with waving flags, and find hundreds of sturdy Knights ready to join us."

But in that twenty miles not a single waving flag did Calhoun see, not a single shout of welcome did he hear. Instead, the inhabitants seemed to be in an agony of fear. They met only decrepit old men and white-faced women and children. Not a single cup of cold water was freely offered them in that twenty miles. If Calhoun could only have seen the welcome given Hobson's men the day after as they came over the same road, the flags that were waved, the shouts of welcome that greeted them, how women and children stood by the roadside with cooling water and dainty food to give them, and sent their prayers after them—if Calhoun could have seen all these things, his heart would have sunk, and he would have known that there was no welcome for Morgan's men in Indiana.

But he was soon to have a ruder awakening. As he neared Corydon, he and his scouts were greeted with a volley, and sixteen of his men went down. The raid for them was over.

"Charge!" shouted Calhoun, and like a whirlwind he and his men were on the little band of [pg 238]home guards, who thought they could withstand Morgan's whole force.

In a few brief minutes the fight was over, and on the sod lay several motionless figures. In spite of himself, Calhoun could not help thinking of Lexington and the farmer minute men who met Pitcairn and his red-coats on that April morning in 1775. Were not these men of Corydon as brave? Did they not deserve a monument as much? He tried to dismiss the thought as unworthy, but it stayed with him for a long time.

A short distance beyond Corydon stood a fine house, which, with all its surroundings, showed it to be the dwelling of a rich and prosperous farmer. When Calhoun came up, the owner, bareheaded and greatly excited, was engaged in controversy with one of Calhoun's scouts who had just appropriated a fine ham from the farmer's smoke-house and was busily engaged in tying it to his saddle-bow.

"You have no business to take my property without paying for it!" the farmer was saying, angrily. "I am a friend of the South; I have opposed the war from the beginning."

Seeing Calhoun, and noticing he was an officer, the farmer rushed up to him, crying, "Stop them! Stop them! they are stealing my property!"

"Well, I declare, if it isn't my old friend Jones!" exclaimed Calhoun. "How do you do, Mr. Jones? Where are those five hundred armed Knights who you said would meet us here? Where is [pg 239]your hat, that you are not throwing it high in air? Why are you not shouting hallelujahs over our coming?"

Jones had stopped and was staring at Calhoun with open mouth and bulging eyes. "Bless my soul," he at length managed to stammer, "if it isn't Mr. Harrison!"

"Lieutenant Pennington, at your service. But, Jones, where are those Knights of the Golden Circle you promised would join us here?"

Jones hung his head. "We—we didn't expect you to come so soon," he managed to answer; "we didn't have time to rally."

"Mr. Jones, you told me this whole country would welcome us as liberators. They did welcome us back there in Corydon, but it was with lead. Sixteen of our men were killed and wounded. Mr. Jones, there will be several funerals for you to attend in Corydon."

"It must be some of those Union Leaguers," exclaimed Mr. Jones. "Glad they were killed; they threatened to hang me the other day."

"They were heroes, compared to you!" hotly exclaimed Calhoun. "You and your cowardly Knights can plot in secret, stab in the dark, curse your government, but when it comes to fighting like men you are a pack of cowardly curs."

But Mr. Jones hardly heard this fierce Phillipic; his eyes were fixed on his smoke-house, which was being entered by some more of the soldiers.

"Won't you stop them," he cried, wringing his [pg 240]hands; "they will take it all! Why, you are a pack of thieves!"

"Boys, don't enter or disturb anything in the house," cried Calhoun, turning to his men, "but take anything out of doors you can lay your hands on; horses, everything."

The men dispersed with a shout to carry out the order. Calhoun left Mr. Jones in the road jumping up and down, tearing his hair and shouting at the top of his voice, "I am going to vote for Abe Lincoln. I am—I am, if I am damned for it!"

In all probability Morgan's raid in Indiana and Ohio made more than one vote for old Abe. Of all the thousands of Knights of the Golden Circle in Indiana and Ohio, not one took his rifle to join Morgan, not one raised his hand to help him.

In speaking of this to General Shackelford, who captured him, Morgan said, bitterly: "Since I have crossed the Ohio I have not seen a single friendly face. Every man, woman, and child I have met has been my enemy; every hill-top a telegraph station to herald my coming; every bush an ambush to conceal a foe."

The people who lived along the route pursued by Morgan will never forget his raid. What happened has been told and retold a thousand times around the fireside, and the story will be handed down not only to their children, but to their children's children. Morgan was everywhere proclaimed as a thief and a robber. They forgot that he had to subsist at the expense of the country, [pg 241]and that he had to take horses to replace those of his own which had broken down. Not only that, but it was life to him to sweep the country through which he passed clear of horses, that his pursuers might not get them. The Federals in pursuit took horses as readily as Morgan's men.

Those who proclaim Morgan a thief and a robber sing with gusto "Marching through Georgia," and tell how "the sweet potatoes started from the ground." They forget how Sheridan, the greatest cavalry leader of the Federal army, boasted he had made the lovely Shenandoah Valley such a waste that a crow would starve to death flying over it. The Southern people look upon Sherman and Sheridan as the people of Ohio and Indiana look upon Morgan. These generals were not inhuman; they simply practised war. It is safe to say that less private property was destroyed in Morgan's raid in Indiana and Ohio than in any other raid of equal magnitude made by either side during the war.

One can now see by reading the dispatches the panic and terror caused by Morgan in this raid. From Cairo, Illinois, to Wheeling, West Virginia, the Federals were in a panic, for they knew not which way Morgan would turn, or where he would strike. From the entire length of the Ohio, the people were wildly calling on the government to send troops to protect them from Morgan. There were fears and trembling as far north as Indianapolis. Governor Tod, of Ohio, declared martial law through the southern part of his state, and [pg 242]called on Morton to do the same for Indiana. But Morton, cooler, more careful, and looking farther ahead as to what might be the effect of such a measure, wisely refused to do so.

From Corydon Morgan rode north to Salem. The Federals now thought for sure that Indianapolis was his objective point, but from Salem he turned northeast and swept through the state, touching or passing through in his route the counties of Jackson, Scott, Jennings, Jefferson, Ripley, and Dearborn, passing into Ohio, in the northwest corner of Hamilton County, almost within sight of the great city of Cincinnati. Turning north, he entered Butler County. Here, as in Indiana, he met only the scowling faces of enemies.

"And here is where they worship Vallandigham!" exclaimed Calhoun, passionately. "Here is where they told me almost every man belonged to the Knights of the Golden Circle, and that the whole county would welcome us. Here is where even the Democratic party meet in open convention, pass resolutions in favor of the South, denounce Lincoln as a monster and tyrant, and demand that the war cease at once and the South go free, saying they will support no man for office who in the least way favors the war. And now not a word of welcome, not a single hand reached out in aid. Oh! the cowards! the cowards!"[3]

Morgan made no bitter reply, but said. "You warned us, Lieutenant, how it would be. I have [pg 243]expected no aid since the first day we entered Indiana. But with God's help we shall yet escape from our foes. Oh, if my gallant men were across the Ohio once more! It is only that river which stands in between us and safety. There is now no hope of securing a steamboat. But at Buffington Island the river is shoal, and can be forded. If we can reach Buffington Island before our enemies, we can laugh at our pursuers."

And for Buffington Island Morgan headed, threatening each place along the way, to keep the Federals guessing where he would attempt to cross. Like a whirlwind he swept through the counties of Warren, Clermont, Brown, Adams, Pike, Jackson, Gallia, Meigs, brushing aside like so many flies the militia which tried to impede his progress.

The goal was nearly reached. Hobson was half a day behind, still trailing, still following like a bloodhound. The Confederates knew of no force in front except militia. Safety was before them. The river once passed, Morgan would have performed the greatest exploit of the war. His men were already singing songs of triumph, for the river was in sight. Night came on, but they marched through the darkness, to take position. In the gray of the morning they would sweep aside the militia and cross over.

In the morning a heavy fog hung over river and land, as if the sun were afraid to look down upon the scene to be enacted. In the gloom, Colonel Duke and the dashing Huffman formed their com[pg 244]mands and moved to the attack. They were received with a fire which surprised them, coming as they supposed from militia. But with loud cheers they swept forward, and the Federals were forced back, leaving a piece of artillery. A little farther and the ford would be won; then there came a crashing volley, mingled with the thunder of artillery, and they saw before them, not militia, but long lines of blue-coated veterans. General Judah's brigade had been transported up the river in steamboats, and landed at Pomeroy. They had marched all night, and were now in possession of the ford.

In vain the gallant Duke and Huffman struggled against that force. They were driven back. Flight was to be resumed up the river, when couriers came dashing in with the news that Hobson was up. They were hemmed in. There was one place yet, a path through the woods, by which a few could escape, if the Federal force could be held back for a time.

"Go!" cried Duke to Morgan, "and I will hold them until you are gone."

"Go!" cried Huffman, faint and bleeding from a wound, "and I will stay and help Colonel Duke."

"Go!" cried Calhoun, "if you are saved I care not for myself."

Then there arose a storm of protests. Who could so well guard and protect the chief as Calhoun and his scouts? And so, against Morgan's will, Calhoun went with him.

"Come, then, we will clear the way," Calhoun [pg 245]cried to his scouts, and before the way was closed, six hundred men with Morgan had escaped.

Hemmed in on every side, the Confederates fought as only desperate men can fight; but as soon as it was known that Morgan was well away, Duke and Huffman, and with them many other gallant officers, saw it would be madness to fight longer, and with breaking hearts they surrendered to their exultant foes. Then it was that some two or three hundred, in spite of shot and shell, in spite of the leaden hail which fell around them, plunged down the bank into the river. The bodies of many floated down, their life blood reddening the water. The current swept many a steed and rider down, and they were seen no more. A few there were who struggled through to safety, and these were all that escaped of the thousands that crossed the Ohio at Brandenburg.

CHAPTER XVIII.
THE RIDE OF THE SIX HUNDRED.

What Morgan's thoughts were, what his hopes were, as he rode away from that fatal field at Buffington Island, no one knows. With him rode six hundred, all that were left of three thousand. He could have had no thoughts of attempting to cross the Ohio anywhere near Buffington Island, for he rode almost due north. It may have been he thought that he might cross near Wheeling or higher up, and escape into the mountains of Western Pennsylvania; or as a last resort, he might reach Lake Erie, seize a steamboat, and escape to Canada. Whatever he thought, north he rode, through the most populous counties of Ohio. And what a ride was that for six hundred men! Foes everywhere; Home Guards springing up at every corner; no rest day or night.

Close in his rear thundered the legions of General Shackelford, a Kentuckian as brave, as fearless, as tireless as Morgan himself. But in spite of all opposition, in spite of foes gathering on right and left and in front, Morgan rode on, sweeping through the counties of Meigs, Vinton, Hocking, Athens, Washington, Morgan, Muskingum, Guernsey, Belmont, Harrison, Jefferson, until he reached Columbiana County, where the end came.

[pg 247]

At almost every hour during this ride the six hundred grew less. Men fell from their horses in exhaustion. They slept as they rode, keeping to their saddles as by instinct. The terrible strain told on every one. The men grew haggard, emaciated. When no danger threatened, they rode as dead men, but once let a rifle crack in front, and their sluggish blood would flow like fire through their veins, their eyes would kindle with the excitement of battle, and they would be Morgan's fierce raiders once more.

As for Calhoun, it seemed as if he never slept, never tired. It was as if his frame were made of iron. Where danger threatened there he was. He was foremost in every charge. It looked as if he bore a charmed life. The day before the end came he was scouting on a road, parallel to the one on which the main body was travelling. Hearing shots, he took a cross-road, and galloped at full speed to see what was the trouble. A small party of Home Guards were retreating at full speed; one far in advance of the others was making frantic efforts to urge his horse to greater speed. Calhoun saw that he could cut him off, and he did so, reaching the road just as he came abreast of it. So intent was the fellow on getting away he did not notice Calhoun until brought to a stand by the stern command, "Surrender."

In his surprise and terror, the man rolled from his horse, the picture of the most abject cowardice Calhoun ever saw. He fairly grovelled in the dust. [pg 248]"Don't kill me! Don't kill me!" he cried, raising his hands in supplication. "I didn't want to come; they forced me. I never did anything against you."

Dismounting Calhoun gave him a kick which sent him rolling. "Get up, you blubbering calf," he exclaimed, "and tell us what you know."

The fellow staggered to his feet, his teeth chattering, and trembling like a leaf.

"Now, answer my questions, and see that you tell the truth," said Calhoun. "Are there any forces in front of us?"

"N—not—not as I know," he managed to say.

"Do you know the shortest road to Salineville?"

"Yes; yes."

"Will you guide us there if I spare your life?"

"Anything, I will do anything, if you won't kill me," he whined.

"Very well, but I will exchange horses with you, as I see you are riding a fine one, and he looks fresh," remarked Calhoun.

The exchange was made, and then Calhoun said, "Now lead on, and at the first sign of treachery, I will blow out your brains. Do you understand?"

"Yes, yes, I will take you the shortest road."

"What's your name," asked Calhoun, as they rode along.

"Andrew Harmon."

"Well, Andrew, I wish all Yankees were like you. If they were, we should have no trouble [pg 249]whipping the North. I reckon you are about as big a coward as I ever met."

Harmon, still white and trembling, did not answer; he was too thoroughly cowed.

Ride as hard as Morgan's men could, when they neared Salineville Shackelford was pressing on their rear. They had either to fight or surrender.

"My brave boys, you have done all that mortals can do. I cannot bear to see you slaughtered. I will surrender."

As Morgan said this his voice trembled. It was a word his men had never heard him use before.

"General, it is not all over for you," cried Calhoun, his voice quivering with emotion. "Think of the joy of the Yankees if you should be captured. Let me take half the men. You take the other half and escape. I can hold the enemy in check until you get well away."

Morgan demurred. "The sacrifice will be too great," he said.

"You must, you shall consent. We will force you," the cry went up from the whole command as from one man.

Morgan bowed his head, he could not speak. In silence he took Calhoun's hand, tears gathered in his eyes, the first tears Calhoun ever saw there. There was a strong clasp, a clasp which seemed to say "It may be the last," then, wheeling his horse, Morgan galloped swiftly away, followed by less than half of his six hundred.

There was not a moment to lose, for the Feder[pg 250]als were already charging down with triumphant cheers, confident of an easy victory. Calhoun had posted his men well, and a withering volley sent the Federals reeling back. They charged again, only to recoil before the fierce fire of the Confederates. There was now a lull in the fighting. Calhoun saw that they were flanking him on the right and left. "Charge!" he shouted, and the little band were soon in the midst of their enemies. The Federals closed in around them. There was no way to retreat. Calhoun's men, seeing how hopeless the fight was, began to throw down their arms.

"Surrender," cried a fine-looking officer to Calhoun, who, well in front, was fighting like a demon. Even in that hell of battle Calhoun knew the officer. It was Mark Crawford, the captain whose horse he had captured in Tennessee, and whom he afterwards took prisoner at Cave City. But the captain was wearing the shoulder-straps of a major now.

"Never!" shouted Calhoun, in answer to the summons to surrender, and with sword in hand, he spurred forward to engage Crawford in single combat. But that officer had a revolver in his hand, and he raised it and fired.

Calhoun felt as if he had been struck on the head with a red-hot iron. He reeled in his saddle, and then fell forward on his horse's neck. His sword dropped from his nerveless hand. His horse, wild with fear and not feeling the restraining hand of a [pg 251]master, broke through the ranks of the Federals, and bore him out of the conflict.

Still clinging to the neck of his horse and the horn of his saddle, he kept his seat. He straightened himself up, but the blood streaming over his face blinded him, and he saw not where he was going. Neither did he realize what had happened, for the shock of his wound had rendered him half-unconscious.

His mind began to wander. He was a soldier no longer, but a boy back in Kentucky running a race with his cousin Fred.

"On! on! Salim," he weakly shouted; "we must win, it is for the Sunny South we are racing."

The horse still ran at full speed, his glossy coat dripping with perspiration, his nostrils widely distended and showing red with blood. But his pace began to slacken. Darkness gathered before the eyes of Calhoun. "Why, it's getting night," he murmured; "Fred, where are you?" Lower still lower he sank, until he was once more grasping the neck of his horse. A deadly faintness seized him, total darkness was around him, and he knew no more.

With Calhoun gone, all resistance to the Federals ceased. Of the six hundred, who had ridden so far and so well, fully one-half were prisoners.

The Federals were greatly chagrined and disappointed when they found that Morgan was not among the prisoners. The man they desired above all others was still at liberty. "Forward," was the command, and the pursuit was again taken up.

[pg 252]

With the remnant of his command, Morgan was nearing New Lisbon. If there were no foes before him there was still hope. From a road to the west of the one he was on, a cloud of dust was rising. His guide told him that this road intersected the one he was on but a short distance ahead. His advance came dashing back, saying there was a large body of Federal troops in his front. From the rear came the direful tidings that Shackelford was near. Morgan saw, and his lip quivered. "It is no use," he said, "it is all over."

The ride of the six hundred had ended—a ride that will ever live in song and story.

"Morgan has surrendered! Morgan is a prisoner!" was the news borne on lightning wings all over the entire North.

What rejoicing there was among the Federals! The great raider, the man they feared more than an army with banners, was in their power.

[pg 253]

CHAPTER XIX.
AN ANGEL OF MERCY.

In front of one of the most beautiful and stately farm-houses in Columbiana County stood a young girl. With clasped hands and straining eyes she was gazing intently down a road which led to the west. The sound of battle came faintly to her ears. As she listened, a shudder swept through her slight frame.

"My brother! My brother!" she moaned, "he may be in it. O God of battles, protect him!"

She would have made a picture for an artist as she stood there. The weather being warm, she wore a soft, thin garment, which clung in graceful folds around her. Her beautifully rounded arm and shapely shoulders were bare. Her luxuriant hair, the color of sun-beams, fell in a wavy mass to her waist. Her eyes, blue as the sky, were now troubled, and a teardrop trembled and then fell from the long lashes.

As she looked, the sound of battle became fainter, and then ceased altogether. But down the road, a mile away, a little cloud of dust arose. It grew larger and larger, and at last she saw it was caused by a single horseman who was coming at a furious pace. Was the rider a bearer of ill tidings? No, there was no rider on the horse. He who [pg 254]rode must have been killed. It might be her brother's horse; she grew sick and faint, but still she gazed. The horse came nearer; he was slackening his speed. Yes, there was some one on the horse—a man—but he had fallen over on the saddle, and his arms were around the horse's neck.

It must be her brother, wounded unto death, coming home to die, and she gave a great convulsive sob. Then like a bird she flew to the middle of the road. She saw that the horse's mane and shoulders were dripping with blood, that the rider's hair was clotted with it.

As the horse came to her it stopped, and the rider rolled heavily from the saddle. With a cry she sprang forward and received the falling man; but the weight of Calhoun, for it was he, bore her to the earth. She arose, screaming for help. There was no one in the house except a colored servant, who came rushing out, and nearly fainted when she saw her mistress. No wonder, for the girl's dress and arms were dripping with blood.

"Oh! Missy Joyce! Missy Joyce!" wailed the colored woman, "what's de mattah? Be yo' killed?"

"No, no, this soldier—he is dead or dying. Oh, Mary, what can we do?"

But help was near. A couple of neighbors had also heard the sound of battle, and were riding nearer that they might learn the result.

"Great heavens! what is this?" exclaimed one, as they rode up. "As I live, that is Andrew Har[pg 255]mon's horse. Well, I never thought Andrew would get near enough to a battle to get shot."

By this time they had dismounted. Going to Calhoun they looked at him, and one exclaimed, "This is not Harmon; it's one of Morgan's men. Got it good and heavy. Served him right."

"Is he dead?" asked the girl, in a trembling voice.

The man put his hand on Calhoun's heart. "No, marm," he answered, "but I think he might as well be."

"Carry him into the house, and send for Doctor Hopkins, quick," she said.

"What! that dirty, bloody thing! Better let us carry him to the barn. It's a blame sight better place than our boys get down South."

"The house, I say," answered the girl, sharply.

"Why, Miss Joyce," said the other man, as he looked at her, "you are covered with blood."

"Yes, I caught him as he fell from his horse," she answered. "I am not hurt."

The men were about to pick Calhoun up and carry him in according to the directions of the girl, when she exclaimed, "There comes Doctor Hopkins now."

Sure enough, the Doctor had heard of the fight, and was coming at a remarkable speed, for him, to see if his professional services were needed. He reined in his horse, and jumping from his gig, ejaculated, "Why! why! what is this? And Miss Joyce all bloody!"

[pg 256]

"I am not hurt. The man, Doctor," she said.

The Doctor turned his attention to Calhoun. "As I live, one of Morgan's men," he exclaimed, "and hard hit, too. How did he come here?"

"His horse brought him," answered one of the men. "He clung to his horse as far as here, when he fell off. Miss Joyce caught him as he fell. That is what makes her so bloody."

"Well! well! well!" was all that the old Doctor could say.

"The queer part is," continued the man, "that the horse belongs to Andrew Harmon. I heard that Andrew had gone out with the Home Guards, but I could hardly believe it. I guess this fellow must have killed him and appropriated the horse."

"What! Andrew Harmon killed in battle?" cried the Doctor, straightening up from his examination of Calhoun. "Don't believe it. He will turn up safe enough."

Then speaking to the girl, the Doctor said, "Miss Joyce, this man has nearly bled to death. I cannot tell yet whether the ball has entered his head or not. If not, there may be slight hopes for him, but he must have immediate attention. It is fortunate I came along as I did."

"Miss Joyce wanted us to take him into the house," said one of the men, "but I suggested the barn."

"The barn first," said the Doctor; "if I remember rightly, there is a large work-bench there. It [pg 257]will make a fine operating-table. And, Joyce, warm water, towels, and bandages."

Joyce Crawford, for that was the girl's name, flew to do the Doctor's bidding, while the men, to their credit be it said, picked Calhoun up tenderly and carried him to the barn, where the work-bench, as the Doctor had suggested, made an operating-table. Joyce soon appeared with the water, towels, and bandages. The Doctor had already taken off his coat and rolled up his sleeves, ready for work. Although he was a country practitioner, he was a skilful surgeon. Carefully he washed away the blood, then clipped away the matted hair from around the wound. It seemed to Joyce a long time that he worked, but at last the wound was dressed and bandaged.

"The ball did not penetrate the brain," he said, as he finished, "nor do I think the skull is injured, although the ball plowed along it for some distance. Fortunately it was a small bullet, one from a revolver, probably, which hit him. It cut a number of small arteries in its course, and that is the reason he has bled so much. An hour more and he would have been beyond my skill."

"Will he live now?" asked Joyce.

"The chances are against him. If saved at all, it will only be by the best of nursing."

"He can be taken into the house now, can't he?" she asked.

"Yes, but you had better first let a tub of water be brought, and clean underclothes, and [pg 258]a night shirt. He needs a bath as much as anything."

Joyce had the men get the water, while she procured some underclothes which belonged to her brother. Calhoun's clothes were now removed, clothes which had not been off him for a month.

"Here is a belt," said one of the men; "it looks as if it might contain money," and he was proceeding to examine it when the Doctor forbade him.

"Give it to Miss Joyce," he said; "the fellow is her prisoner."

The belt was handed over rather reluctantly. Calhoun having been bathed, Joyce was called, and told that her prisoner was ready for her.

"Bring him in, the chamber is all prepared," was her answer.

Calhoun was brought in and placed in a large, cool upper chamber.

"This is mighty nice for a Rebel," said one of the men, looking around. "My Jake didn't get this good care when he was shot at Stone River."

"Too blame nice for a Morgan thief," mumbled the other.

"Shut up," said the Doctor; "remember what Miss Joyce has done for our boys. Worked her fingers off for them. This man, or rather boy, for he can't be over twenty, was brought to her door. Would you have him left to die?"

The men hung their heads sheepishly, and went [pg 259]out. They were not hard-hearted men, but they were bitter against Morgan, and any one who rode with him.

"Now I must go," said the old Doctor kindly, taking Joyce's hand. "You have done to this young man as I would have one do to my son in a like extremity."

The old Doctor's voice broke, for he had lost a son in the army. Recovering himself, he continued, "I must go now, for I may be needed by some of our own gallant boys. I will drop in this evening, if possible, and see how your patient is getting along. God bless you, Joyce, you have a kind heart."

Joyce looked after the old Doctor with swimming eyes. "One of God's noblemen," she murmured.

She took the belt which had been taken from Calhoun, and which had been handed her by the Doctor, and put it carefully away. She then began her vigil beside the bedside of the wounded man. The Doctor had given her minute directions, and she followed them faithfully. It was some hours before Calhoun began to show signs of consciousness, and when he did come to, he was delirious, and in a raging fever.

The Doctor returned as he had promised. He shook his head as he felt Calhoun's pulse, and listened to his incoherent mutterings.

"This is bad," he said. "It is fortunate he lost so much blood, or this fever would consume him. [pg 260]But we must hope for the best. Only the best of nursing will bring him through."

"That he shall have," said Joyce. "I have sent for Margaret Goodsen. You know she is an army nurse, and knows all about wounded men."

"Yes, Margaret is good, none better," replied the Doctor.

All through that night Joyce sat by the bedside of Calhoun cooling his fevered brow, giving him refreshing drinks. He talked almost continually to himself. Now he would be leading his men in battle, cheering them on. Then he was a boy, engaged in boyish sports. The name of Fred was uttered again and again.

"I wonder who Fred can be?" thought Joyce; "a brother, probably."

Joyce Crawford was the only daughter of the Hon. Lorenzo Crawford, one of the most prominent citizens of Columbiana County. Mr. Crawford had served two terms in Congress, and was at the time of the war a member of the state senate. He had one child besides Joyce, his son Mark, who we have seen was a major in the Federal army.

Mr. Crawford lost his wife when Joyce was three years old; since that time his house had been presided over by a maiden sister. This lady was absent in Steubenville when Morgan appeared so suddenly in the county; thus at the time of Calhoun's appearance only Joyce and the servants were at home, Mr. Crawford being [pg 261]absent in the east on duties connected with the Sanitary Commission.

Mr. Crawford was what is known as an original Abolitionist. Before the war his house was one of the stations of the underground railroad, and many a runaway slave he had helped on the way to Canada. Twice he had been arrested by the United States officials for violation of the fugitive slave law, and both times fined heavily. He believed there could be no virtue in a slave-owner; such a man was accursed of God, and should be accursed of men. His daughter had to a degree imbibed his sentiments, and the idea of slavery was abhorrent to her; but her heart was so gentle, she could hate no one. Calhoun's helplessness appealed to her sympathies, and she forgot he was one of Morgan's raiders. Although young, only eighteen, she had admirers by the score, but her father so far had forbidden her receiving company, considering her as yet only a child.

Joyce's beau ideal of a man was her brother Mark, and he was worthy of her adoration. Several years her senior, he had watched over and guided her in her childhood, and never was a brother more devoted.

The next morning the news came that Morgan was captured, and the scare in Columbiana County was over. The morning also brought Miss Crawford, who had come hurrying home on receipt of the news that Morgan was in the county. She nearly went into hysterics when she learned that one of [pg 262]the dreadful raiders was in the house. "How could you do it, child?" she cried to Joyce; and "Doctor, why did you let her?" she added to Doctor Hopkins, who had just come in to see his patient.

"Madam, it was a case of life or death," replied the Doctor. "Joyce did right. We are not heathens in Columbiana County."

"But you will take him right away?" pleaded the lady.

"It would be death to move him."

"But he might murder us all," said Miss Crawford.

The Doctor smiled. "If he lives, it will be weeks before he will have the strength to kill a fly," he answered.

Miss Crawford sighed, and gave up the battle. She was not a hard-hearted woman, but the idea of having one of Morgan's dreadful raiders in the house was trying on her nerves.

The afternoon brought Major Crawford. The story of Joyce's capture of a raider had travelled far and wide, and the Major had already heard of it. "So you captured a prisoner, did you, Puss?" he exclaimed, kissing her, as she threw herself in his arms. "Is he a regular brigand, and bearded like a pard?"

"No, no, he is young, almost a boy," she answered. "Margaret Goodsen is taking care of him now. Come and see him, but he is out of his head, and raves dreadfully."

She led the way to the chamber where Calhoun [pg 263]was. No sooner did Major Crawford see him than he turned pale and staggered back, "Great God!" he exclaimed.

What fate was it that had led the man he had shot to the house to be cared for by his sister?

"What is it, Mark? What is it?" she cried, seeing his agitation.

Should he tell her? Yes, it would be best. "Joyce, you will not wonder at my surprise, when I tell you it was I who shot him."

"You, brother, you!" she cried, and instinctively she shrank from him.

Mark saw it, and exclaimed, "Great God! Joyce, you don't blame me, do you? I had to do it to save my life. He was about to cut me down with his sword when I fired."

"No, no," she cried, "I don't blame you, but it was so sudden; it is so dreadful. I never before realized that war was so terrible."

"Well, Joyce, save the poor fellow's life if you can; I don't want his death on my hands if I can help it. Do you know who your prisoner is?"

"No, you see the condition he is in."

"His name is Pennington, Calhoun Pennington. He is one of Morgan's bravest and most daring officers. I ought to know him, he took me prisoner twice."

"You, Mark, you?"

"Yes, you remember I told you how I lost my horse in Tennessee. He is the fellow who took it. He afterwards captured me at Cave City."

[pg 264]

"Mark, what will become of him if he gets well?" she asked.

"The United States officials will take him," he answered. "His being here must be reported."

"And—and he will be sent to prison?"

"Yes, until he is exchanged."

"But you were not sent to prison when you were captured," she protested.

"No, I was paroled; but I hardly believe the government will parole any of Morgan's men."

"Why?" she asked.

"They have given us too much trouble, Puss. Now we have them, I think we will keep them."

"Mark, Aunt Matilda don't like my taking this Pennington in. She says father will not like it at all."

"I will see Aunt Matilda, and tell her it is all right. I will also write to father. No, Joyce, I don't want Pennington to die. It is best, even in war, to know you have not killed a man. So take good care of him, or rather see he has good care. Get a man to nurse him nights."

"I will look out for that," said Joyce.

"Well, Puss, good-bye, keep me posted. I had leave of absence only a few hours, so I must be going."

"Oh, Mark, must you go so soon?" And she clung to him as if she would not let him go. Gently disengaging her arms, he pressed kiss after kiss on her brow and was gone. She sank into a chair weeping, and for a time forgot her prisoner.

The next day Joyce had another visitor, in the person of Andrew Harmon. He had heard that his horse was at Crawford's, and that the officer who took him was there desperately wounded. He made his visit with pleasure, for of all the girls in Columbiana County, she was the one he had selected to become Mrs. Harmon. He had no idea he would be refused, for was he not considered the greatest catch in the county?

Harmon had two things to recommend him—good looks and money. He was accounted a handsome man, and was as far as physical beauty was concerned. He had the body and muscle of an athlete, but there was nothing ennobling or inspiring in the expression of his countenance. By nature he was crafty, mean, cruel, and miserly, and was one of the biggest cowards that ever walked.

Like many others, he was a great patriot as far as talk was concerned. He had been so unfortunate as to be drafted at the first call, and had promptly furnished a substitute. He was fond of boasting he was doing double duty for his country, not only was he represented in the army, but he was doing a great work at home. This work consisted in contracting for the government, and cheating it at every turn. Many a soldier who received shoddy clothing, paper-soled shoes, and rotten meat had Mr. Harmon to thank for it. But he was piling up money, and was already known as one of the richest men in the county. When he went out with the Home Guards, he had no idea of getting near [pg 2766]Morgan; he would look out for that. But his party ran into Morgan's advance unexpectedly, and as has been related, he was captured by Calhoun. It was a most wonderful story he had to tell.

He had been beset by at least six of Morgan's men. A desperate conflict followed, and he had killed, or at least desperately wounded, three of his assailants, and it was only after he had not a single shot left in his revolver and was surrounded that he had surrendered.

"So enraged were they at my desperate defence," said he, "that the officer in charge pulled me from my horse, brutally kicked and struck me, threatened to kill me, and then appropriated my horse. He is a desperate fellow, Miss Joyce; I would not keep him in the house a single moment."

Joyce, who had listened to his account much amused, for she had heard another version of it, said, "I do not think, Mr. Harmon, he could have beaten you very hard, for I see no marks on you, and you seem to be pretty lively. As for sending Lieutenant Pennington away, the Doctor says it would be death to move him."

Mr. Harmon shifted uneasily in his chair as Joyce was saying this, and then asked to see Calhoun, as he wished to be sure whether he was the one who had captured him. This Joyce consented to, provided he would be careful not to disturb him. Harmon promised, and he was taken into the room. Calhoun was tossing on his bed, as he entered, and no sooner did his wild eyes rest on [pg 267]Harmon than he burst into a loud laugh, "Oh! the coward! the coward!" he shouted, "take him away."

Harmon fled from the room white with rage. "Miss Joyce, that fellow is shamming," he fumed. "I demand he be delivered to the United States officials at once."

"The Doctor thinks differently; he says it will kill him to be moved," she answered.

"Let him die, then. It isn't your business to nurse wounded Rebels, especially one of Morgan's cutthroats."

"I do not have to come to you to learn what my business is," answered Joyce, haughtily, and turned to leave the room.

Mr. Harmon saw that he had made a mistake. "Joyce! Joyce! don't go, hear me," he exclaimed.

"You will find your horse in the stable," was all she said, as she passed out.

He left the house vowing vengeance, and lost no time in informing the Federal authorities that the wounded officer at Crawford's was shamming, and would give them the slip if not taken away. Two deputy marshals came to investigate, and went away satisfied when Doctor Hopkins promised to report as soon as his patient was well enough to be removed.

In due time Joyce received a letter from her father. He had not heard that Morgan had come as far north as Columbiana County, until after he was captured. As all danger was now over, he [pg 268]would not be home for some time. The thousands who had been wounded in the great battle of Gettysburg were occupying his attention. He also had to make a visit to Washington and Fortress Monroe, and might go as far south as Hilton Head. As for the wounded Rebel at his house, Joyce had done right in not letting him die in the road, but that he should be turned over to the military authorities at the earliest possible moment. Little did Mr. Crawford think what the outcome of the affair would be.

Contrary to her aunt's protest, Joyce insisted on taking most of the care of Calhoun during the day. Margaret Goodsen was all the help she needed. She had engaged a competent man to care for him nights. Had not Mark told her to save the life of the man he had shot, if possible?

CHAPTER XX.
CALHOUN AWAKES TO LIFE.

For two weeks Calhoun hovered between life and death; but at last his rugged constitution conquered. During this time Joyce was unremitting in her attention. "I must save him for the sake of Mark," she would say, "I cannot bear to have his blood on Mark's hands."

In speaking to Joyce's aunt, Matilda Goodsen said: "The poor child will hardly let me do anything; she wants to do it all."

Miss Crawford fretted and fumed, but it did no good. In this Joyce would have her way.

Calhoun's fever had been growing less day by day, and the time came when it left him, and he lay in a quiet and restful slumber. But his breathing was so faint, Joyce was almost afraid it was the sleep which precedes death.

It was near the close of an August day. The weather had been warm and sultry, but a thunder shower had cooled and cleared the atmosphere, and the earth was rejoicing in the baptism it had received. The trees seemed to ripple with laughter, as the breeze shook the raindrops from their leaves. The grass was greener, the flowers brighter on account of that same baptism. The birds sang a [pg 270]sweeter song. What is more beautiful than nature after a summer shower!

It was at such a time that Calhoun awoke to life and consciousness. A delicious lethargy was over him. He felt no pain, and his bed was so soft, he seemed to be resting on a fleecy cloud. He tried to raise his hand, and found to his surprise he could not move a finger. Even his eyes for a time refused to open. Slowly his memory came back to him; how in the fierce conflict he tried to break through the line and sought to cut down an officer who opposed him. Then there came a flash, a shock—and he remembered nothing more. Where was he now? Had he passed through that great change called death? By a great effort he opened his eyes, and was bewildered. He was in a strange room. By an open window sat a young girl. She had been reading, but the book was now lying idly in her lap, and she was looking apparently into vacancy. The rays of the setting sun streamed in through the windows, and touched hair and face and clothes with its golden beams. Calhoun thought he had never seen a being so lovely; her beauty was such as he fancied could be found only in the realms above, yet she was mortal. He could not take his eyes from her. She turned her head, and saw him gazing at her. Uttering a little exclamation of surprise, she arose and came swiftly but noiselessly to his side.

"Who are you? Where am I?" Calhoun whispered, faintly.

[pg 271]

"Hush! hush!" she said, in low, sweet tones, "you must not talk. You have been sick—very sick. You are better now."

She gave him a cordial. He took it, and with a gentle sigh, closed his eyes, and sank to sleep again. Before he was quite gone, it seemed to him that soft, tremulous lips touched his forehead, and a tear-drop fell upon his cheek. Its memory remained with him as a beautiful dream, and it was long years before he knew it was not a dream.

Doctor Hopkins was delighted when he called in the evening and learned that his patient had awaked with his fever gone, and in his right mind. "All that he needs now," he said, "is careful nursing, and he will get well. But mind, do not let him talk, and tell him nothing of what has happened, until he gains a little strength."

From that time Calhoun gained slowly, but surely. When he became strong enough to bear it, Joyce told him all that had happened. He could scarcely realize that over a month had passed since he had been wounded.

"Then that stand of mine did not save Morgan," said Calhoun, sorrowfully.

"No, he was taken a few hours afterwards," answered Joyce. "He and his officers are now in the penitentiary at Columbus."

Calhoun could hardly believe what he heard. "Then we are to be treated as felons, are we?" he asked, bitterly.

"They are afraid he might escape from a military [pg 272]prison," replied Joyce. "But the people are very bitter against him. Some are clamoring that he be tried and executed."

"They will not dare do that," exclaimed Calhoun, excitedly.

"No, I do not think there is any danger that way," replied Joyce; "but they want to keep him safe."

"Well they may, but Morgan will yet make them trouble. No prison will hold him long."

"There, there, don't let us talk about it any more," said Joyce; "it will worry you back into a fever."

"You have saved my life," said Calhoun, fervently. "How can I ever repay you for what you have done?"

Joyce did not reply.

Calhoun lay silent for some time, and then suddenly said: "I am one of Morgan's hated officers, and yet you are caring for me as for a brother. What makes you do it?"

"Why shouldn't I?" said Joyce; "I have a dear brother in the army. I am only doing by you as I would have him done by, if he should fall wounded. And then—" Joyce stopped; she could not tell him it was her brother who had shot him.

A great light came to Calhoun. "Joyce! Joyce!" he cried, "I now understand. It was your brother who shot me."

"Oh! forgive him! forgive him!" cried Joyce. [pg 273]"He told me it was to save his own life that he did it."

"Why, Joyce, there is nothing to forgive. Your brother is a brave, a gallant officer. Then he has been here?"

"Yes, and knew you. He bade me nurse you as I would nurse him in like condition."

"Just like a brave soldier; but are there none who find fault with my being here treated like a prince?"

"Yes, one. His name is Andrew Harmon. It was his horse you were riding when you came here. He seems to hate you, and is doing all he can to have you taken to Columbus. He says you treated him most brutally when he was captured."

"I did kick him," answered Calhoun, laughing; "he was on the ground bellowing like a baby. I never saw a more abject coward. I kicked him and told him to get up."

"He has a different story," said Joyce, smiling; and then she told the wonderful story of Harmon's capture as related by himself.

"His capacity for lying is equalled only by his cowardice," said Calhoun, indignantly.

"Yet he is a man to be feared," said Joyce, "for he is rich and has influence, although every one knows him to be a coward."

The days that passed were the happiest Calhoun had ever spent. He told Joyce of his Kentucky home, of his cousin Fred, how noble and true he was, and of his own adventures in raiding with [pg 274]Morgan. She never tired of listening. Is it strange that these two hearts were drawn close to each other. They lived in a sweet dream—a dream which did not look to the future. But almost unknown to them Cupid had come and shot his shafts, and they had gone true.

The day came when Calhoun was able to be placed in an easy-chair and drawn to an open window. It was a proud day to him, yet it was the beginning of sorrow. The Doctor came and congratulated him on his improvement.

"Doctor Hopkins, how can I thank you for your kindness?" he said; "you have done so much for me."

"You need not thank me, thank that young lady there," replied the Doctor, pointing to Joyce. "She it was who saved your life."

"I know, no reward I could give would ever repay her," answered Calhoun. "I can only offer to be her slave for life."

"Your offer is not accepted; you are well aware I do not believe in slavery," replied Joyce, with a merry laugh.

When the Doctor was ready to go, he asked for a private interview with Joyce. It was hard work for him to say what he had to say. He choked and stammered, but at last Joyce understood what he meant. He had promised the government officials to inform them when Calhoun could be moved without endangering his life. That time had come. "But," said he, as he noticed the white face of [pg 275]Joyce, "I shall recommend that he be allowed to remain two weeks longer, as there is no danger of his running away in his weak condition."

But Joyce hardly heard him. "And—and—this means?" she whispered.

"The penitentiary at Columbus."

Joyce shuddered. "And—and there is no way to prevent this?"

"None. God knows I would if I could."

"Thank you, Doctor; I might have known this would have to come, but it is so sudden."

The Doctor went out shaking his head. "I am afraid harm has been done," he said to himself.

Just as he was getting into his gig to drive away Andrew Harmon came riding by. He glanced up and saw Calhoun sitting by the window. "So, your patient is able to sit up," he exclaimed, with a sneer. "About time he were in the penitentiary, where he belongs, isn't it?"

"I don't know how that concerns you," replied the Doctor, coldly, as he drove away.

"Oh ho! my fine fellow. I will show you whether it concerns me or not?" muttered Harmon, looking after him.

That night Harmon wrote to the authorities at Columbus, stating it as his opinion that there was a scheme on foot to detain Lieutenant Pennington until he was well enough to slip away. He was not aware that Doctor Hopkins had reported on the condition of his patient every week, and had already sent a letter saying he could be moved with [pg 276]safety, but recommending he be allowed to remain two weeks longer, on account of his weak condition. Harmon not only wrote to Columbus, but also to Mr. Crawford, hinting that it was dangerous for his daughter to care for Calhoun longer. "You know," he wrote, "that girls of the age of Joyce are inclined to be romantic."

As for Joyce, when the Doctor left her she sank into a chair weak and faint. She saw Andrew Harmon gazing up at the window where Calhoun was, and a terror seized her. She now knew that she loved Calhoun, but with that knowledge also came the thought that her love was hopeless, that even if Calhoun returned her love, her father would never consent to their union. He would rather see her dead than married to a Rebel, especially a hated Morgan raider. Long did she struggle with her own heart, her sense of duty, her ideas of patriotism; and duty conquered. She would give him up, but she would save him.

It was evening before she could muster strength to have the desired interview with Calhoun. When she did enter the room it was with a step so languid, a face so pinched and drawn, that Calhoun stared in amazement.

"Joyce, what is it?" he cried. "Are you sick?"

"Not sick, only a little weary," she answered, as she sank into a chair and motioned for the nurse to leave them. No sooner was she gone than Joyce told Calhoun what had happened. Her voice was so passionless that Calhoun wondered if she [pg 277]cared, wondered if he had been mistaken in thinking she loved him.

"Joyce, do you care if I go to prison?" he asked.

"Care?" she cried. "The thought is terrible. You shall not go, I will save you."

"Joyce! Joyce! tell me that you love me, and it will make my cell in prison a heaven. Don't you see that I love you, that you saved my poor life only that I might give it to you? Joyce, say that you love me!"

For answer she sank on her knees by his bedside and laid her head on his breast. He put his weak arms around her, and held her close. For a while she remained still, then gently disengaging his arms, she arose. There was a look on her face that Calhoun did not understand.

"The first embrace, and the last," she sighed. "Oh, Calhoun, why did we ever meet?"

166

"What do you mean?" he asked, his lips growing white.

"I mean that our love is hopeless. Father will never consent to our marriage. I feel it, know it. Without his consent I shall never marry. But save you from prison I will."

"Joyce, you do not love me!" said Calhoun bitterly.

"As my life," she cried.

"Yet you say you can never marry me!"

"Without my father's consent I cannot."

"Joyce, let us not borrow trouble. Even with [pg 278]your father's consent we could not marry now. I am a prisoner. The war is going on, but it cannot last forever. When it is over, when peace is declared, I will come to you. Then, and not till then, will I ask your father for your hand. Let us hope the skies will be brighter by that time—that to be one of Morgan's men will not be a badge of dishonor, even in the North."

"Oh, Calhoun, if I could only hope! I will hope. Come to me after the war is over. Father's consent may be won. But now the prison, the prison. I must save you. I have thought it all out."

"How can you save me, a poor, weak mortal, who cannot take a step without help?" asked Calhoun.

"Put you in a carriage to-morrow night and take you where they cannot find you."

"So soon? The Doctor said he would ask for two weeks. Two more weeks with you, Joyce—I could afford to go to prison for that."

"Don't talk foolishly. I feel if I don't get you away to-morrow night, I cannot at all."

"But you—will it endanger you, Joyce?"

"Not at all!"

"But how will you explain my disappearance?"

"Suppose you have been shamming, better than we thought you were, and so you gave us the slip."

"A right mean trick," said Calhoun.

"No, a Yankee trick, a real good one. Now listen, Calhoun, and I will tell you all about how I [pg 279]am going to get you away. Some six miles from here a colored man lives whom my father has greatly befriended. He will do anything for me I ask. I shall tell him you are a sick soldier, and for good reasons wish to remain in hiding until you get well."

"Will he know I am one of Morgan's men?" asked Calhoun.

"No, he will think you are a Federal soldier. Calhoun, as much as you may hate it, you must don the Union Blue."

"That would make a spy of me. No, it wouldn't either, if I kept clear of any military post."

"That's good. I have a Federal uniform in the house, which will about fit you. A friendless soldier died here a short time ago. We took him in and cared for him during his last sickness. He had been discharged for wounds received at Fair Oaks. Here is the discharge. I think it fits you close enough, so it may be of use to you."

She handed him the discharge; he took it and read: "James Brown, age nineteen; height five feet nine inches; weight one hundred and sixty pounds; complexion dark; hair and eyes black."

"Why, Joyce, with that in my pocket, and wearing a Federal uniform, I could travel anywhere in the North."

"So I thought. We will cheat that old prison yet. But it is time you were asleep."

"God bless you, Joyce," replied Calhoun. "Give me a kiss before you go."

[pg 280]

She smiled and threw him one as she went out and he had to be content with that. She had not stopped to consider what the result might be if she helped Calhoun to escape. Her only thought was to save him from going to prison. To do this she would dare anything.

The colored man of whom she spoke was to be at the farm in the morning to do some work. A fear had seized her that she might be too late. The fear was well grounded. The authorities at Columbus had resolved to move Calhoun at once. The request of Doctor Hopkins, that he be allowed to remain two weeks longer, although he said he could be removed without danger, aroused their suspicion. Not only that, but the letter of Andrew Harmon to Mr. Crawford had alarmed that gentleman, and he was already on his way home.

Abram Prather, the colored man, was seen by Joyce as soon as he made his appearance.

"Missy Joyce, I jes' do enything fo' yo.' Me an' de ol' woman will keep him all right."

168

So everything was arranged. Joyce breathed freer, yet she waited impatiently for the night.

CHAPTER XXI.

THE ESCAPE.

The day was a long and weary one to Calhoun. Between the joy of knowing he was to be free and his misery over the thought that he must part with Joyce, his soul was alternately swept with conflicting emotions. Then he had seen so little of her during the day; she seemed more distant than she did before she declared her love. How he longed to take her in his arms, to have her head rest on his breast once more! But she had said that although it was the first it was to be the last time. What did she mean? Ah! it must be that he could never embrace her again, never touch her lips again, until her father had consented to their marriage. When the war was over he would wring that consent from him.

The thought brought contentment. Yes, it was better that they should part. Then the news of the terrible battle of Chickamauga had just come, and it had fired his very soul. The South had won a great victory. Surely this was the beginning of the end. Independence was near, the war would soon be at an end, and he longed to be in at the finish. The excitement of war was once more running riot through his veins.

He little thought of the sacrifice Joyce was mak[pg 282]ing, of the fierce conflicts she was having with her conscience. She knew that she was doing wrong, that she was proving a traitor to the flag she loved, that she was aiding and abetting the enemy; but it was one, only one man, and she loved him so. Surely this one man, sick and wounded, could do no harm. It was cruel to shut him up in prison. Thus she reasoned to silence conscience, but if her reasons had been ten times as weak, love would have won.

All through the day she was making preparations for Calhoun's departure. Fortunately the young man who had been engaged to nurse Calhoun during the night had been taken sick a couple of days before, and as Calhoun rested well, another had not been engaged. Thus one of the greatest obstacles to the carrying out of Joyce's plans was out of the way. She could easily manage Miss Goodsen. Joyce's only confidant was the faithful Abe, who obeyed her without question. In his eyes Missy Joyce could do nothing wrong. He had been drilled by Joyce until he knew just what to do. He was to go home, but as soon as it was dark, he was to return, being careful not to be seen. After he was sure the household was asleep he was to harness a span of horses, being careful to make no noise, and have a carriage waiting in a grove a short distance back of the house. Here he was to wait for further orders from Joyce. Being well acquainted with the place, and Joyce promising to see that the barn and the carriage-house were [pg 283]left unlocked, he would have no trouble in carrying out his instructions.

Night came, and Joyce was in a fever of excitement. Would anything happen to prevent her carrying out her plans? If she had known that Andrew Harmon had hired a spy to watch the house she would have been in despair. But the spy was to watch the window of Calhoun's room, and was concealed in a corn-field opposite the house. If he had watched the back instead of the front of the house, he would have seen some strange doings.

Margaret Goodsen was told that as Calhoun was so well, she could lie down in an adjoining room. If he needed anything, he could ring a little bell which stood on a table by his side. The nurse gladly availed herself of the opportunity to sleep. When the nurse retired Joyce came into the room, and speaking so that she could hear her, said, "Good night, Lieutenant Pennington; I hope you will rest well." Then she whispered, "Here is the Federal uniform. Have you strength to put it on?"

"Yes, but oh, Joyce—"

She made a swift gesture and pointed to the door of the nurse's room.

"Here is some money," she continued, in the same low whisper. "Now, don't refuse it; you will need it."

"I had plenty of money in a belt around me when I was wounded," whispered Calhoun.

"The belt, oh, I forgot! The Doctor gave it to [pg 284]me for safe keeping." Noiselessly she moved to the bureau, opened a drawer, and returned with the belt.

"Joyce, I shall not need your money now, but I thank you for the offer."

"It was nothing. Be sure and be ready," and she glided from the room.

The minutes were like hours to Calhoun. At one time he had made up his mind not to accept his proffered liberty, as it might bring serious trouble on Joyce; but he concluded that he must accept.

As for Joyce, she went to her room and threw herself down on a lounge. Her heart was beating tumultuously; every little noise startled her like the report of a gun. She waited in fear and apprehension. At length the clock struck eleven. "They must be all asleep by this time," she thought. She arose and softly went downstairs, carrying blankets and pillows. She stopped and listened as she stepped out of doors. There was no moon, it was slightly cloudy, and darkness was over everything. Without hesitating she made her way through the back yard and the barn lot to the grove, where she had told Abe to be in waiting. She found that the faithful fellow had everything in readiness.

"Abe, I want you to come with me now and get the sick soldier. Drive through the lane until you reach the road; then drive straight to your house. The road is not much frequented, and you will not be apt to meet any one at this time of night. [pg 285]If you do, say nothing. Leave the soldier when you get home, drive straight back the way you came. Turn the horses into the pasture, put the harness and carriage where you found them. Be careful and make no noise. When you have done this go home again and be sure you get there before daylight. It's a hard night's work I have put on you, Abe, but I will pay you well for it. Now, take off your boots and come with me."

The obedient fellow did as he was bid, and followed Joyce into the house and to Calhoun's room.

"Take him to the carriage," whispered Joyce.

The stalwart Abe took Calhoun in his arms as if he had been a child, and carried him to the carriage.

"Now, Abe, remember and do just as I told you," said Joyce.

"Yes, Missy, I 'member ebberyting."

She went to the side of the carriage, arranged the pillows and comforts around Calhoun, and then gave him her hand. "Good-bye," she whispered; "may God keep you safe."

The hand was cold as death, and Calhoun felt that she was trembling violently.

"Joyce! Joyce! is this to be our leave-taking?"

"Yes," she whispered.

"Are you not coming to see me where I am going?"

"No, I dare not; we must not see each other again until—until the war is over."

"Without a kiss, Joyce. Joyce, I—"

"Hush! you have no right to ask for one, I [pg 286]much less right to give it. Come when the war is over, and then"—Her voice broke, and she turned and fled into the darkness.

How Joyce got back into the house she never knew. She fell on her bed half-unconscious. The strain upon her had been terrible, and the effect might have been serious if tears had not come to her relief. After a violent paroxysm of sobbing, she grew calmer, and tired nature asserted itself, and she fell asleep.

It was yet early morning when she was aroused by a cry from Miss Goodsen, and that lady came rushing into her room, wringing her hands and crying, "He is gone! He is gone!"

"Who is gone?" asked Joyce, springing up as if in amazement.

Miss Goodsen, in her excitement did not notice that Joyce was fully dressed. "The wounded Rebel, Lieutenant Pennington," she fairly shrieked. "Oh! what shall I do? What shall I do?" and she wrung her hands in her distress.

Joyce ran to Calhoun's room; sure enough it was empty. "Stop your noise," she said, sharply, to Miss Goodsen. "If any one is to blame, I am. They will do nothing with you. It may be he became delirious during the night and has wandered off. We must have the house and premises searched."

The noise had aroused the whole household. The utmost excitement prevailed. Miss Crawford was frantic. She was sure they would all be sent [pg 287]to prison, and she upbraided Joyce for not getting another male nurse to watch him during the night. The house and the premises were thoroughly searched, but nothing was found of the missing man. The neighborhood was aroused and a thorough search of the surrounding country began.

Joyce took to her room with a raging headache. The afternoon brought a couple of deputy marshals from Columbus. They had come to convey Calhoun to prison, and were astonished when told that the prisoner had escaped. Miss Goodsen was closely questioned. She had looked in once during the night. The Lieutenant was awake, but said he was comfortable and wanted nothing. She then went to sleep and did not awake until morning. She found Joyce in her room, who was overcome when told that her patient was gone. She had not heard the slightest sound during the night.

Doctor Hopkins was summoned. The old Doctor was thunderstruck when he heard the news. He could scarcely believe it. To add to the mystery, Calhoun's Confederate uniform was found. Apparently he had gone away with only his night clothes on. Doctor Hopkins at once gave it as his opinion that Calhoun had been seized with a sudden delirium and had stolen out of the house and wandered away; no doubt the body would be found somewhere. His professional services were needed in the care of Joyce, for she seemed to be completely prostrated, and had a high fever.

"Poor girl," said the Doctor, "the excitement [pg 288]has been too much for her." If he suspected anything he kept his secret well.

The spy employed by Andrew Harmon reported that he had not seen or heard anything suspicious during the night, so that gentleman concluded to say nothing, as he did not wish it to be known that he had had the house secretly watched.

Mr. Crawford returned the day after the escape. He was greatly exercised over what had happened, and blamed every one that Calhoun had been kept so long as he had. Poor Joyce came in for her share, but she wisely held her peace. The country was scoured for miles around, but nothing was seen or heard of the escaped prisoner, and at last the excitement died out.

Joyce did not lack news from Calhoun. The faithful Abe kept her fully informed. Joyce told him that both of them would go to prison if it was known what they had done, and he kept the secret well. He reported that Calhoun was gaining rapidly, and would soon be able to go his way. "He want to see yo' awful bad befo' he goes," said Abe.

But Joyce resolutely refused. It would not do either of them any good. One day the negro brought her a letter. It was from Calhoun, telling her that when she received it he would be gone. He thought it cruel that she had not come to see him just once. He closed as follows:

"Joyce, I feel that my life is yours, for you saved it. Not only that, but to you I now owe my [pg 289]liberty, and I realize the struggle you have had to do as you have done. But be of good cheer. When the war is over the thunder of the last cannon will hardly have died away before I shall be at your side. Till then adieu."

That letter was very precious to Joyce. Before the war was over it was nearly worn out by being read and reread.

Shortly after Mr. Crawford's return he was asked by Andrew Harmon for permission to pay his addresses to his daughter. Harmon hoped that if he had her father's permission to pay his addresses to her, Joyce's coldness might disappear.

Mr. Crawford did not like the man, but he was rich and had a certain amount of political influence. Mr. Crawford was thinking of being a candidate for Congress at the approaching election, and he did not wish to offend Harmon, but he secretly hoped that Joyce would refuse him; in this he was not disappointed. She was indignant that her father had listened to Harmon, even to the extent that he had. "Why, father, I have heard you call him cowardly and dishonest," she exclaimed, "and to think that you told him you would leave it entirely to me."

"I did not wish to offend him," meekly replied Mr. Crawford, "and I had confidence in your judgment. I was almost certain you would refuse him."

"Will you always have such confidence in my judgment?" asked Joyce, quickly.

"What do you mean?" asked her father.

"Suppose I should wish to marry one of whom you did not approve?"

"That is another proposition," said Mr. Crawford. "You might have been so foolish as to fall in love with that Morgan Rebel and horse-thief you took care of so long. If so, I had rather see you dead than married to him."

Poor Joyce! Did her father suspect anything? She caught her breath, and came near falling. Quickly recovering herself, she answered. "At least he was a brave man. But everybody says he is dead, and mortals do not wed ghosts."

"It is to be sincerely hoped he is dead," replied Mr. Crawford, for he had noticed his daughter's confusion, and an uneasiness took possession of him. But much to Joyce's relief he did not question her further.

Andrew Harmon was beside himself with rage when told by Mr. Crawford that, while his daughter was sensible of the great honor he would bestow upon her, she was still very young, and had no idea of marrying any one at present.

Harmon determined to have revenge on Joyce, and began slyly to circulate reports that Joyce Crawford, if she chose, could tell a great deal about the escape of the Rebel officer. In fact, half of his sickness was shammed.

These rumors came to the ears of Mark Crawford. He had been promoted to a colonelcy for gallantry at Chickamauga. During the winter, [pg 291]while the army lay still around Chattanooga, he had come home on furlough. While at home he sought out Harmon and gave him as fine a thrashing as a man ever received, warning him if he ever heard of him connecting his sister with the escape of Calhoun again he would break every bone in his body. The only revenge Harmon durst take was to defeat Mr. Crawford in his aspirations for a nomination for Congress.

CHAPTER XXII.
PRISON DOORS ARE OPENED.

When Calhoun parted from Joyce he sank back in the carriage and gave himself up to the most gloomy thoughts. The sorrow of parting from her took from him the joy of his escape. During the journey his dusky driver did not speak a word. The drive seemed a long one to Calhoun, and he was thoroughly wearied when the carriage drew up by a log house, surrounded by a small clearing.

"Heah we be, Massa," said Abe, as he alighted from his seat. "Hope Massa had a good ride."

The door of the house was opened by a motherly looking colored woman, and Abe, taking Calhoun once more in his arms, carried him into the house. Aunt Liza, as the wife of Abe was called, seeing Calhoun looking so pale and thin, put her fat, black hand on his forehead, and said, "Po' chile, po' chile, don't yo' worry. Aunt Liza take good care ob yo'."

Calhoun felt that he was among friends—friends that would prove faithful and true. He was carried up a ladder to a chamber. The upper part of the house was all in one room, rather low, but the rough walls were whitewashed, and everything was neat and clean. He was placed on a snow-white bed, and soon sank into a peaceful slumber. When [pg 293]he awoke the sun was shining in at the window and Aunt Liza appeared with a breakfast good enough to tempt the appetite of one far more particular than Calhoun.

The invalid remained with his kind friends two weeks, treated like an honored guest, and protected from every inquiring eye. He gained strength rapidly, and at the end of a week was able to walk out evenings, when there was no danger of being seen. Once men who were searching for him entered the house, and Calhoun could hear every word that was said. His heart beat painfully, for it entered his mind that Abe and his wife might betray him for the sake of the reward offered. But the thought did injustice to these simple-minded people. As for the searchers, the loft of the house of a poor negro who had run away from slavery was the last place they thought of looking for an escaped Confederate.

Through Abe Calhoun often heard from Joyce. She cheered him with words of love and comfort, but absolutely refused to come and see him, saying it would be dangerous. In this she was right, for Andrew Harmon was alert. He believed that Joyce had had something to do with the disappearance of Calhoun, and had her closely watched. Fortunately his suspicions did not extend to Abe, so that communication between Joyce and Calhoun was not interrupted. At the end of two weeks he felt able to leave his place of concealment. But where should he go? He longed to be South, in the [pg 294]midst of the strife, but his heart was drawn toward Columbus, where his comrades lay languishing in prison. What could he do at Columbus? He did not know, but something might transpire that would enlighten him. At least he would go and look over the field. Once out of the neighborhood, in his Federal uniform and with Brown's discharge in his pocket, there would be little fear of detection. He made his preparations to go, wrote Joyce the letter which she prized so highly, and bade his kind protectors farewell, placing in their hands a hundred dollars. Their surprise and joy over the gift were about equal.

"De Lawd keep yo'!" said Aunt Liza, wiping her eyes.

Calhoun had determined to start early in the evening, travel all night, lie concealed during the day, and travel the next night. By that time he thought he would be so far away from the place of his escape that he could venture to take the cars without danger. Aunt Liza had supplied him with ample provisions for the two days. He carried out his programme, and on the morning of the second day found himself near a small town where he concluded to take the cars, but deemed it safer to wait for the night train. The conductor eyed him sharply when he paid his fare instead of showing a pass, for soldiers generally travelled on Federal transportation. But the conductor took the money and passed on without remark.

[pg 295]

Opposite Calhoun in the car sat a gentlemanly looking man, and much to Calhoun's surprise, when the conductor passed, he saw the gentleman make the sign of recognition of the Knights of the Golden Circle, and it was answered by the conductor. When the conductor next passed Calhoun gave the sign. The man stared, but did not answer. But he seemed to be troubled, and passed through the cars frequently, and Calhoun saw that he was watching him closely. At length, in passing, the conductor bent down and whispered to the gentleman opposite. Calhoun now knew another pair of eyes were observing him.

Watching his opportunity, Calhoun gave this gentleman the sign of recognition. The gentleman shifted uneasily in his seat, but did not answer.

"I will give you something stronger," thought Calhoun, and the next time he caught the gentleman's eye, he gave the sign of distress. This was a sign no true knight could afford to ignore. Leaning over, the gentleman said, "My boy, you look pale. Have you been sick?"

177

"Very, and I now need friends," answered Calhoun.

"Come over here and tell me about it," said the gentleman.

Calhoun took a seat by his side, and the man whispered, "Are you a deserter, and are they after you?"

"Yes," said Calhoun.

"Where are you going?"

[pg 296]

"To Columbus."

"That is a poor place to go to keep out of the hands of Lincoln's minions," answered the man.

"I am not afraid," said Calhoun. "What I want to know is where I can find friends in Columbus whom I can trust—true, firm friends of the South."

"My name is Pettis," replied the man. "I reside in Columbus. Once let me be satisfied as to who you are and what you are wearing that uniform for and I may be able to help you."

"That is easily answered," said Calhoun; "but first I must be fully satisfied as to you. Let me prove you, my brother."

Calhoun found that Mr. Pettis was high up in the order, and was violent in his hatred of the Lincoln government. He could be trusted.

"I am not a Federal soldier," said Calhoun after he had fully tested him. "I am wearing this uniform as a disguise. I am a Confederate officer."

"What! escaped from Johnson's Island?" asked Mr. Pettis, in astonishment.

"No, I am one of Morgan's officers."

Mr. Pettis nearly jumped off the seat in surprise.

"Morgan's officers are all in the penitentiary," he gasped.

"One is not and never was," answered Calhoun.

Mr. Pettis regarded him closely, and then said: "It can't be, but it must be. Is your name Pennington?"

"It is," replied Calhoun.

[pg 297]

"Why, the papers have been full of your escape. But the general opinion seemed to be that you wandered away in a delirium and died."

"Which you see is not so," said Calhoun, with a smile.

178

"How in the world did you get away?"

"That is a secret which I cannot tell even you."

"Very well; but, Mr. Pennington, you must come home with me. You will find friends in Columbus, many of them, who will be delighted to meet you."

When Columbus was reached, Calhoun, on advice of Mr. Pettis, bought a suit of citizen's clothes, for, said he, "We Knights hate the sight of that uniform; it's the badge of tyranny."

Calhoun saw that he had found a friend indeed in Mr. Pettis. No Southerner could be more bitter toward the Lincoln government than he. He fairly worshipped Vallandigham, and said if he would only return to Ohio, he would be defended by a hundred thousand men. He was especially indignant over the way Morgan and his officers were treated.

"We have schemed and schemed how to help him," said he, "but see no way except we storm that cursed penitentiary as the Bastille was stormed. And," he added, with emphasis, "the day is fast approaching when we will do it."

For three days Calhoun remained at Mr. Pettis's, wearying his brain as to how he might help his general, but every plan proposed was rejected as impracticable. On the third morning he happened [pg 298]to pick up a paper, and glancing over its columns, saw an advertisement which caused every nerve in his body to tingle. It was an advertisement for a boy to work in the dining-room and wait on the table at the penitentiary. The advertisement stated that the sole duty of the boy was to wait on the table when the Confederate officers ate, as they objected to being waited upon by convicts. In less than five minutes Calhoun was in his Federal uniform and on his way to the penitentiary to apply for the position.

"You do not look very strong," said the warden, kindly; "do you think you could fill the bill?"

"I am sure I can," said Calhoun. "Only try me and see."

"Well," replied the warden, "I had rather hire a boy who has served his country, as you have, and I will give you a trial."

Thus to his great joy Calhoun found himself hired to wait upon his old comrades in arms. With what feelings he commenced his duties can be imagined. Would they recognize him, and in their surprise give him away? No, he thought not. They knew too well how to control themselves for that. It was with a beating heart that Calhoun waited for the time of the first meal. It came, and the Confederate prisoners came marching in. How Calhoun's heart thrilled at the sight of his old comrades! But if they recognized him they did not show it by look or sign.

When the meal was finished and the prisoners [pg 299]marched out, Calhoun managed to give Morgan a little slip of paper. On it was written: "I am here to help you if I can. Be of good cheer."

But how could Calhoun help them? Even at meal-time guards stood everywhere watching every move. His duties did not take him out of the dining-room. Calhoun began by making a careful survey of the building in which the prisoners were confined. Fortune favored him. One day he made a remark to one of the employees of the prison that the floor of the building seemed to be remarkably dry and free from damp.

"It should be," was the reply; "there is an air chamber under the floor."

Like a flash there came to Calhoun a plan for escape. If this air chamber could be reached a tunnel might be run out. He took careful note of all the surroundings, and drew a plan of the buildings and surrounding grounds. These he managed to pass to Morgan unobserved. At the next meal-time as Morgan passed him, he said, as if to himself, "No tools."

This was a difficult matter. Nothing of any size could be passed to them without discovery. But in the hospital Calhoun found some large and finely tempered table-knives. He managed to conceal several of these around his person, and one by one they were given to Morgan.

Calhoun now waited in feverish excitement for the success of the plan. He had done all he could. The rest depended on the prisoners themselves. [pg 300]Through the shrewdness and indomitable energy of Captain Thomas H. Hines the work was carried to a successful termination inside the prison wall.

General Morgan occupied a cell in the second tier, and could do nothing. Only those who occupied cells on the ground floor had any hopes of escaping. Captain Hines, with infinite labor made an opening through the floor of his cell into the air chamber. Once in the air chamber they could work without being discovered. With only the table-knives to work with, these men went through two solid walls, one five feet, and the other six feet in thickness. Not only that, but they went through eleven feet of grouting. Then, working from under, they went through the floors of six cells, leaving only a thin scale of cement, which could be broken through by a pressure from the foot. The work was commenced November 4, and finished November 24. Thus in twenty days seven men, working one at a time, had accomplished what seemed almost impossible.

During these days Calhoun could only wait and hope. As the prisoners passed him in the dining-room, all they could say was "Progressing," "Not discovered yet," "All is well so far." At last, on the 24th, Calhoun heard the welcome words, "Finished. First stormy night."

Calhoun now examined the time-tables and found that a train left Columbus for Cincinnati at 1:15 A. M.; arriving in Cincinnati before the prisoners were aroused in the morning. So he wrote on [pg 301]a slip of paper: "Escape as soon after midnight as possible." He believed that train could be taken with safety. The afternoon of November 27, the weather became dark and stormy. At supper-time Calhoun heard the glad word, "To-night."

As soon as his duties were done he hurried to the home of Mr. Pettis, exchanged his uniform for citizen's clothes, telling Mr. Pettis his work at the penitentiary was done, and he had decided to leave. "Ask no questions; it is better that you know nothing," said Calhoun.

Mr. Pettis took his advice, but he was not surprised in the morning when he heard that Morgan had escaped. For General Morgan to escape, it was necessary for him to occupy a lower cell. His brother, Captain Dick Morgan, occupied the cell next to Captain Hines. The Captain, giving up his chance of escaping, effected an exchange of cells with his brother. This was easily accomplished, as they were about of a size, and it was quite dark in the cells when they were locked in.

The General had been allowed to keep his watch. When a few minutes after twelve came, he arose, fixed a dummy in his bed to resemble a man sleeping, and breaking through the thin crust over the opening with his foot, slipped into the air chamber. He gave the signal, and was quickly joined by his companions. Captain Morgan had made a ladder out of strips of bed-clothing, and by the aid of this ladder they hoped to scale two walls, one twenty [pg 302]feet high, which would stand between them and liberty, after they had emerged from the tunnel.

A little before midnight Calhoun made his way as close as he durst to the place where he knew the wall must be scaled. Not three hundred feet away several guards were gathered around a fire. The night was cold, and the guards kept close to the fire. Slowly the minutes passed. The city clocks struck half-past twelve. Would they never come? Had their flight been detected?

Suddenly a dark spot appeared on top of the wall. Then another, and another, until Calhoun counted seven. They were all there. Silently they slid down the rope ladder, the talk and laughter of the guards ringing in their ears. But noiselessly they glided away, and the darkness hid them.

"This way," whispered Calhoun. When out of hearing of the guards, they stopped for consultation. It would not do to keep together. They decided to go two and two. Calhoun handed each a sum of money. There was a strong clasping of the hands, a whispered farewell, and they who had dared so much separated.

The next morning there was consternation in the penitentiary at Columbus. The news of Morgan's escape was flashed over the country. The Federal authorities were astonished, dumbfounded. A reward of five thousand dollars was offered for his recapture. Every house in Columbus was searched, but to no purpose. John Morgan had flown.

ESCAPE OF MORGAN FROM PRISON

CHAPTER XXIII.

THE FLIGHT TO THE SOUTH.

The 1:15 train from Columbus to Cincinnati was about to start. "All aboard," shouted the conductor.

Two gentlemen sauntered into one of the cars, to all appearances the most unconcerned of individuals. They took different seats, the younger just behind the older. General Morgan and Calhoun had reached the train in safety; had purchased tickets, and taken their seats without exciting suspicion. A moment more and they would be on their way South.

A Federal major came hurrying in and seated himself beside Morgan, and the two entered into conversation. On the way out of the city the train had to pass close to the penitentiary. The major, pointing to the grim, dark pile, and thinking he might be imparting some information, said: "There is where they keep the notorious John Morgan."

"May he always be kept as safe as he is now," quickly replied the General.

"Oh! they will keep him safe enough," said the major, complacently stroking his chin. The major better understood the Delphic answer of the General the next morning.

All went well until Dayton was reached, where [pg 304]by some accident the train was held over an hour. It was an anxious hour to Morgan and Calhoun. It meant that the train would be late in Cincinnati, that before they arrived there the Federal authorities of the city might be informed of the escape. It would never do for them to ride clear into the city. As the train slowed up as it entered the suburbs, the General and Calhoun both dropped off without being noticed.

Morgan being well acquainted with the city, they quickly made their way to a ferry, and by the time the escape had been discovered at the penitentiary, Morgan's feet were pressing the soil of Kentucky. Calhoun's heart thrilled as he once more breathed the air of his native state. He felt like a new being, yet he knew that it was hundreds of miles to safety. They must steal through the states of Kentucky and Tennessee like hunted beasts, for the enemy was everywhere. But friends there were, too—friends as true as steel. And hardly had they set foot in Kentucky before they found such a friend, one who took them in, fed them, and protected them. He gave them horses, and sent them on their way. Slowly they made their way through the state, travelling all night, sent from the house of one friend to that of another. At last they reached

183

the Cumberland River near Burkesville, where they had crossed it at the beginning of their raid. To Calhoun it seemed that years had passed since then, so much had happened.

On entering Tennessee, their dangers thickened. [pg 305]They did not know friend from foe. On entering a house they did not know whether they would be protected or betrayed. The country was swarming with Federal cavalry. It was rumored that Morgan was in the country making his way south, and every officer was eager to add to his laurels by capturing him. In the mountains Morgan and Calhoun met a party of forty or fifty Confederates who were making their way to the Confederate lines. In the party were a number of Morgan's old men, who hailed their chief with the wildest delight. Morgan assumed command of them. But few of the party were mounted, consequently their progress was slow and their dangers were augmented.

All went well until the Tennessee River was reached, a few miles below Kingston. The river was high and there was no means of crossing. A rude raft was constructed, and with the horses swimming, they commenced crossing. When about half were across a company of Federal cavalry appeared and attacked those who were still on the northern bank. On the frail raft, Morgan started to push across to their aid.

"Are you crazy, General," cried Calhoun; "you can do no good, and will only be killed or captured. See, the men have scattered already, and are taking to the woods and mountains."

It was true, and Morgan reluctantly rode away. He had the satisfaction afterwards of learning that most of the men escaped.

The next day was the last day that Calhoun [pg 306]ever rode with Morgan, but little did he realize it at the time. Along in the afternoon they became aware of the close proximity of a squadron of Federal cavalry. Morgan and those with him took shelter behind a thick growth of cedars, while Calhoun rode ahead to investigate. He discovered no enemy and was coming back when he ran squarely into the Federals. The foremost of them were not ten feet from Morgan, he still being screened from view by the cedars. Without hesitation, Calhoun cried, "This way, Major. Hurry up, they have gone this way," pointing the way he had come.

The major took Calhoun for a guide, and giving the command, "Forward," rode rapidly after Calhoun, and Morgan was saved. For half a mile they rode, when a stream was reached, and it was seen no horseman had crossed it. The major drew rein and turned to Calhoun in fury.

"You have deceived me, you dog!" he cried.

"Yes, I am one of Morgan's men," calmly replied Calhoun.

The anger of the major was terrible. He grew purple in the face. "Yes, and you have led me away from Morgan," he hissed. "You will pay for this."

Calhoun still remained calm. "That was not Morgan," he said; "I ought to know Morgan, I have ridden with him for two years."

"I know better," roared the Major, thoroughly beside himself; "you are a lying scoundrel; I will fix you."

[pg 307]

"What are you going to do?" asked Calhoun, with apparent calmness, but a great fear coming over him.

"Hang you, you lying devil, as sure as there is a God in heaven! I would not have had Morgan slip through my fingers for ten thousand dollars. It would mean a brigadier generalship for me if I had caught him. String him up, men."

One of the soldiers coolly took the halter off his horse, fastened it around Calhoun's neck, threw the other end over the projecting limb of a tree, and stood awaiting orders.

Once more an ignominious death stared Calhoun in the face, and there was no Captain Huffman near to rescue him. It looked as if nothing could save him, but his self-possession did not forsake him.

"Major, before you commit this great outrage—an outrage against all rules of civilized warfare—let me say one word." Calhoun's voice did not even tremble as he asked this favor.

"Be quick about it, then, but don't think you can say anything that will save your cursed neck!"

"Major, if that was General Morgan, as you say, and I have been one of Morgan's men, as I have confessed, ought I not to be hanged if I had betrayed him into your hands?"

The fire of anger died out of the major's eyes. He hesitated, and then said: "You are right. If that was General Morgan, and you are one of his men, you should be hanged for betraying him, not for saving him." Then to his men he said: "Boys, [pg 308]take off that halter; he is too brave and true a man to be hanged."

Calhoun drew a long breath. He had appealed to the major's sense of honor, and the appeal had not been made in vain.

The major kept Calhoun for three days, and during that time treated him more like a brother than a prisoner. Calhoun never forgot his kindness. At the end of the three days Calhoun was placed under a strong guard with orders to be taken to Knoxville. He resolved to escape before Knoxville was reached, or die in the attempt. Never would he live to be taken North in irons, as he would be when it became known that he was one of Morgan's officers.

At the end of the first day's journey the prisoners, of whom there were several, were placed in the tower room of a deserted house. Three guards with loaded muskets stood in the room, another was just outside the door. Calhoun watched his chance, and when the guards inside the room were not looking, he dashed through the door, closing it after him. The guard outside raised his musket and fired. So close was he that the fire from the muzzle of the gun burned Calhoun's face, yet he was not touched. Another guard but a few feet away saw him running, and fired. The ball tore its way through the side of his coat. But he was not yet out of danger. He had to pass close to two picket posts, and as he neared them he was saluted with a shower of balls. But he ran on unharmed. One [pg 309]of the pickets with fixed bayonet took after him. He came so close that Calhoun could hear his heavy breathing. Calhoun ran as he had never run before. A turn in the road took him out of sight of his pursuers, and he sprang to one side and began to climb the mountain. A squad of cavalry dashed by in pursuit; they had missed him. With a thankful heart Calhoun saw them disappear.

But darkness came on and he had to feel his way up the mountain on his hands and knees. His progress was so slow that when morning came he had only reached the top of the mountain. He could hear the shouts of the soldiers searching for him. Near him was a growth of high grass. Going into this he lay down; and here he remained all day. At one time the soldiers in search of him came within twenty feet of where he lay.

It was the longest and dreariest day that Calhoun ever spent. Hunger gnawed him, and he was consumed with a fierce thirst. It was midwinter, and the cold crept into his very bones. The warmth of his body thawed the frozen ground until he sank into it. When night came it froze again, and when he tried to rise he found he was frozen fast. It was with difficulty that he released himself without sacrificing his clothing. For the next seven days he hardly remembers how he existed. Travelling by night and hiding by day, begging a morsel of food here and there, he at last reached the Confederate lines near Dalton.

CHAPTER XXIV.
CHIEF OF THE SECRET SERVICE.

"Is this General Shackelford?" asked Calhoun of a distinguished-looking Confederate officer.

"It is; what can I do for you, my boy? You look as if you had been seeing hard times."

"I have," answered Calhoun; "I have just escaped from the North. I am one of Morgan's men."

"Are you one of the officers who escaped with Morgan?" asked the General, with much interest.

"Yes and no. I was not in prison with Morgan, but I escaped South with him."

"I had a nephew with Morgan," continued the General. "We have not heard from him since Morgan was captured. The report is that he was killed in the last fight that Morgan had before he was captured. Poor Cal!" and the General sighed.

"Uncle Dick, do you not know me?" asked Calhoun, in a broken voice.

General Shackelford stared at Calhoun in astonishment. "It cannot be, yes, it is Cal!" he exclaimed, and the next moment he had Calhoun by the hand, and was nearly shaking it off.

"And you have been in a Northern prison, have you?" asked the General.

[pg 311]

"No, but I was wounded near unto death. Fortunately I fell into kind hands."

"But your looks, Cal; you are nothing but skin and bones."

"No wonder. I have not had enough to eat in the last seven days to keep a bird alive. Then I was none too strong when I started on my journey south."

"Tell me about it some other time," said the General. "What you want now is rest and something to eat."

And rest and food Calhoun got.

When he came to tell his story it was listened to with wonder. He was taken to General Joseph E. Johnston, then in command of the Confederate forces around Dalton, and the story was repeated.

"You know, I presume," said Johnston, "that Morgan escaped, and is now in Richmond."

"Yes, I long to be with him," answered Calhoun. "I feel as strong as ever now."

"Do not be in a hurry to report," said Johnston. "Wait until you hear from me."

In a few days Calhoun received a message from General Johnston saying he would like to see him. Calhoun lost no time in obeying the summons. He was received most cordially.

"In the first place, Captain," said the General, "allow me to present you this," and he handed him his commission as captain in the Confederate army.

Calhoun choked, he could only stammer his thanks. But what came next astonished him still [pg 312]more. "I now offer you the position of Chief of the Secret Service of my army," said the General. "After listening to your story, although you are young, I believe there is no officer in the army more capable of filling it."

Calhoun knew not what to say; it was a place of the greatest honor, but he hated to leave Morgan. "Will you let me consult my uncle before I give an answer?" asked Calhoun.

"Most certainly," replied the General.

"Accept it, by all means, Cal," said General Shackelford when Calhoun appealed to him. "In the first place, it is your duty to serve your country in the place where you can do the most good. There is no question but that at the head of the Secret Service you can render the country vastly better service than you can riding with Morgan. In the next place, I fancy it will not be exactly with Morgan as it was before his unfortunate raid. His famous raiders are prisoners, or scattered. It will be impossible for him to gather another such force. They understood him, he understood them. This will not be the case with a new command. Then, this is for your ear alone, Calhoun, the authorities at Richmond are not satisfied with Morgan. In invading the North he disobeyed orders; and this, those high in authority cannot overlook."

So, with many regrets, Calhoun decided to accept the offer of General Johnston; but for many days his heart was with his old chieftain. The [pg 313]time came when he saw the wisdom of his uncle's remarks. General Morgan never regained his old prestige. It is true the Confederate government gave him the department of Western Virginia, but they so hampered him with orders that any great success was impossible.

In June, 1864, Morgan made his last raid into Kentucky. At first he was successful, sweeping everything before him. He had the pleasure of taking prisoner General Hobson, the man who had tracked him all through his

Northern raid. But at Cynthiana he met with overwhelming defeat, his prisoners being recaptured, and he escaping with only a small remnant of his command.

On the morning of the 4th of September, 1864, the end came. General Morgan was slain in battle at Greenville, East Tennessee. Calhoun mourned him as a father, when he heard of his death. It was long months afterwards before he heard the full particulars, and then they were told him by an officer who was with the General on that fatal morning.

"We marched into Greenville," said the officer, "and took possession of the place on the afternoon of the 3d. There was a small company of Yankees within four miles of us, but there was no considerable body of Yankees nearer than Bull's Gap, sixteen miles away. The General established his headquarters at the house of a Mrs. Williams, the finest house in the little city.

"In the evening a furious storm arose and con[pg 314]tinued most all night. The rain fell in torrents. The lightning flashed incessantly, and there was a continual crash of thunder. It seemed impossible that troops could move in such a storm, and we felt perfectly safe.

"But there were traitors in Greenville, and they carried the news to the little company of Yankees four miles away that Morgan was in the city, and told at what house he lodged. Two daring young cavalrymen volunteered to carry the news to General Gillem at Bull's Gap. Talk about the ride of Paul Revere, compared to the ride of those two Yankees! Buffeted by wind and rain, one moment in a glaring light and the next in pitch darkness, with the thunder crashing overhead, in spite of wind and rain, those two cavalrymen rode the sixteen miles by midnight.

"The command was aroused. What if the rain did pour and the elements warred with each other? Morgan was the prize, and by daylight Gillem's soldiers had reached Greenville. So complete was the surprise that the house in which the General slept was surrounded before the alarm was given. Then thinking only of joining his men, the General leaped out of bed, and without waiting to dress, seized his sword and dashed out of the house, seeking to escape by the way of the garden. But he was seen by a soldier and shot dead. The news that Morgan was killed seemed to go through the air. It was known in an incredibly short time by both sides.

[pg 315]

"Now," said the officer, "occurred one of the most singular circumstances I know of during the war. There was no flag of truce, no orders to cease firing, yet the firing ceased. The Confederates gathered together, and marched out of the city; the Federals marched in; the two were close together, within easy musket range, but not a shot was fired. It seemed as if both sides were conscious that a great man had fallen, a gallant soul fled, and that even grim war should stay his hand."

It is not within the scope of this book to follow Calhoun through the last year of the war. Suffice it to say, that in the enlarged sphere of his new position, his genius found full scope. He was all through the Atlantic campaign, where for four months the thunder of cannon never ceased, and where seventy-five thousand men were offered as a sacrifice to the god of war. He followed Hood in his raid to the rear of Sherman's army, and then into Tennessee. He was in that hell of fire at Franklin, where fell so many of the bravest sons of the South. At Nashville he was among those who tried to stem the tide of defeat, and was among the last to leave that fatal field. When the remnants of Hood's army were gathered and marched across the states of Alabama and Georgia into North Carolina, hoping to stay the victorious progress of Sherman, Calhoun was with them.

Not until the surrender of Lee and Johnston did Calhoun give up every hope of the independence of the South. But the end came, and in bitter anguish [pg 316]he laid down his arms. He had given his young life to his country when only seventeen years of age. For four years he had fought and hoped. When the end came it seemed to him the sky was darkened, that every hope had perished, that everything worth living for was gone. Oh, the bitterness of defeat! Strong men wept like children.

Even the victors stood in silence over the grief of those whom they had met so many times in battle. They were brothers now, and they took them by the hand and bade them be of good cheer, and divided their rations with them. The soldiers who had fought each other on so many bloody fields were the first to fraternize, the first to forget.

When Calhoun gave his parole, he met his cousin Fred, who was on General Sherman's staff. The meeting was a happy one for Calhoun, for it served to dispel the gloom which depressed his spirits. It seemed to be like old times to be with Fred again. Nothing would satisfy Fred, but that Calhoun should return home by the way of Washington. He consented, and was in Washington at the time of the Grand Review. All day long he watched the mighty armies of Grant and Sherman, as with steady tread they marched through the streets, showered with flowers, greeted with proud huzzahs. And then he thought of the home-coming of the ragged Confederates, and the tears ran down his cheeks. But as he looked upon the thousands and thousands as they marched along, and remembered [pg 317]the depleted ranks of the Southern army, his only wonder was that the South had held out so long as it did. Defeated they were, but their deeds are carved deep in the temple of fame, never to be erased.

[pg 318]

CHAPTER XXV.
THE LONE RAIDER.

It was near the close of a beautiful day in early June that Joyce Crawford was once more standing by the gate, looking down the road. It is nearly two years since we saw her last. She has grown taller, more womanly, even more beautiful, if that were possible. The sound of war had ceased in the land. No longer was the fierce raider abroad; yet Joyce Crawford stood looking down that road as intently as she did that eventful evening when Calhoun Pennington came riding to the door.

She had not heard a word from him since his escape; nor had she expected to hear. All that she could do was to scan the papers for his name among the killed or captured Confederates. But the Northern papers published few names of Confederates known to have been killed, except the highest and most distinguished officers.

During these two years Joyce's heart had been true to her raider lover. He had said that he would come when the war was over, that the thunder of the last cannon would hardly have ceased to reverberate through the land before he would be by her side. It was two months since Lee had surrendered yet he had not come. That [pg 319]he had been untrue she would not admit; if such a thought came to her, she dismissed it as unworthy. No! Like his general, he was lying in a soldier's grave; or he might be sick, wounded, unable to come.

This June evening, as she stood looking down the road, her thoughts were in the past. Once more, in imagination, Morgan's raiders came riding by; she beheld the country terror-stricken; men, women, and children fleeing from— they hardly knew what. Once more she heard the sound of distant battle, then down the road that little cloud of dust which grew larger and larger, until the horse with its stricken rider came to view. How vividly she remembered it all, how real it seemed to her! She actually held her breath and listened to catch the sound of battle; she strained her eyes to catch a glimpse of that little cloud of dust.

SHE HELD HER BREATH AND LISTENED TO CATCH THE SOUND OF BATTLE

No sound of battle came to her ears, but away down the road, as far as she could see, arose a little cloud of dust. Her heart gave a great throb; why she could not tell, for she had seen a thousand clouds of dust arise from that road, as she watched and waited. The little cloud grew larger. Now she could see it was caused by a single horseman, one who rode swiftly, and sat his horse with rare grace. She stood with hands pressed to her bosom, her eyes dilating, her breath coming in quick, short gasps.

Before she realized it, the rider had thrown himself from his horse, and with the cry of "Joyce! [pg 320]Joyce!" had her in his arms, kissing her hair, her brow, her lips. For a minute she lay at rest in his arms; then, with burning brow and cheek and neck, she disengaged herself from his embrace, and stood looking at him with lovelit eyes. Could this be he whom, two years before, she had taken in wounded nigh unto death? How manly he had grown! How well his citizen suit became him!

"Were you watching for me, Joyce?" asked Calhoun.

"I have watched for you every night since Lee surrendered. I began to think you had forgotten—no, not that, I feared you had been slain," she exclaimed, in a trembling voice.

"Death only could have kept me from you, Joyce. In camp and battle your image was in my heart. The thought of seeing you has sweetened the bitterness of defeat. The war did not end as I thought it would, but it has brought me to you—to you. Now that the war is over, there is nothing to separate us, is there, Joyce?"

She grew as pale as death. She had not thought of her father before—he believed that the South had been treated too leniently, that treason should be punished. All that the South had suffered he believed to be a just punishment for her manifold sins. If the Rebels' lives were spared, they should be thankful, and ask nothing more. Joyce knew how her father felt. Not a word had ever passed between them relative to Calhoun since his escape; but the father knew much more than Joyce [pg 321]thought. He had kept still, thinking that time would cure his daughter of her infatuation, for he considered it nothing else.

Calhoun saw the change in Joyce, how she drew from him, how pale she had grown, and he asked, "What is it, Joyce? Why, you shrink from me, and tremble like a leaf. Tell me, Joyce, what is it?"

"My father!" she whispered, "Oh, I fear—I fear!"

"Fear what, darling?"

"That he will drive you from me; that he will forbid me seeing you!"

"For what?"

"Because you fought against your country; because you were one of Morgan's men."

"What would he do? Hang me, if he could?" asked Calhoun, bitterly.

"No, no, but—oh, Calhoun, let us hope for the best. Perhaps when he sees you it will be different. You must see him. He and aunt have gone to New Lisbon; but they will be at home presently."

With many misgivings Calhoun allowed his horse to be put up, and he and Joyce enjoyed an hour's sweet converse before her father and aunt returned.

When her father entered the room Joyce, with a palpitating heart, said: "Father, let me introduce you to Mr. Calhoun Pennington, of Danville, Kentucky. He is the young officer whom we cared for when wounded. He has come to thank us for the kindness shown him."

[pg 322]

Mr. Crawford bowed coldly, and said, without extending his hand, "Mr. Pennington need not have taken the trouble; the incident has long since been forgotten. But supper is ready; I trust Mr. Pennington will honor us by remaining and partaking of the repast with us."

Calhoun could do nothing but accept, yet he felt he was an unwelcome guest. As for Joyce, she knew not what to think; she could only hope for the best. The meal passed almost in silence. Mr. Crawford was scrupulously polite, but his manner was cold and constrained. Poor Joyce tried to talk and appear merry, but had to give it up as a failure. Every one was glad when the meal was through. As they arose from the table, Mr. Crawford said: "Joyce, remain with your aunt, I wish to have a private conversation with Mr. Pennington." Calhoun followed him into the parlor. He knew that what was coming would try his soul more than charging up to the mouth of a flaming cannon.

The first question asked nearly took Calhoun's breath away, it was so sudden and unexpected. It was, "Young man, why am I honored with this visit?"

"As your daughter said, to thank you for the kindness I received while an enforced guest in your house," answered Calhoun, and then he mentally cursed himself for his cowardice.

"Guests who leave as unceremoniously as you did do not generally return to express their thanks," answered Mr. Crawford, dryly. "It was [pg 323]a poor return you gave my daughter for her kindness."

"What do you mean?" asked Calhoun, in surprise.

"I mean that leaving as you did subjected my daughter to much unjust criticism. An honorable man would have gone to prison rather than subjected the young lady to whom he owed his life to idle remarks."

Calhoun felt every nerve in him tingle. His hot blood rushed through his veins like fire, he clenched his hands until his nails buried themselves in the palms. How he longed to throttle him and force the insult down his throat! But he was an old man; he was Joyce's father. Then, as Joyce had never told him it was she who had planned the escape, it was not for him to speak. Controlling

195

himself by a mighty effort, he calmly said: "Mr. Crawford, I am sorry you think so poorly of me, for I came here to ask of you the greatest boon you have to give on earth, that is your consent that I may pay my addresses to your daughter, and in due time make her my wife. I love her with my whole soul, and have reason to know that my love is returned."

"And I had rather see my daughter dead than married to a Rebel and traitor, especially to one of Morgan's men. You have my answer," said Mr. Crawford, angrily.

"Why call me Rebel and traitor?" asked Calhoun. "Whatever I may have been, I am not that [pg 324]now. The government has pardoned; can you not be as generous as the government? as generous as your great generals, Grant and Sherman?"

"And the government will find out its mistake. Your punishment has not been what your sins deserve. Your lands should be taken from you and given to the poor beings you have enslaved these centuries. But we need not quarrel. You have had my answer concerning my daughter. Now go, and never let me see you again."

"Mr. Crawford," said Calhoun, rising, "you have been very outspoken with me, and I will be equally so with you. As to the terms you say should have been given the South, I will say that had such been even hinted at, every man, woman, and child in the South would have died on their hearthstones before yielding. But this is idle talk, as I trust there are but few in the North so remorseless as you. Now, as to your daughter; if she is willing, I shall marry her in spite of you. There is one raider of Morgan still in the saddle, and he will not cease his raid until he has carried away the fairest flower in Ohio."

"Go," cried Mr. Crawford, losing his temper, "go before I am forced to use harsher means."

Before Calhoun could reply, before he could take a step, there was a swish of woman's garments, and before the father's astonished eyes there stood his daughter by the side of her lover. Her form was drawn to its full height, her bosom was heaving, her eyes were flashing. Taking her lover's hand, [pg 325]she cried: "Father, what have you done? I love this man, love him with all my heart and soul, and he is worthy of my love. If I can never call him husband, no other man shall ever call me wife."

The father staggered and grew deadly pale.

"O God," he moaned. "I have no daughter now. Child, child, much as I love you, would that you were lying beside your mother."

Leaving the side of Calhoun, Joyce went to her father, and taking his hands in hers said, "Father, grant me but a few moments' private interview with Captain Pennington, and I promise I will never marry him without your free and full consent. Nay, more, without your consent I will never see him again or correspond with him."

"Joyce, Joyce!" cried Calhoun, "what are you doing? What are you promising?" and he started toward her, but she motioned him back.

"Father! Father!" she wailed, "don't you hear?"

Mr. Crawford looked up.

"Joyce, what did you say? What do you mean?" he whispered.

Joyce repeated what she had said.

"And you mean it, Joyce? you are to stay with me?" he asked, eagerly.

"Yes, but I must have a private interview with Captain Pennington before he goes. Then it is for you to say whether I shall ever meet him again or not."

Calhoun stood by while this conversation was [pg 326]going on, the great drops of perspiration gathering on his forehead. Was he going to lose Joyce after all?

The father arose and left the room. No sooner was he gone than she turned, and with a low cry sank into her lover's arms.

"Joyce, Joyce, what have you done?" cried Calhoun. "Fly with me now! Let me take you to my Kentucky home. Father will welcome you. You will not lack the love of a father."

Joyce raised her head, her eyes swimming in tears, but full of love and tenderness. "Hear me, Calhoun," she said, "and then you will not blame me. We cannot marry now, we are both too young. You told me that you and your cousin were to go to Harvard. That means four long years. Before that time my father may give his consent to our union."

"But you told him you would not see me, would not even write. That means banishment."

"Not from my heart," she whispered. "Calhoun, for you to attempt to see me now, or to write to me, would be but to increase my father's opposition. I trust to time, and by filial obedience to win him. It is a fearful thing, Calhoun, to be disowned by one's own father, and by a father who loves one as I know my father loves me. It would kill him if I left him, and the knowledge would make me unhappy, even with you. Calhoun, do you love me?"

"As my life," he answered, clasping her once more to his breast. "And to be banished entirely [pg 327]from your presence is more than I can bear. It is cruel of you to ask it."

"Calhoun, did you love me when I aided you to escape?"

"You know I did, why do you ask?"

"Yet you left me for two long years, left me to fight for principles which you held dear. What if, for love of me, I had asked you to resign from the army, to forsake the cause for which you were fighting?"

"I couldn't have done it, Joyce. I couldn't have done it, even for your love. But you would not ask me to do such a craven act."

"And yet you ask me to forsake my father, to be false to what I know is right."

"Joyce, how can I answer you? I am dumb before your logic. But how can I pass the weary years which are to come?"

"You have passed two since we parted, and your college years need not be weary. They will not be weary. Have faith. When father learns how good, how noble, how true you are, he will give his consent. And Mark, my brother Mark, he will plead for me, I know."

"Joyce, I am like a criminal awaiting pardon—a pardon which may never come."

"Don't say that. Now, Calhoun, we must part. Remember you are not to try to see me or write to me. But the moment father relents I will say, Come. It will not be long. Now go."

Calhoun clasped her once more in his arms, pressed the farewell kiss on her lips, and left her.

[pg 328]

CHAPTER XXVI.
"COME."

Calhoun found his life in the university delightful. He was a good student, and a popular one. The black-haired young Kentuckian who had ridden with Morgan was a favorite in society. Many were the languishing glances cast upon him by the beauties of Cambridge and Boston, but he was true to Joyce. In the still hours of the night his thoughts were of her, and he wondered when he would hear that word "Come." But months and years passed, and no word came. He heard that her father was still obdurate. He would wait until his college course was finished, and then, come what would, he would see Joyce and try to shake her resolution. He would carry her off *vi et armis* if necessary.

The day of his graduation came. It was a proud as well as a sad day to him. Sad because friendships of four years must be broken, in most cases never to be renewed; and sadder yet because no word had come from Joyce. She must know that he was now free, that of all things he would long to come to her. Why should she longer be held by that promise to her father? For the first time he felt bitterness in his heart.

Twilight, darkness came, still he sat in his apart[pg 329]ments brooding. From without came the shouts and laughter of students, happy in the thought of going home; but their laughter found no echo in his heart. A step was heard, and his cousin Fred came dashing into the room. "Why, Cal," he exclaimed, "why sit here in the darkness, especially on this day of all days? We are through, Cal, we are going back to Old Kentucky. Don't the thought stir your blood?"

"Go away and leave me, Fred. I am desperate to-night. I want to be alone," replied Calhoun, half despondently, half angrily.

Fred whistled. "Look here, old fellow," he said, kindly, "this won't do. It's time we met the folks down at the hotel. By the way, here is a telegram for you. A messenger boy handed it to me, as I was coming up to the room."

Calhoun took the yellow envelope languidly, while Fred lighted the gas; but no sooner had he glanced at his telegram, than he gave a whoop that would have done credit to a Comanche Indian.

"Fred, Fred!" he shouted, dancing around as if crazy, "when does the first train leave for the west? Tell the folks I can't meet them."

"Well, I never—" began Fred, but Calhoun stopped him by shaking his telegram in his face.

It read:

"Come.

"Joyce."

That was all, but it was enough to tell Calhoun that the long years of waiting were over, that the little [pg 330]Puritan girl had been true to her lover, true to her father, and won at last. The first train that steamed out of Boston west bore Calhoun as a passenger, and an impatient passenger he was.

How had it fared with Joyce during these years? If Calhoun had known all that she suffered, all her heartaches, he would not have been so happy at Harvard as he was. The fear of losing his daughter being gone, Mr. Crawford, like Pharaoh, hardened his heart. He believed that in time Joyce would forget, a pitiable mistake made by many fathers. A woman like Joyce, who truly loves, never forgets. It is said that men do, but this I doubt.

The troublesome days of Reconstruction came on, and Mr. Crawford felt more aggrieved than ever toward the South. He believed that the facts bore out his views, that the North had been too lenient. As for Joyce, she gave little thought to politics. She believed that her father would surely relent before Calhoun had finished his college course; but as the time for his graduation approached, and her father was still obdurate, her courage failed. Her step grew languid, her cheeks lost their roses, the music of her voice in song was no longer heard.

Strange that her father did not notice it, but there was one who did. That was her brother Mark. He was now a major in the Regular Army, had been wounded in a fight with the Apaches, and was home on leave of absence. To him Joyce confided all her sorrows, and found a ready sym[pg 331]pathizer, for he was as tender of heart as he was brave.

He went to his father and talked to him as he had never talked before. "Your opposition is all nonsense," said Mark. "Young Pennington is in every way worthy of her. I have taken pains to investigate."

The old gentleman fairly writhed under his son's censures, and tried to excuse himself by saying, "Mark, I have said I had rather see her dead than married to a Rebel, one of Morgan's men."

"Well, you will see her dead, and that very soon," retorted Mark, thoroughly aroused. "Have you no eyes? Have you not noticed her pale cheeks, her languid steps? Is she the happy girl she was? Your foolish, cruel treatment is killing her."

Mr. Crawford groaned. "Mark, Mark," he cried, "I can't bear to hear you talk like that, you my only son. I have only done what I thought was right. You must be mistaken about Joyce."

"I am not; look at her yourself. Never was there a more dutiful daughter than Joyce. She would rather die than break her promise to you. Free her from it. Make her happy by telling her she can see Pennington."

"Mark, don't ask too much. Joyce is all I have to comfort me. When I am gone you will be the head of the family. You can then advise her as you please."

[pg 332]

"Better be kind to her and give her your blessing while you live," said his son, turning away, believing that his words would bear fruit.

What Mark had said deeply troubled Mr. Crawford. He now noticed Joyce closely, and was surprised that he had not perceived the change in her. He meant to speak to her, but kept putting it off day by day, until sickness seized him. The doctor came, and told him he had but a short time to live. Mr. Crawford heard the verdict with composure. The Puritan blood in his veins led him to meet death as he would meet any enemy in life. But he would do justice to his daughter before he died. Calling Joyce to him, he took her hand in his, and said: "Joyce, you have been all that a daughter should be to me, but to you I have been a hard, cruel father."

"No, no, you have been the kindest of fathers," she cried, her tears falling fast. "Father, don't talk so, or you will break my heart."

"Listen, Joyce. I now know how much suffering I have caused you. I drove from you the man you loved. Do you still love him, Joyce?"

"Father, I love him, I shall always love him, but I have been true to my promise. I—"

"There, child," broke in Mr. Crawford, "say no more. I know how true you have been, how sacred you have kept your word, while I—oh, forgive me, Joyce!"

"Don't, father, don't, you only did what you thought was right."

[pg 333]

"But Pennington, Joyce—has he been true all these years?"

"I charged him not to see or write to me until I bade him, and that was to be when I had your free and full consent. Father, have I that consent now?"

"Yes, yes, tell him to come."

With her feet winged with love Joyce flew to send the glad message. But that night Mr. Crawford became much worse. It was doubtful if he would live until Calhoun could arrive.

Once more the sun is sinking in the west; again is Calhoun galloping up the road which leads to the Crawford residence. But Joyce is not standing at the gate watching for him. The little cloud of dust grows larger and larger, but it is not noticed. In the house a life is ebbing away—going out with the sun. Calhoun is met by Abe, who takes his horse, and points to the house. "Massa Crawford dyin'," is all he said.

He is met at the door by Joyce. "Come, father wants to see you," she says, and leads him into the chamber where the dying man lies.

"Father, here is Calhoun," she sobbed.

Mr. Crawford opened his eyes, stretched forth a trembling hand, and it was grasped by Calhoun. In that hour all animosity, all bitterness, was forgotten.

Joyce came and stood by the side of her lover. Her father took her hand and placed it in that of Calhoun. "God bless you both, my children," he whispered. "Forgive!"

[pg 334]

"There is nothing to forgive," replied Calhoun, in a choking voice.

A look of great contentment came over the dying man's face. "Sit by me, Joyce," he whispered. "Let me hold your hand in mine."

Joyce did so, her tears falling like rain. For some time she held her father's hand, and then his mind began to wander. It was no longer Joyce's hand he held, but the hand of her mother, who had lain in the grave for so many years. Once he opened his eyes, and seeing the face of Joyce bending over him, murmured, "Kiss me, Mary."

Brushing aside her tears, Joyce kissed him, not once, but again and again.

He smiled, closed his eyes—and then fell asleep.

A year has passed since the death of Mr. Crawford. Calhoun has come to claim his beautiful bride. He is making his last raid; but this time no enemy glowers upon him. Instead, flowers are scattered in his path; glad bells are ringing a joyful welcome. He is fully aware that the war has left many bitter memories; yet when the words are spoken which link his life to Joyce's forever and forever (for true love ends not in the grave), he clasps her to his heart, and thanks God that Morgan made his raid into Ohio.

Lightning Source UK Ltd.
Milton Keynes UK
UKHW011948270622
405049UK00002B/62

9 783752 376135